T0196822

Retired high school teacher Gwen Franklin has a new pet valet business with her BFF, and a whole new leash on life. But a killer is about to come sniffing around . . .

Gwen Franklin is looking forward to spending her retirement drinking her favorite coffee and reading mystery novels. Those peaceful plans are brought to heel by her best friend, Nora. Sporting stiletto heels, leggings, and a "more is better" makeup routine, fifty-something Nora Goldstein has a penchant for marrying—and divorcing—rich men. Now that Gwen's got free time, Nora figures they should start a dog-walking and pet-sitting service together.

But it's far from a walk in the park when the corpse of Linda Fletcher is found in Nora's kitchen. Linda was Nora's nemesis, and the large knife protruding from her chest points to murder. With no doubt that her bestie's being framed, Gwen puts her sleuthing skills—acquired from reading every Agatha Christie mystery—to the test as she digs through suspects, including four disgruntled ex-husbands, ten greedy ex-stepchildren, not to mention all her exes' exes. But with death threats and another body surfacing, can Gwen curb a killer before her own (dog) days come to an end?

Books by Dane McCaslin

The Proverbial Crime Mysteries
A Bird in the Hand
When the Cat's Away
You Can Lead a Horse to Water

The 2 Sisters Pet Valet Mysteries
Doggone Dead*

Coming in 2021
Cat's Meow*

*Published by Kensington Publishing

Doggone Dead

Dane McCaslin

LYRICAL PRESS
Kensington Publishing Corp.
www.kensingtonbooks.com

LYRICAL UNDERGROUND BOOKS are published by
Kensington Publishing Corp.
119 West 40th Street
New York, NY 10018

All Kensington titles, imprints, and distributed lines are available at special quantity discounts for bulk purchases for sales promotion, premiums, fund-raising, educational, or institutional use.

Special book excerpts or customized printings can also be created to fit specific needs. For details, write or phone the office of the Kensington Sales Manager: Kensington Publishing Corp., 119 West 40th Street, New York, NY 10018. Attn. Sales Department. Phone: 1-800-221-2647.

Lyrical Underground and Lyrical Underground logo Reg. US Pat. & TM Off.

First Electronic Edition: August 2020
ISBN-13: 978-1-5161-1014-8 (ebook)
ISBN-10: 1-5161-1014-5 (ebook)

First Print Edition: August 2020
ISBN-13: 978-1-5161-1017-9
ISBN-10: 1-5161-1017-X

Printed in the United States of America

This book is dedicated to my mother, 1944-2010
"Her children arise up, and call her blessed..."
—Proverbs 31:28

Chapter 1

What woke me wasn't the insistent ringing of my alarm clock or the sound of the wind that blew in from the Willamette River. Instead, the first official day of my retirement began with an early morning phone call from my best friend, Nora Goldstein.

"What do you want?" I sounded as surly as I felt. I'd been looking forward to this first late morning from the moment I'd announced my intention to retire early from a wonderful but exhausting career as a high school teacher. I wanted to sleep in, get up and have coffee, and go right back to bed, preferably with a book. "This had better be really good."

"And a good morning to you too, Gwen." She gave a short bark of a laugh that echoed in my ear in the most irritating way. "What's better than two besties spending some time together?"

Besties? *Besties*? This woman was way too awake for my liking.

"Nora, you sound like a geriatric teenager—and, in case you didn't notice, I'm not hanging out with that particular age group anymore."

"Oh, poo on you, spoilsport." Again that laugh. Maybe she was on something.

I'd heard stories of seniors baking brownies with marijuana in them and passing them around to their pals. I made a mental note to check up on Nora's latest whereabouts.

"Besides, I've got a great idea I want to share."

I groaned at her words. "Fabulous. As great as the last one? Please say no."

I could almost hear her disdainful expression.

"It's not my fault the city wouldn't let me start a fish pedicure salon. You'd think it'd be a slam dunk, what with all the fish we've got around here."

What Nora lacked in common sense, she made up for in dollar bills. As in millions of them, all tucked securely away in various banks, thanks to a rather extensive lineup of ex-husbands.

"I'm pretty sure the fish used in those types of salons aren't of the largemouth bass variety." My tone was as dry as a lecture on the finer points of comma usage. "Look, I don't want to spend my first real morning of no more school talking on the phone, even with my best friend."

Sometimes Nora could be as thick as the pea soup fog that rolled in from the rivers. Plain talking was the only way to get through to her. To my surprise, this morning it worked on the first try.

"My thoughts exactly." She spoke briskly, as if suddenly noticing the time. "Get yourself up and meet me at The Friendly Bean in one hour sharp."

And with that, the phone went dead. I let it fall out of my hand onto the fluffy comforter, one arm slung across my eyes. I loved that gal like a sister—I really did—but occasionally her timing could make me crazy.

There was no going back to dreamland now. I was wide awake and, knowing Nora, she'd probably march over here and drag me out of bed if I didn't show up. Sighing deeply, I flung the covers back and shuffled toward the bathroom.

Living in Portland suited me. I liked the climate, the surrounding mountains, the rivers. I liked hiking at Multnomah Falls, even when it was full of selfie-taking tourists. I even liked the rain—as long as I was indoors, preferably with a mug of coffee and a good book.

Being retired suited me as well. I'd planned on reading through my extensive collection of mysteries, beginning with the dame herself, Agatha Christie. Why Nora thought I needed anything else to do was as nebulous as she was, hard to pin down and always changing. It was a good thing that we were as close as we were, better than real-life sisters, as Nora had said more than once. She'd even taken to calling me "Sis" when we were much younger, something that could confuse those who didn't know us and put a smile on my face whenever I heard it.

Except, of course, when I got pulled into one of her nutty ideas.

Within the prescribed hour, I was showered, dressed, and walking toward The Friendly Bean, our neighborhood coffee spot with some of the best blends around town. It was a coffee kind of day, no doubt about it, but most of them were here in the great Northwest. Clouds that had earlier looked like soft pillows were now turning bruised faces towards the darkening Columbia River. Rain had already begun its daily drizzle shortly before I left my small bungalow, a soft prelude to a larger battering to come.

True to their promise, the skies opened up as I walked, drenching me and every other unfortunate person who happened to be outdoors. We were in for a day of what we called "weather" here in Portland. I yanked up the hood on my jacket and scurried for cover, my Birkenstocks flapping on the wet pavement like a pair of stranded fish.

Nora was sitting near the rear of the small café, one arm draped in a proprietary fashion around the back of the only empty chair in the place. Ignoring the frowns of those having to drink their coffee standing at the various tall tables that dotted the room, I hurried toward her, flinging raindrops as I did.

"It's already getting messy out there." I hung my wet jacket on the back of the saved chair and slipped damply into it.

The coffee shop was full of the sound of hissing espresso machines and baristas calling out orders, almost masking the noise of the rain as it hurled itself against the windows that streamed with condensation. Portland, I'd heard one tourist say, tended to rain both inside as well as out.

"I'm glad I Ubered here." Nora reached up to pat her hair, a smug expression on her thin face. "Rain and hairspray aren't a good mix." She inclined her head at the two mugs already sitting in front of me. "I got you the usual, Sis."

"Thanks. Some days I feel like I need coffee more than food." I took an exploratory sip and winced. The coffee was hovering somewhere near molten. "And why in the world did you use a taxi? You live closer than I do."

"Because I didn't want to get my new shoes wet."

I leaned over to stare at a pair of bright pink sky-high heels, each one sporting a lacey bow on top. Typical Nora. Ostentatious and girly in one fell swoop.

"And you do know, don't you, that fifty is the new thirty?" Taking a sip of her drink, a chocolaty concoction that could have doubled as a dessert, Nora dropped one frosted eyelid in a wink. "I mean, just look at Julia Roberts. And me."

I couldn't unsee her if I wanted to. Her hair, or what was left of it after a recent disastrous bout with perming rods and an overzealous hairdresser, was teased to within an inch of its blonded life and tucked underneath a hefty "fall" of fake hair. She favored clothes a few decades too young, especially the type made from the stretchy, tight material that would have been at home in a yoga studio. It always amazed me I couldn't read the care tag stitched into the seams of her clothes. Her makeup routine was based on the "more is better" mind-set, and her shoes were usually of the stiletto heeled variety. Altogether, Nora was a conglomerate of styles that defied age and common sense, in my humble opinion.

I, on the other hand, favored a bare face and shoes as flat as I wished my stomach was. I made up in real estate what Nora lacked. I was wide where she was thin and rounded where she was angled. Life, as far as I was concerned, had been so much better before the advent of irritants such as cholesterol and calories, back when a little puppy fat never did a girl any harm.

I sighed, shook my head, and took another tentative taste of my coffee. Good to go. It was a real woman's drink: dark roast, black as ink, and guaranteed to put hair on my chest. As if that would even matter. I glanced at my unshaven legs, where they poked out from a pair of old denim capris, scratchy with stubble and white enough to use as nighttime beacons in the harbor. Retirement chic in all its glory.

But if I was honest, I'd preferred a slap-dash approach to fashion my entire life. Nora, in contrast to my choices, had been a fashionista even in kindergarten.

"Oh, come on, you. Cheer up already. Just think, no more grading papers, no more whining parents, no more doing anything you don't want to do." Nora held her mug out and clinked it against mine, causing a small tidal wave of coffee to spill on the table. "Here's to a whole new Gwen Franklin!" She gave my current ensemble a critical look, sweeping her gaze from stem to stern. "And we've got to do something about that wardrobe of yours."

I cautiously waved my mug in her direction, careful to keep the dripping coffee away from my lap. On top of everything else, I didn't want to walk around town looking like I had an issue with incontinence.

"Just because you've got the wherewithal to do whatever you'd like doesn't mean I can. Really, Nora. Have you seen the size of a teacher's paycheck these days? How big do you think my retirement checks will be?" I leaned in, catching an enticing whiff of chocolate. "And when it comes to choosing between having the lights on and buying clothes, well, let's just say I prefer to see what I'm doing."

Although, running around sans garments in a lighted house might not improve my standing with the neighbors. We had children in the neighborhood, for goodness' sake.

"Whatever." She brushed my comment aside as if it was a troublesome fly. "Look, I've been thinking, Gwen. What you need is a hobby."

I snorted, earning a frown from Nora.

"And no, I don't mean doing the daily crossword. I mean a *real* hobby. One that'll make you some money."

I had to laugh. Sometimes Nora's thought processes were difficult to follow. And sometimes they were downright comical, like now.

"I'm pretty sure that's called a 'job.'" I set my still-dripping mug on the table. "And I didn't retire from one only to get another." I slumped back against my chair. "Besides, I can only work a few hours a week anyway before they start docking my monthly check."

"Not if they don't know you're working." Nora's smile could have given the Cheshire Cat a run for its money. "The way I see it, we could do a few things around this place that you don't need to report."

That last statement had me worried. Not the fact that I wouldn't be reporting the income of whatever it was she had in mind, but the "we" part of it. Clearing my throat, I leaned in closer, crooking one finger at her.

"And who's this 'we,' if you don't mind sharing?" My voice was a shade above a whisper, a little teacher trick I'd used whenever I needed someone's attention. "Are you talking 'we' like the queen, or 'we' as in you and me?"

"As in us, of course." She tossed her head, sending the faux ponytail bouncing.

I watched, fascinated, as it settled back into place, this time a good inch lower than it had been.

"I've been doing some thinking," she began, and I cringed inwardly. Nora had her manicured fingers in a lot of financial pies, mostly from an investor's standpoint, but she'd recently begun a one-woman dog walking service for some of the residents in her luxury apartment building, just to "help out the poor dears," as she liked to say. I'd noticed, however, that her idea of "help" came with a price tag. So much for being altruistic.

If she thought that I was going to join her—well, she had another think coming.

And of course she did. My throat began itching as I listened to her enthusiastically describing our new partnership. I was allergic to all things furred and feathered, and not just a little bit. It was a full-fledged reaction to any type of dander that could begin with a runny nose and end with my eyes swollen almost shut. Benadryl was my friend, and I made sure to steer clear of anyone with a pooch or a cat. Working with them was completely out of the question.

"Nora, has it slipped that mind of yours that I'm horribly allergic to animals, especially those of the pet variety? Cats make me sneeze, dogs are worse, and even rabbits can make me break out in hives."

"Oh. That's right. Dang." She looked down, tapping a long fingernail—fake, of course—against her chin and then straightened with a bright smile. "Well, you'll just have to wear one of those mask things, the kind doctors wear when they're getting ready to operate. Besides, it'll keep your face hidden in case the folks from the state come looking for you. Just kidding."

I glared at her. "Not funny." My momentum plunged as I recalled all the dire warnings we'd been given. In every one of the pre-retirement meetings I'd attended, we'd been cautioned about The State, capitals implied, and what might happen to our annuity if we got caught working outside of the prescribed limitations. I was pretty sure that one of Dante's infamous circles in you-know-where had been reserved for all retired teachers who tried to beat the system.

"Oh, get a sense of humor, girl. Who's really going to check to see what you do with your time? They don't own you anymore." The fake hair slid another inch as she shook her head. "And besides meeting me for coffee, what else were you planning to do today?"

She had a point. And I did need something to do with all the time I'd have on my hands, besides rearranging my bookcases.

I gave a small shrug and tipped my head back, emptying the cooling coffee in one gulp. Placing the thick white mug back on the table, I looked at Nora and lifted my chin. Chins. All right, I lifted my chins. I was ready. "Okay, let's hear it. I guess I'm in."

The exaggerated whoop of delight Nora let fly was just this side of a sonic boom. Before I could say "boo," she leaned across and wrapped me in her arms, rocking me back and forth like a crazed wind-up toy.

I managed to catch her ponytail as it slid from its pins, holding it in place with one hand and attempting to free myself from her grasp with the other. I'd never had a problem when thirty pairs of juvenile eyes stared at me in the classroom, but there was something uncomfortable about having a dozen grown people in a coffee shop gawking at the sight that was Nora with her arms wrapped around me, especially when I had one hand on the back of her head while she was hugging me like a long-lost friend.

"Nora, get a grip," I hissed in her ear, a line of tiny gold loops nearly catching in my teeth. "You've lost your, uh, your hair, and everyone is staring at us."

By the time we left, Nora's hair was somewhat back in order. I'd never seen a ponytail look like that before, and, judging by the expressions on the other faces, nobody else had either. If this was going to be the start of something big, at least we were going to do it in unforgettable style.

At Nora's insistence, we took an Uber for the short ride from The Friendly Bean to her apartment building. We needed to head for her place first, she'd decided, so we could talk about our plans for our newly hatched partnership.

"The way I see it, there are at least three pets per floor in my building, not to mention the ones I see every day at the dog park. I've been walking one or two a day, tops, but between the two of us, we can double that." Nora grabbed at the sissy bar above her door as our driver took a sharp turn in front of a rather large logging truck. "If we live, that is. Young man, if you want me to give you a tip, I wouldn't drive like that. Besides, you might give my friend here a relapse, and trust me when I say you don't want that to happen."

Just what it was I was supposed to relapse back into, I had no idea, but I played along, letting my eyelids hang at half-mast while I collapsed against the seat and clutched feebly at the front of my jacket. Nora looked back at me approvingly, reaching over to pat my hand as though I was really ailing.

"You hang in there, Gwennie girl. We'll get you home and you can put your feet up if we aren't killed first." She twisted around to frown at the driver.

"I'm not gonna get us killed," he protested, sounding as young as one of my high school students. "Miss Franklin, is that you back there?"

Fabulous. I bolted upright, my eyes now wide open, trying desperately to recall his name. After twenty-something years of teaching, though, most faces looked the same. Unless, of course, they'd made some sort of impression on me, usually that of the negative kind.

"Oh, hey you." I spoke weakly, resorting to my tried and true greeting of forgotten students. "How are things?"

"I'm great." He fixed his gaze on the rearview mirror and narrowly missed a bicyclist that had swerved into our lane. "Sorry to hear you aren't feeling so good. Is that why you quit teaching?"

"Something along those lines." I tried to glare at a grinning Nora and smile at the driver simultaneously. I was saved from further conversation by a cacophony of horns as we zipped into the only empty space in front of Nora's luxury apartment building.

"Thanks for the ride. It was really good to see you again."

"Yeah, you too. Gimme a call whenever you need to go somewhere." He reached into the middle console and fished out a grubby card. "Use this number and I'll let you know if I'm available, okay?"

I grabbed it out of his hand before Nora's fingers closed on it. Brent Mayfair. That was his name. Smiling at him as I opened the back door, I waved the card at him.

"Well, thanks again, Brent." I felt smug when I said his name. "Please say hello to your mom for me."

"Will do, Miss F. See ya." And with a screech of tires, he shot back into traffic millimeters ahead of a fully loaded passenger van.

"If that kid makes it to his next birthday without causing an accident, I'll personally bake him a cake." Nora started to shake her head but reached up one hand instead to explore the ponytail. "Well, come on, partner. We've got big plans to make."

The big plans entailed making a pot of coffee, slicing a Danish pastry— cream cheese, my favorite—and thumbing through Instagram and Pinterest. By the time I'd looked at a million videos of cute kittens and puppies and commented on a handful of posts, I was ready to go home. All of that screen time, plus a few bites of pastry, and I was ready for a nap. Nora hadn't even touched her Danish. That probably had something to do with why I was a bit broader in the beam than she was.

"Nora, it's been a blast, but I need to get going." I stood and stretched, stiff from sitting curled up on one of Nora's overstuffed linen-covered sofas. "So much for our business planning session." I stifled a yawn, glad I could fall back into bed if the spirit moved me. Maybe I did need to get a hobby.

Nora looked at me, one eyebrow lifted in that half-questioning, half-mocking way she'd perfected over the years.

"What do you mean, 'so much for our business yadda yadda'? I got most of it done while you were playing on your phone." Holding her iPad up so I could see the screen, she gave me a smug smile. "And here's what I'm calling it. Two Sisters Private Services. Whaddaya think?"

"Nora, that 'private services' bit makes us sound, I don't know, a tad sleazy, don't you think?" I held out one hand for the iPad, visions of what our uniform might entail nearly giving me the heart attack I'd feigned in the Uber.

She leaned over and poked me in the arm, a mischievous glint in her eyes. "I'm just kidding, Sis. How about Two Sisters Pet Valet Services? I think that has a classy ring to it, don't you?"

I sat back down with a relieved thump, rubbing my arm where she'd hit it. "Much better. I don't think it would be good for my reputation to be part of a 'private services' gig anyway." I glanced at the iPad, noting she'd listed her name first. Fair enough. "Any idea how we might start rounding up a few takers?"

She gave a nonchalant shrug, a too-casual dip of one shoulder that had me instantly on high alert.

"Easy enough. I'll print up a few business cards and slide them underneath the doors in this building while you canvas the dog park across the street."

She started walking toward the desk that peeked out from behind a Japanese silk screen in one corner of the room, the latest in desktop computers and printers sitting primly side by side on its polished surface.

"Hold up." I stared at her, my hands lifted and eyes narrowed. "How come you get to stay inside and I have to go out? It's raining cats and dogs out there, in case you didn't notice."

"All the better to snag a few clients."

"Oh, hardee har har. I'm serious."

"So we both go. Gwen, if we're going to be successful pet sitters, we've got to get used to being outside."

She had a point. Just as sure as God made those little green apples, Portland skies would always be ready to dump something on our heads.

I was ready to give in gracefully when another thought crossed my mind. I bounced to my feet, hands on my hips, a suspicious expression on my face.

"Nora, exactly how much experience have you had in, uh, dealing with animal waste? I mean, you do realize that we have to clean up after the little darlings, right?" I pointed to her stilettos, one eyebrow lifted in question. I could practically see the steaming ooze left behind by one of our clients. The pets, not the owners. And definitely *not* a pleasant visual, I can tell you that.

"Me?" She gave a laugh as she quickly tapped on the keyboard, glancing at the computer's wafer-thin monitor as she typed. "I'm not the poop scooping type. Not one bit. My last husband, or was it the one before, always employed someone to clean up after his precious yappy dogs." She glanced over at me. "And my parents were too busy for me to have any pets of my own."

"I hate to break it to you, but that someone is going to be *us* in this little business venture." A thought occurred to me and I said, "You haven't been picking up after the dogs you've been walking, have you."

She stopped typing and stared across the room at me, eyebrows drawn together in consternation.

"Well, no, but…" Her voice trailed off and then her face brightened, the lines smoothing out. "But we can hire someone to do that part of it. Easy peasy. How about that kid that drove us here? He needs something else to do besides trying to cause a wreck."

I let my hands drop to my thighs, wincing as I hit a bruise I'd collected from a recent round with the lawn edger. That was Nora's answer to everything. Hire someone. Throw money at them. How we were going to pay for all of this and still make any money was beyond me. Before I could get any further with these rather dismal thoughts, Nora looked at me, smiling and waving a handful of newly printed business cards.

"Aaand here we go, Sis! It's time to get this show on the road to fame and fortune."

Two hours and fifteen floors later, plus a brief jaunt across the street to the Portland Pooch Park during a break in the rain, we had collected four new clients.

And a few other souvenirs as well.

I examined the bottoms of my Birkenstocks before wiping them on a patch of grass outside of the apartment building. I'd have to hose them off before I could wear them again in polite company.

Nora, of course, had managed to navigate the puppy pitfalls in her sky-high heels.

"This could really turn into something big, Gwen. Really big." She tossed the leftover cards onto the concierge's desk as we walked back into the luxury apartment building, ignoring the irritated expression on the woman's face. I walked behind Nora and scooped the cards up again with an apologetic smile. Sometimes going places with Nora made me feel like a pet owner in training: I always had to clean up her messes. And judging by the way the woman's face wrinkled in revulsion, she thought so as well.

Or maybe it was my shoes.

"So, what's the schedule?" I hurried to catch up with Nora, shoving the cards into my jacket pocket. "Did we say I'd be starting tomorrow?"

"Tomorrow?" Nora snorted, giving her head a hair-wrecking toss. "You're starting today, hon." She looked at me with a critical eye, her nose wrinkling as her glance swept over my sandaled feet. "I guess I'll have to loan you something to wear."

I looked down and saw the dark streak that stretched from the bottom of the shoe to the side of my sock. It was pretty repugnant. I really hoped I wouldn't have to toss out the shoes. They'd been faithful companions for at least ten years. Maybe more. And were much less critical than some folks, that was certain. They never uttered a peep, no matter the weather, and were always ready to roll for any occasion. Sigh. Maybe it was time to retire them. Kind of like me, come to think of it. Was that how an old teacher was viewed? As a worn-out shoe with disgusting things stuck all over the bottom?

"Gwen? You all right?" Nora was leaning toward me, a concerned expression on her face. "I didn't mean I don't like your sandals, I really didn't. It's that they've got, well..." She let her words trail off into midair as the elevator came to a juddering halt.

Forcing myself to smile, I straightened my shoulders, hopefully adding an inch or three to my height and subtracting a few unnecessary pounds from around my middle. "Not a problem. I'll take them off before we go inside." "And I know just the place you can leave them, too." Nora giggled, pointing down the carpeted hallway. "That snotty Linda Fletcher needs a surprise package, wouldn't you say?"

Dealing with Nora was like handling a roomful of hormone-crazed teens. The best way to do that, I'd always found, was to respond firmly but kindly and to redirect their risk-taking brains in another direction.

"Why don't we leave her a business card instead?" I pulled one out of my pocket. "She can give it to someone who has a pet." Or not. She'd probably tear it up and sprinkle the pieces in front of Nora's door.

The ongoing feud between Nora and Linda was something out of a soap opera. Or an elementary playground. I didn't know the entire story, but I did know there was something to do with a man, of course, and maybe a few mean-spirited tricks or two that Nora might have played on her.

"You're no fun. How'd you ever survive teaching high school?"

"Because I wasn't any fun." I said it solemnly, only half in jest, and she began laughing, pulling me inside behind her.

"Oh, you. You probably had them falling out of their desks. And kick off those sandals," she called over her shoulder as she headed to the kitchen. "I think there's an extra pair of house slippers under the couch. Coffee? Or hot tea?"

"Tea, please." I bent down to fish out the slippers. I'd taken my socks off for good measure, holding them by the cuff before tucking them inside the sandals. Might as well go whole hog and dump the lot. Maybe I could have a farewell, a send-off, Viking style. It might smell pretty bad, though. Tossing them in the nearest dumpster was probably the best bet. Sighing morosely, I slipped my bare feet inside the pair of fuzzy shoes and shuffled toward the kitchen.

And froze.

Nora was standing in the middle of the room, both hands covering her mouth, eyes opened as wide as they'd go. Stretched out on the floor, a large knife protruding from her chest, was Linda Fletcher. And, judging by the pool of blood on the floor surrounding her, this was no joke.

Chapter 2

"Oh, Gwen, what'll we do?"

Nora's face was paler than the average northwestern complexion, and I could tell even from where I was standing that she was trembling all over. I made myself ignore Linda's body and marched over to where Nora stood, grabbing her by the elbow and steering her back toward the living room. It was bad enough having a body in the kitchen, and I surely didn't need Nora fainting in there as well.

"You sit right here. I'm going to call the cops." I pushed her down onto the sofa and fished in my jacket pocket for my cell phone.

As cool as I was trying to be, I was still all thumbs as I tried punching in the simple numbers for the emergency services. Nine-one-one suddenly seemed like a complicated algebraic formula.

By the time I'd gotten through to an emergency dispatcher, had explained the situation, and had given the location, I'd calmed down enough to tiptoe back into the kitchen for a closer look. It wasn't a ghoulish streak that made me do this. Instead, I wanted to see if I could figure out what in the world Linda was doing in Nora's kitchen in the first place.

That she was actually inside the apartment wasn't a surprise to me. No one, especially Nora, locked their doors in this building unless they were going out for more than a few hours. Taking a quick walk to the mailbox or having coffee with a neighbor wasn't a good enough reason for locking a door. Still, I had questions. Had Linda known Nora had stepped out, or had she simply barreled inside, spoiling for an argument?

A loud thump on the apartment door roused me from my contemplation of Nora's unwelcomed guest, and I went back into the living room. Nora had stirred herself enough to answer the door, and now she was standing in front of two very large men, one of whom looked like he could moonlight as an Ironman competitor while the other one looked more like a contestant on *Iron Chef.* Drawing in a steadying breath, I addressed my comments to him, trusting that a soft belly equaled a soft heart.

"Thanks for getting here so quickly." I held out one hand in greeting. Both officers merely glanced down as though expecting the proverbial smoking gun. Or bloody knife, in this case. My ears grew warm as I dropped my hand, but whether it was from embarrassment or an errant hot flash, I couldn't tell.

Crossing my arms, I gave both officers the stare I'd perfected from years of dealing with the occasional impossible student. Firm and unwavering, unsmiling and mute. Unless one of them chose to speak up, I could do a silent standoff for as long as necessary. Finally, Ironman—Officer Taylor, according to the shiny brass name badge pinned to his uniform—gave a great sigh, moving his gaze from me to Nora and back.

"We were told you found a body? In your kitchen?" This was directed to the air somewhere between Nora and me, but I jumped in with the answer, not sure of her ability to string together a coherent sentence at the moment.

"Yes." I started toward the kitchen and beckoned them to follow. "She's in here, Officers."

"Ma'am, if you could stop right there?" Apparently Officer Taylor could only communicate via questions.

I wanted to give him a lesson in sentence structure on the spot. Instead, I froze in place and watched as he walked into the kitchen, one hand resting lightly on the black Taser that hung from a wide leather belt.

Iron Chef—Officer Reinhart—remained behind, presumably to keep an eye on the two suspects. That would be Nora. And me. The mere thought that I could be seen as a dangerous criminal almost made me smile.

Almost. One glance at Nora told me she was close to collapsing, and I moved quickly toward her, reaching out to steady her with one hand.

"You need to sit down." I guided her over to the sofa nearest the kitchen door and gently pushed her onto the cushions. "I need to get my friend some hot tea or something, or I'm afraid she's going to faint." This comment was directed to Reinhart, who had been watching the two of us with suspicion as if we were orchestrating some great escape plan right under his rather fleshy nose.

By the time both officers had decided that yes, indeed, we *did* have a dead body in the kitchen and had called for the necessary folks to join us, Nora looked as though she needed a month-long rest any place else but Portland, preferably someplace with lots of sun. And mojitos. And a cute waiter to keep them coming. Since I was officially retired, without a set schedule, I could offer to go with her, purely out of the goodness of my heart, of course.

"You know we're going to have to reschedule all those jobs, right?" I stared blankly at Nora, my mind still occupied with sunshine and sassy pool boys.

"What jobs?" I paused a moment while my brain played catch-up and then groaned, "Oh, you mean *those* jobs." I'd completely forgotten about Two Sisters Pet Valet Services. "Can't we cancel them?"

She gave a vigorous shake of her head and the fake ponytail gave up its tentative grasp on her head, falling to the floor like a dead ferret. Ignoring the wide-eyed stare from Officer Reinhart and a smothered laugh from Officer Taylor, Nora shoved the offending article under the couch with one foot.

"Let's give that horrible driver a call. My gut tells me he'll do it."

"His name is Brent." I fished in my jacket pocket for the crumpled card. "And what should I say?"

"Ask him—no, *tell* him we need someone to help us out. And remind him not to cause a wreck on the way over here, please."

"What'll I say about pay? You know he'll ask."

Nora gave a one-shouldered shrug as if letting the question slide off her back. "Whatever he wants. Within reason, of course. Tell him I'll negotiate."

Brent Mayfair had been a mediocre student but a sweet kid, always anxious to include everyone in whatever class project we had going on at the moment. No one had had a bad word for him, except for the football coach, and even then it was full of regret.

"That kid is built like a Mack truck, but he's got instincts like a teddy bear made from marshmallow," Coach Freeman had said. "I'd love to have him on the team. Heck, he'd be able to run over every last player out there, but he won't do it. I've started calling him 'Ferdinand' because he's too nice."

I'd been with a group of teachers standing on the edge of the football field before the season's first game, talking about the various players and just how far they'd go. Everyone agreed with Coach's assessment of Brent, though, and I was secretly glad. I really hated it when my student athletes got injured and had to miss school, which to me meant missed assignments and falling grades.

"Gwen? Snap out of it and call the boy already." Nora's words broke into my reverie and I was happy to hear the typical brusqueness back in her voice. She'd clearly recovered from finding Linda's body in her kitchen. Or maybe it was the prospect of a) making more money and b) bossing someone else around. "We need to get this pet sitting business up and running."

"Aye, aye, Cap'n." I snapped off a salute with one hand while tapping in Brent's cell phone number with the other.

"This is Brent's phone. Leave a message."

I held the cell phone away from my ear and turned to Nora, still trying to push the ferrety hairpiece farther under the couch with her foot. "He's not answering. Should I leave a message?"

"Yep. And tell him not to call you while he's driving."

I rolled my eyes at her words. "I think he's smarter than that. Besides, I saw a hands-free device in his ear."

"Oh, fabulous. That means he *will* call you while he's driving. Well, keep your ears open for the sound of a pile-up out there. That'll be the kid."

Hoping his voicemail hadn't picked up Nora's commentary, I said brightly into the phone, "Brent, it's Miss Franklin calling. Could you please call me back at..."

I broke off with a squawk as someone began speaking in my ear.

"Miss F? This is Brent. Did I really sound like an answering machine?"

I closed my eyes and slumped back against the couch's cushioned back. "Very funny, Brent, very funny."

"I do that so I can see who's on the line." Had the boy no concept of how voicemail worked? Knowing Brent, it was entirely possible. "So, what is it you need me for?"

I cringed at his words and nearly corrected his grammar but stopped myself in time. I was retired, for heaven's sake. Besides, if we didn't get someone here in a hurry, the newly hatched business was going to die a painful death. Like Linda.

"Mrs. Goldstein and I would love to have you join us in a new business venture," I began in a somewhat formal tone that earned my own eye roll from Nora.

"Oh, give me the phone." She impatiently stuck out one hand, fingers motioning for my cell.

I meekly passed it over, glad to let her take care of business. A tremor began in my hands, and when another knock sounded at the apartment door, it made me spring to my feet in alarm, knees trembling. Was this a delayed reaction after finding Linda, or had I overdone the caffeine bit?

A phalanx of white-suited folks stood there, looking like refugees from a sci-fi space movie. Officer Taylor waved them in, and I watched as they moved across the living room to the kitchen, carrying what looked like oversized tackle boxes and tripod stands.

"Don't you dare get my kitchen all dirty," Nora called after them, one hand covering the cell's mouthpiece. "My housekeeper will have your hides, I can promise you that." With a follow-up glare that made Officer Reinhart start and then scuttle after them to the relative safety of the kitchen, Nora sighed and went back to her conversation with Brent.

"Don't wear anything too good, but make sure you comb that rat's nest hair of yours. And wear a tie." After delivering that last order, she stabbed the "end" button and handed the phone back to me.

"A tie? Whatever for?" I glanced at the cell's screen to make sure it was indeed disconnected before slipping it back into my jacket. "He's going to be cleaning up after dogs, Nora, not serving dinner. At least I hope not," I added with a shudder and a slightly queasy feeling. Sometimes words made pictures in my head that needed no further exploration.

"Don't be silly." I could tell her heart wasn't in the rebuke. Instead, she was already on her feet, peeking around Officer Taylor's bulk as she tried to see what was happening. "You there! The one in white. No, not you, the other one. Get that tripod off my counter this minute! I prepare my food there, young man. Would you want me to go to your house and start putting foreign objects all over your counters?"

There was the sound of shuffling and movement from the kitchen as Nora supervised the Portland Police Department's forensic team. I sat back against the sofa cushions and watched in amusement as Officer Taylor tried to wrench control from her stubborn hands. Nora in action was always worth a ticket.

"Ma'am?" He was back in questioning mode, "Are you aware this is a crime scene?"

She stared at him, head tilted to one side as though she'd just discovered the earth wasn't flat. I watched the scene unfolding in front of me and wanted to tell the unsuspecting officer he'd better watch his back. I'd seen Nora act just that way right before she'd all but skewered someone with a rapier-like response.

"Don't be an idiot, Officer," snapped Nora. "Of course I know. I found the body, didn't I?" She turned around and surveyed the kitchen, a smile replacing the scowl. "Now, that's much better. Would anyone like coffee?"

I smiled. Classic Nora Goldstein. She used the "carrot and stick" approach with aplomb and got great results as well. I'd have to be careful, or she'd be using it on me too.

There was the rattle of ceramic mugs as the coffee maker gurgled into life. I could hear someone protesting that the mugs were contaminating the scene, and Nora retorting that "the body is lying on the floor, not my kitchen counters."

Amidst all the action, I'd almost forgotten that Linda Fletcher was still in the kitchen. I shivered suddenly and superstitiously mumbled the only prayer I could recall from my childhood. "Now I lay me down to sleep, I pray the Lord my soul to keep. If I should die..."

I was pretty sure Linda hadn't gotten up that morning with her mind on death. But someone had. And were they after Linda or Nora? And if it was Nora, what was the reason? She might not be everyone's favorite person—all right, she could be downright abrasive—but her heart was as wide as the Pacific Ocean, and almost as deep.

And if they were going to come after Nora, they'd have to deal with me as well. With a bracing resolve underpinning my shaky emotions, I jumped to my feet as the front door opened once more.

Standing there was a woman I'd never seen. She was dressed as if going to a fancy party, even though it wasn't quite noon, a pair of ankle-breaking stilettos on her feet and an ermine coat sliding from a pair of very bony shoulders. And when she opened her mouth to speak, I nearly fell back onto the sofa in shock.

"Oh, my God! I just heard! My stepmama's dead!"

Stepmama? Dead? Judging by the astonishment on Nora's face, this was news to her as well.

"Officer, could you help me a moment? Someone just let an entire batch of crazy into my apartment." Nora was glaring at the woman, hands on hips as she blocked the apartment's doorway. "And in case you can't tell, Phoebe, I'm very much alive." She paused a moment, her eyes narrowing in a way that I recognized as a danger signal. "And who told you I was dead, anyway?"

I missed the rest of the conversation as Officer Taylor joined the two women, stepping between them like a boxing match referee.

"Sorry, Miss F. I couldn't stop her."

Brent Mayfair, a sheepish expression on his face and a ratty tie hanging from his neck, moved around the woman and headed to where I sat. My mouth, I hated to admit, was hanging open in a most unteacherly—my word, not Webster's—manner, but Brent didn't seem to notice.

"That's all right." I spoke automatically, patting the sofa and motioning for him to take a seat. "How did she know where to go?"

"I guess she heard me ask that woman downstairs where Mrs. Goldstein's apartment was. And she kinda followed me." Brent gave his broad shoulders a shrug, straining the buttons of a very wrinkled dress shirt. "And you know me, Miss F. I don't like putting my hands on no one, especially a lady." He glanced over where the lady in question was still ranting at Nora as the officer attempted to calm her down, moving her back into the hallway. Judging by the salty vocabulary I was hearing, I was fairly certain the description of "lady" needed to be applied loosely.

"Anyone," I corrected him automatically. "And you did nothing wrong." I gave his arm a reassuring pat. "Would you like coffee while you wait to speak with Mrs. Goldstein?"

Nora had followed Taylor and the woman, firmly shutting the apartment door behind them.

"A soda, if she's got some." He paused, his grin lopsided. "I've had so much coffee today it's a wonder you don't hear me sloshing when I walk."

I had to take a moment to process this logic. Wouldn't any type of liquid add to the sloshing? Still, his expression was so hopeful that I nodded as I rose.

"I'll see if Nor...Mrs. Goldstein has any." I glanced over to where Officer Reinhart stood in the kitchen's doorway, his bulk effectively blocking any entrance. "Or I can ask him to check the fridge. He's probably not going to let me in there."

"Yeah, what's with all the police, Miss F.? You two been selling drugs outta here or something?" This was followed by a wide grin that crinkled his entire face.

"Not this time." I managed to keep my tone light. "Just a visit from our friendly neighborhood cops, checking to make sure the oven is safe to use."

"Whoa, that's cool." Brent looked duly impressed. "Maybe they need to go to my mom's kitchen and check on our stove. It's always burning our food."

This kid was too gullible for his own good. He was going to make the perfect pooper scooper for the Two Sisters Pet Valet Services.

There was a momentary scuffling noise heard from the kitchen and Reinhart moved back from the doorway. The white-suited crime scene folks were packing up and leaving, hauling out the cases and tripods that they'd carried in with them. Brent's eyes were so wide I was afraid he'd suffer permanent damage to his eye sockets.

"Wow, Miss F." He turned to look at me, letting out a low whistle. "They really don't fool around, do they?"

"Absolutely not," I agreed solemnly. "A safe oven is a healthy oven."

How I'd explain a dead body when they came to remove it was another issue entirely.

Thankfully, Brent was out on the first of four dog-walking assignments when the medical examiner's office came to remove Linda Fletcher's body. I'd already concocted a story of sorts that focused on the oven angle, but I was glad I didn't have to use it. My ability to tell a whopper of a lie was becoming somewhat disconcerting, especially for someone who saw herself as a truth-loving, God-fearing, salt-of-the-earth woman.

"Good work." Nora turned to me, holding up one hand for a high five. This was an action that always struck me as juvenile, but I dutifully held my own hand up and slapped Nora's open palm. "You can be the marketing expert."

"Marketing expert?" I was puzzled, trying to link telling lies and promoting a business. "As in rhetorical devices?" I was beginning to realize that my teacher brain was having a hard time shutting off. Just how long it would take to return to normal, I had no idea.

Nora didn't bother answering. Instead, she walked to the kitchen doorway, shaking her head as she observed the detritus left by the police department. "I need to call my housekeeper pronto." She shook her head some more as she peered around the room. "And who's going to want to clean up after Linda? I swear, Gwen, that woman is as much trouble dead as she was alive."

"Well, don't tell her. Your housekeeper, I mean," I added, clarifying my statement. "Or call one of those crime scene cleaning crews."

"Or I could ask knucklehead to do it when he gets back." Nora turned to look at me, a mischievous grin on her face. "You could tell him that's where you fainted because the oven was so bad."

"He's such a nice kid." I walked over to join Nora in the doorway. "I hate to keep lying to him just to get him to do our dirty work."

Nora snorted. "That's called being a boss, Gwen. Ever heard of it?"

I thought about the various administrations I'd worked with over the years and had to agree.

"Dirty work it is," I agreed. There was a knock at the door and I headed over to answer it. "And just in time, too. I think he's back."

It wasn't Brent Mayfair, though. Instead, it was a rather stern-faced plainclothes officer, his badge clipped to the waistband of his immaculate chinos. Behind him stood Officer Reinhart and another cop, a woman with both hands resting on rather substantial hips.

Flashing his I.D. in a manner normally reserved for fast-paced cop shows, the plainclothes officer said, "Nora Goldstein? We need you to come with us downtown."

Chapter 3

"That's Nora Goldstein." I gestured helpfully over my shoulder to where Nora stood, her mouth hanging open. "I'm her friend."

"Oh, thanks a lot, *friend*," Nora hissed as she walked past me. "Come in, won't you?" This last comment was directed toward the three officers in her doorway, but they remained where they were, the Three Fates of law enforcement, waiting to spin the outcome for another suspect. Nora gave a great sigh. "Well, can I at least get my bag?"

While they waited for Nora to retrieve the leather messenger bag she liked to carry, I tried to make small talk.

I gave the three officers my brightest "end of the year" smile, the one that usually felt like it stretched from ear to ear. They stared silently back at me like a class full of students unprepared for a pop quiz. Well, if it was a test they wanted, I had question *numero uno* locked and loaded.

"Wouldn't it make sense for me to go with Nora? After all, I was with her when we found—found the, you know." I lamely gestured behind me. "Besides, she's my best friend. I know she'll want me there."

Still nothing from the three amigos. Maybe they hadn't studied before showing up. I sighed and folded my arms, waiting for Nora to get back in here and save me from feeling as though I'd been ambushed by an unannounced visit from the principal.

"All righty, folks. Let's get this show on the road." Nora was back, brown leather bag slung across her body, its somber style clashing horribly with the neon spandex outfit she'd changed into.

The bright blue stilettos she'd put on in place of house slippers gave her another three inches in height and an extra wiggle in the hips. All together, she was going to give the Portland Police Department something to look at. And, judging by the expressions on their faces, the three officers were already enthralled by the Nora Goldstein show.

"Nora, I'll go with you, share the load, so to speak." I detected the slightest quaver in my voice and cleared my throat, throwing my shoulders back hard enough to pop my neck. Ignoring it, I said, "Two heads are better than one and all that jazz, right?" There. I was going to play the part of the loyal friend to the hilt, even if it meant the hilt was buried in my chest too. And I'd make sure Nora remembered this.

"Only if you're confessing that you've got something to do with the death, Miss—Ms." One of the officers elbowed the other, a wide grin on his round face.

My cheeks burned. "Absolutely not." I was as indignant as a cat with its tail caught in a screen door and my voice was almost as screechy. I modulated my tone, conscious of the amused expression in the officer's eyes. "And it's Miss Franklin to you, young man." I drew myself up to my full height of five feet nothing, my chin jutting out like the bow of a ship sailing full tilt into harbor. "I had nothing to do with it and neither did Mrs. Goldstein. And you can put that in your pipe and smoke it. If you smoke, that is. Personally, I've always found it to be a disgusting habit."

I shot Nora a triumphant glance, ignoring the stifled snort of laughter coming from one of the officers. My brilliant repartee would send them packing, their proverbial hats in their hands. This would be even better than Holmes and Watson or Poirot and Hastings. Franklin and Goldstein—another dynamic duo, Portland style.

"Yeah, yeah. That's what they all say." The detective motioned impatiently for Nora to step into the hall, rudely imploding my dream. "Mrs. Goldstein, we need to go." He craned his neck around to stare directly at me. "And for your information, I don't—oh, never mind. If I find out you had something to do with this, Miss Franklin, you can bet I'll be back for you."

"It'll be okay, Sis. Don't you worry. And just ignore Mister Sunshine there." Nora patted her frizzy hair into submission, her fingers lingering for a moment over the spot where the fake ponytail had been. "Make sure you send the boy to the next job, all right?"

"And what job might that be?" the plainclothes officer asked as they walked off. I heard Nora laughingly reply, "Scooping poop, Officer. Scooping poop." What did he think she meant? Another murder?

Closing the door behind them, I slowly turned around and faced the empty room. I was alone in Nora's apartment. Alone with a recent crime scene. Where someone had died. Quite messily. My stomach lurched and

I hastily took a drink of my cold coffee. I didn't believe in ghosts. I really didn't, but I wouldn't put it past Linda Fletcher to hang about, if only to give Nora a hard time. Eternal feuding, Portland style.

A loud knock on the door sent me to my feet as though there was an ejector button in the sofa. With a trembling hand, I opened the door to see a grinning Brent standing there with a small puppy wriggling in his arms.

"Look what I found, Miss F." He held out the dog for me to see, a proud smile on his broad face. "Wanna hold her?"

"Keep that thing away from me." I quickly backed away from Brent and his furry companion. "I'm allergic to dogs. And you can't bring it in here. Where'd you get it, anyway?" I stared at the small puppy, its eyes a warm brown in a rather endearing face. It was cute enough to make me wish I *could* hold it.

"It's a her. See?" He held the puppy up so I could view its nether regions.

I backed up even farther. "I'll take your word for it, and it's a she, not a her." I watched as he cuddled the tiny dog close to his dress shirt, now wrinkled beyond redemption. "And you still can't keep it—her."

"That's what I said, a her. And I know. I'm watching her for the client." He spoke the last word with relish. "So, you wanna watch her while I go on the next job?"

"Absolutely not." My voice was firm and the smile slid off his face. "You either take her with you or back to her owner. Bringing animals to Mrs. Goldstein's apartment is not part of the agreement."

"Speaking of, where is Mrs. G?" He stepped farther into the apartment, bending down to set the puppy on the ground. It instantly squatted, leaving a small wet spot on Nora's immaculate carpet.

"Brent, get that creature out of here! I not only need to clean up after a dead body, I've now got to clean up after a dog." I glared at him, hands on my hips.

"Dead body? What dead body?" He grabbed the puppy to his broad chest as though it could act as a shield, staring at me with both eyebrows hovering around his hairline.

Oh, fabulous. I'd let slip exactly what we'd wanted to keep from him. So much for my carefully concocted oven inspection story.

"It's complicated." I sighed as I flopped back onto the sofa, patting the cushion beside me. "Here, sit down while I explain. Staring up at you is giving me a neck ache. And keep that dog on your lap." I gave the adorable bundle of fur a hard stare. I didn't want this one to leave its calling card on Nora's carpet.

With as little fanfare as possible, as Brent was the type of student who needed only the basics in order to comprehend a new concept, I told him about the ongoing clash of personalities between Nora and Linda and the many nasty tricks they'd played on one another.

"And to be honest, Brent, I wouldn't have put it past her to fake her death in Nora's kitchen to give us a heart attack." I clutched at the front of my shirt, recalling the ride to the apartment from the coffee house. "It's almost how I feel when you drive."

"What's wrong with my driving?" He sounded hurt, a great big child sitting there clutching his puppy.

It made me feel guilty. For about a second.

"Let's say I hope you clean up after dogs better than you navigate Portland's roads." I slapped my palms against my thighs and stood, gesturing to the front door. "Now get that dog back to her owner and make sure you take care of the rest of the jobs, all right?"

With a pouting Brent sent on his way, I worked on scrubbing up the evidence of the dog's visit, glancing occasionally over my shoulder toward the kitchen. I hated the idea of the mess I knew was in there, but I wasn't that enthusiastic about cleaning it up either.

"Yoo hoo! Is anyone home?"

Nora's apartment was busier than The Friendly Bean on payday. I turned around from where I was working on restoring the carpet to its pre-puppy state to see the building's concierge standing there, her eyes wide as she stared at me.

"Can I help you?" I managed to get to my feet without falling over, each knee sending out a warning shot as I straightened my legs. "Nora isn't here at the moment." I stared back at her, noting her hair looked worse than Nora's did, if that was even possible. I made a mental note to find out whether they saw the same stylist.

"Actually, I ran up here to see if there was anything I could do to help you. To help Nora, I mean." She edged farther inside the living room, looking around curiously as she did. "So, where did she find the body?"

"Body?" I managed to insert an element of surprise into my voice, tilting my head to the side like an inquisitive robin. Or maybe a tropical bird. I was beginning to feel very much out of my comfort zone, what with Phoebe Hayward, the Portland PD, and now the concierge moving in and out of Nora's apartment like some Neil Simon farce. "What body might that be? And I'm sorry, but I didn't catch your name. I'm Gwen Franklin." Rubbing my damp hand against my leg, I held it out.

"I'm Patsy, Patsy Reilly." She took my hand and gave it a brief shake before dropping it and tucking her hands inside her pockets. "And I'm talking about the body they hauled out of here not too long ago."

"Oh, *that* body." I gave a short laugh, trying to sound as if there were so many bodies in and out of here I couldn't keep track of them. "She was in the kitchen. The body was, I mean. And Nora was as well. In the kitchen." I was babbling now, but I was darned if I was going to give out any more information. "It was Linda Fletcher," I added helpfully and then could have bit my tongue.

"Really? Linda Fletcher, huh?" Patsy started toward the kitchen, her face avid with interest. "Those two hated each other. Are you sure Nora didn't do it?"

I hurried after her and jumped in front of her to stand in the kitchen's doorway, effectively blocking her from going any farther without physically moving me out of the way.

"I'm positive she didn't do it. And if you aren't going to help me with the cleaning, you should probably go back downstairs and do whatever it is you do." I folded my arms across my chest and affixed my sternest expression on my face, the one that could quell an entire classroom full of rowdy teens. "Now, please."

"Fine." She gave an injured sniff, turning around and heading across the room. "You think you can keep the riffraff out of here by raising the rent, but it still doesn't work."

"If you're referring to Nora, she isn't riffraff! And I'll thank you to knock next time," I yelled as I charged to the front door, giving it a hearty slam behind her retreating back.

Feeling suddenly exhausted, I walked over to the couch and dropped down, curling my legs up and closing my eyes. Dealing with bodies and puppies, not to mention crazy stepchildren and the police department, had worn me out.

I woke to see Nora's face bending close to mine, a concerned expression in her eyes. Startled, I sat up and managed to bump my forehead against her chin, sending me back against the cushions in a daze.

"Gwen? How many fingers am I holding up?"

I opened my eyes, squinting at Nora's hands waving in front of my face.

"I have no idea, especially since you won't keep your hand still." I struggled back up, this time more slowly, and waited until the room came back into focus. "So, how'd the PD visit go?"

"Fine." She shrugged, bending down to unfasten the straps on her shoes as she kicked them off. "That's better." She groaned as she sank down beside me. "I swear, I think I'm getting too old to wear those things." "Never," I replied promptly. "You'll be wearing stilettos when you're eighty."

"Which is exactly how old I'm feeling at the moment." She bent over and rubbed her toes, giving them each a tug until they popped. "That's better. And I need some decent coffee pronto. The stuff they gave me at the police department looked and tasted like last year's river sludge."

"No problem." I got to my feet and then paused, cognizant of the newly cleaned spot in front of the couch. Should I tell her? No. I headed toward the kitchen. It could wait. I'd let Brent tell her so he could take the blame and the fallout. With that cheery thought, I made a fresh pot of coffee, determinedly ignoring the crime scene leftovers behind me.

Once Nora had gotten one cup of coffee in her and started on the next, I broached the topic buzzing in my head like a crazed wasp. Why had they focused in on her? Did they think she killed Linda Fletcher?

"Oh, that." Nora impatiently batted away my questions. "Apparently, they start with the nearest person to the crime scene, and, since it's my apartment, that would be yours truly. Believe you me, Gwen, by the time I got finished with those clowns, they didn't know which end was up." She smiled suddenly, that mischievous glint I recognized back in her eyes. "I did kinda point out that you were on the scene as well."

"Hang on there a minute, 'bestie.'" I spoke automatically, using the air quotes that usually made me cringe. "I had nothing to do with your little tiff with Linda. If anyone is a suspect here, it's you."

Nora gave a head toss, acting as though the faux rattail was still in place. It made her look like she had a bad case of nervous tics in her neck. "Just returning the favor, sweetie. Now, how about more coffee?" She held out her empty mug, her smile as bright as the sun on a beautiful Portland day.

Oh, Nora. I had to love the gal. I really did. We might butt heads, but we were fiercely loyal to each another, jealously guarding our friendship against outside disruptions— like a visit to the Portland Police Department.

She'd come back with a new dose of energy, sore feet aside, and now was beginning to get a good-sized caffeine buzz as well. The woman would be climbing the walls soon if I didn't rein her in quickly.

"It's been a long day for me." I surprised myself with a wide yawn. "I'm going to need to get some shut-eye soon or I won't be good for anything tomorrow."

"Party pooper," objected Nora. "It's only seven thirty. And speaking of pooper, how'd our boy do today?"

"It's already past my bedtime." I stood, swaying slightly. Maybe I did need to see a doctor. I'd heard of athletes getting concussions from tripping over untied shoelaces. "And Brent did fine. In fact, he did better than fine. In my opinion, if we can figure out how to swing it, money-wise," here Nora gave a deprecatory snort, "I vote we take him on as a full-time employee."

"There's no issue with the money. And I'll take your word for it since you know him better than I do." To my amusement, she yawned loudly as well, tapping her mouth with shiny fake nails. "Oh, stop grinning, you. I need oxygen, that's all."

"If that's what you think." I reached out one hand and pulled my visibly tired pal to her feet. "Come on. Walk me to the door and lock it behind me, okay?"

"How're you going to get home?" Nora let me lead her to the door, her words almost swallowed up by another gaping yawn. "And don't tell me you're calling Brent. I won't be able to rest if you do."

I laughed, shaking my head as I stepped into the hall.

"I'll walk. It's not that far, and, besides, I need to sort things out in my head or I'll be the one not sleeping."

"Well, be careful out there. I don't want to lose my best friend because she gets hit by a crazy Uber driver."

"I'll try to stay on the sidewalks and out of the street, all right?"

"As if that would make a difference with the kid driving." Nora smiled at me and I could see the bags under her eyes. Knowing Nora, they'd be designer bags, of course. "I'll see you in the bright and early."

"Absolutely. And I'll bring breakfast."

Her door was already closing, and I waited a moment longer to listen for the sound of the safety lock being turned. Satisfied, I walked toward the elevator, purposely keeping my eyes averted from Linda Fletcher's empty apartment.

* * * *

I managed to combat next morning's sluggishness with a cup of Organic Sumatra from Portland Coffee Roasters. Dark and perfectly smooth, it provided the figurative kick in the pants I needed after a rather restless night. I flipped on the radio to the local news station, only half listening, as I threw together an easy breakfast casserole to share with Nora and Brent.

"…helping the police with their initial investigation. Mrs. Goldstein said as she was leaving the police station, 'If you want to catch a killer, you need to be a little quicker than these guys,' followed by a laugh. We asked Portland PD if they had a response but so far have heard nothing. Back to you, Brian."

I had to smile. Only Nora could get away with saying something that far out, and in front of the media to boot. Of course, only Nora had been targeted by the police at this point. Who would be next? I'd lain awake longer than I'd wanted to last night, despite the walk home, trying to figure out who might want Linda Fletcher dead, or—and this troubled me far worse—who might want Nora dead and had killed her verbal sparring partner by mistake.

I was still thinking along these depressing lines when Brent arrived to drive me to Nora's.

"Good morning, Miss F."

Brent's greeting was cheerful and I answered in kind, trying to set aside my current worries.

"How did the rest of your day go after you left Mrs. Goldstein's apartment yesterday?"

"It was cool." He pulled out into the road without checking his mirrors or looking over his shoulder. I shut my eyes and held onto the casserole dish as if it was a lifeline. "And guess what? That last lady told me that I could have one of her new puppies! Now how's that for a work bonus?"

"Very cool, as long as your mom's okay with it. That might be two dogs too many, in my opinion. And just an FYI, Brent. I didn't mention anything to Nor—Mrs. Goldstein about that puppy accident, all right?"

"No worries. I wasn't planning on saying nothing either."

He looked over at me and grinned, completely missing the stop sign at the end of my normally quiet street. I didn't bother pointing it out, or the grammar issue, but held on tightly, muttering my one and only prayer as we sped towards Nora's luxury apartment building and another day of mayhem.

Chapter 4

"I swear I'm going to start walking over here." I spoke under my breath as we sat watching Brent shovel in a third helping of my hash brown and egg casserole. "Either that, or I'm going to learn how to magically transport myself to your place and save the daily carnival ride with that kid."

I shot Brent a look that could subdue the most truculent student, but he took no notice. Maybe if I'd suddenly turned into a large breakfast burrito or a gallon of milk, he might have noticed me. I'd never seen someone so intent on his food before. If he drove with that same concentration, he'd be the safest driver in Portland.

"You made it here in one piece, so that's a plus." Nora reached around her own plate and gave my arm a pat. "First things first, though. We need to get a cleaning crew in here to give this place a good once-over, and then we need to make a few phone calls to set the day's appointments."

"And who's this 'we,' woman? Have you suddenly got a mouse in your pocket?" I turned a glare on her, still fuming from my daily dose of nearly being killed.

"Sounds like someone's sense of humor got up on the wrong side of bed this morning." Nora pushed back her chair and carried her plate over to the sink. "I'm merely suggesting that one of us make the phone calls and the other one handle the cleanup crew, that's all."

"Well, why didn't you say so?" I reached over to hand my plate to her as well. "I volunteer for phone duty."

Portland folks liked to get up early and get their coffee quotient started well before breakfast, so I wasn't surprised to find that all four of that day's clients were already up and running. With three of them opting for a thirty-minute dog walk and the other asking for a four-hour pet sitting session, Two Sisters Pet Valet Services was fully booked until three. That would give us plenty of time to do a little digging into Nora's background and see if we could turn up anyone who might want her dead.

Brent had finally stopped eating, scraping the last portion of the casserole from my baking dish with his fork. I checked the pan carefully to make sure he hadn't scraped any of the Teflon coating off as well. He'd also drunk three glasses of milk and eaten four pieces of buttered toast. In my opinion, he had more than enough food in him to last through the pet sitting assignment. I hoped.

"Brent, you're in luck." Nora handed him the list of pet walking jobs, along with a big smile. "All three of these are right here in the building, so you can take the little darlings across the street to the dog park to do their business."

"So, what're you two gonna be doing while I'm out there doing all the work?" His tone was suspicious, and I instantly adopted an injured expression.

"Brent Mayfair, how do you think the paperwork gets done? By magic?" I snapped my fingers in his face, making him jump back. "No, sir, it doesn't. Someone has to stay here and work on that. Of course, if you'd rather do that instead of getting some fresh air, Nor—Mrs. Goldstein and I can take over." I managed to give my shoulders an extra droop and noticed Nora was doing the same. Between the two of us, we looked like a pair of down-and-outs without one thin dime between us.

"Nah, that's okay, Miss F." He'd backed another step away from me, hands held up in front of him as if to ward off a case of hard work. "Besides, my gramma always said that when folks get to a certain age, they can break a lot of bones. I'd sure hate for you two fine ladies to break anything out there."

And with that, he was gone.

"I can see exactly why you enjoyed teaching high school so much." Nora's words were underpinned with admiration, and I couldn't help preening inwardly. "They're so easily outsmarted, aren't they?"

"You have no idea." My voice and expression were as enigmatic as the Mona Lisa. "Okay, partner, what's next?"

"I got a hold of some outfit called Karen's Kleen-Up Krew and she promised to be here by ten." Nora shook her head in disgust. "Just why it is that people feel the need to have a cutesy name, I'll never understand."

"Maybe it's because she didn't have a 'sister' to run the business with her." I bracketed the word "sister" in a set of air quotes.

Nora snorted, then turned to look around the kitchen. "Well, they won't have much to do in here, except some disinfecting and some stain removal." She bent over to take a closer look at the floor where Linda's body had lain. "At least she didn't bleed out that much." She snickered. "I always knew she wasn't human."

I had to roll my eyes. From everything that Nora had told me about their ongoing feud, and from the few incidents I'd witnessed, I had to agree. No one with that much vitriol in their system could be a member of the human race.

That thought was interrupted by a tentative knocking on the front door. Nora and I stared at each other, neither of us making a move to answer it.

"It's your apartment." I swept out one arm in an extravagant gesture, giving her a mocking bow. "Your place, your door."

"I'll remember that. And the way you shopped me yesterday as well."

"I did *not* 'shop you.' I simply pointed you out."

My words bounced off her back as I followed her into the living room. Nora yanked open the door and revealed a pair of nervous women, each one clutching a large handbag as though it carried precious cargo. She took one look at them and gave a great groan as she grabbed her chest. I rushed over to her, afraid that she was having a heart attack.

"First Phoebe and now you two. And get off me, Gwen." She shook her arm away from me and stepped back from the doorway with a sigh. "Might as well come in. But no coffee," she added in a warning tone. "You're not staying that long." She turned and looked at me, her tone and expression exasperated, as if she'd just discovered gum on the bottom of a pair of Jimmy Choos. "Meet my stepdaughters, the Terrible Twosome."

"How do you do." I spoke automatically, proffering my hand to the air between them.

They each shook it in turn, their own hands feeling as insubstantial as bird wings. Come to think of it, they reminded me of birds. Two tiny wrens, each one dressed in brown, light brown hair piled atop their heads like nests. I could almost see them pecking at the ground in an eager search for a morning bug or two. Maybe they thought Nora would be a wormy jackpot, so to speak.

I shook my head, trying to dispel the visual. Not everyone was out to get Nora. This could, in fact, be an innocent visit by a pair of gals who were truly concerned about their stepmother's well-being.

And pigs might fly.

"Nice to meet you," they both tittered back at me, and I couldn't resist a sideways glance at Nora. She was staring impatiently at the three of us, practically tapping one foot as she waited.

"If I can interrupt this charming display of niceties, I'd like to close the door. If that's all right with you," she said with exaggerated politeness to the two women.

"Oh, that's perfectly all right, isn't it, Mercy?"

"It most certainly is, Grace."

More tittering and head bobbing. I had to hide a smile behind a sudden fit of coughing.

"Mercy and Grace are...were...my stepdaughters from my second marriage. Or maybe it was my third."

The two small women set up a small protest at her words.

Nora rolled her eyes. "All right, it was my second. Whatever. Anyhoo, these two haven't shown their faces for, what, girls? At least ten years? Or twenty?"

"Nora, why don't you and your guests come in and have a seat?" I stepped back and indicated the nearest sofa.

Mercy and Grace looked gratefully at me and began inching inside.

Nora promptly walked over and plopped down in the exact middle, forcing our visitors to sit down on either side of her. I shot her a look that said 'play nice'—at least that's the message I hoped I was sending. Nora, on the other hand, didn't seem intent on being anything at the moment except her snarkiest self. The two sisters looked as though they'd already shrunk a couple inches each.

Sighing, I sat across from the trio, affixing a pleasant expression on my face. I was becoming used to being Nora's emotional counterweight, the nice cop to her very, very bad one, the sugar to her spice. Or maybe it was vinegar. An old saying about honey and vinegar and flies slipped into my head, and I completely missed Nora's opening gambit.

"How can you say that!" exclaimed Mercy, her eyes wide in shock. "We would never want that to happen. Would we, Sister?"

"Absolutely not," agreed Grace in a pious tone. "We are lifetime volunteers at St. Bridget's Family Center."

She said that as if it was the mark of someone with a spotless reputation, someone as clean and pure as the driven snow. Having seen quite a bit of snow in my lifetime, though, I was well aware of what it could conceal underneath. Rocky soil. Trash piles. Dead bodies.

"And I could really give a rat's a...patootie what you two nutcases do all day." Nora examined her nails as if they were the most important things in the room.

I groaned inwardly; I knew that tone. It generally heralded the storm's imminent arrival. Jumping to my feet, I redoubled my smile and stared hard at Nora. "Nora, dear, why don't I make us some tea?"

"Not on your life, Gwen. These two imbeciles were leaving."

To my surprise, the sisters rose as one, each clasping her handbag to her scrawny chest like a shield. In less than ten seconds, they were gone.

Nora slumped back against the sofa's cushions, and I was concerned to see how much that little exchange had taken out of her. Of course, it must have been unpleasant, seeing two reminders of a past failure on top of the visit from Phoebe.

Then I remembered her bank account. If anything, Nora had come out of all of her marriages more than a conqueror. In fact, she was quite the modern Viking. Plundering and pillaging wherever the latest husband's money was kept.

Still, I didn't like the way she looked at the moment and told her so.

"I'm taking stock." She sat with her head back and eyes closed. "Don't get your panties all bunched up, Gwen."

"Whether you like it or not, I'm getting you some tea." I headed for the kitchen, my back stiff at her last words.

"Put some brandy in it," she called after me. "I could use a hefty dose after those two. For medicinal purposes, of course."

"You're going to become a raving alcoholic," I muttered to myself as I rattled the mugs against the counter. "That'll go nicely with your raving lunatic mind."

"I heard that! And I don't care what time of the day it is. Folks can get sick at all hours." There was a slight pause. "And I am *not* a lunatic. *I* was not the one teaching adolescent maniacs all those years."

"Blah, blah, blah. Fine." I reached for the bottle of brandy, my lips folded together as I added a slosh to her teacup. If my best friend was going to go all alcoholic on me, she'd better be ready for an intervention. I could do it, too. I'd seen the shows on television where a person's loved ones ganged up on them and offered an ultimatum.

Besides, Brent was big enough to haul her skinny butt out of here and to rehab if I asked him to.

"Ah, that's better." Nora took an exaggerated slurp from her cup and smiled at me. "You should try it. It'll make you relax."

"I don't need to relax." I spoke through gritted teeth as I sat ramrod straight on the edge of my chair. "What I need to do right now is figure out why someone wants you dead." I raised my voice as she began a halfhearted protest. "And if there's going to be a parade of stepchildren coming through that door, I think I'll go back to my own place, thank you very much."

To my surprise, Nora began to giggle. It couldn't be the brandy. I hadn't put that much in her tea. Carefully placing her cup on a nearby table, she leaned back against the sofa and howled with laughter.

Standing, I glared at her, hands planted firmly on my hips. That way, I wouldn't be tempted to kill her.

"I don't know what's so funny about wanting to keep you safe." My voice was stiff with hurt pride. "It's your life, though. You can count me out of this circus."

"It's not you." She managed to gasp the words out between bouts of hilarity. "Did you see them? That hair! And those handbags!" She went off into another fit of laughter, wiping her streaming eyes.

"And their names." I gave a tentative smile. "Who in their right mind names their kids Mercy and Grace?" It suddenly struck me as hilarious. I'd only had one tiny sip of brandy, cross my heart. I joined Nora on the sofa, unable to control a fit of giggles.

"Are you two all right?"

In all the noise we were making, neither one of us had heard the Boy Wonder come in. I took one look at his concerned face and began giggling again. I felt as unrestrained as if I'd been the one drinking the brandy.

"Miss F? Should I call someone?" Brent stood there uncertainly, staring at the two of us as we writhed about in a rather undignified manner.

I suddenly noticed he was trying to hold something small and wiggly next to his chest and sat up, wiping my eyes.

"Brent Mayfair, what in heaven's name do you think you're doing? I told you that you couldn't bring that thing back here." I pointed at the tiny puppy, its soft snout emerging from behind his large hands. "I don't think Mrs. Goldstein is going to appreciate you bringing work back to her apartment."

"But the lady said I could keep her."

I thought I could hear tears in his voice.

"And my mom won't let me keep her at my house, so she's got to go somewhere."

"Absolutely. Right back to her owner. That's where."

I pointed at the door, ignoring the look of despair on his face. Large shoulders sagging, he turned and began a pitiful shuffling toward the door.

"Oh, quit your blubbering and get back in here, boy," Nora called after him and turned to glower at me, her happy mood evaporated. "So you knew about this already?"

I shrugged. "Maybe. I can't say you've given me a lot of chances to tell you, though." I crossed my fingers mentally. It was only a tiny lie, wasn't it? Crossed fingers should take care of that.

"And she didn't even tell you about the puppy doing a number one on your carpet, either." Brent sounded proud, looking at me as though I was his hero. "She cleaned it up good, too."

"It's 'well,' not 'good.'" I corrected him automatically, keeping one eye on Nora as I slithered to the farthest end of the sofa. "And yes, it did come out of the carpet without much effort." I shot Nora a quick glance. "Of course, Karen's Kleen-Up Krew can take a look at it, if you ask them."

"Oh, my word!" Nora slapped her forehead. "I completely forgot about that. Thanks for reminding me." She glanced at her cell phone. "They should be here in the next ten minutes or so. Brent, did you get the potty patrol finished?"

Glad to have the topic changed, I reached for my cup and took the last sip of very cold tea. "Should we be here while they're cleaning up in there?" I pointed my chin toward the kitchen.

"Why not?" Nora gave a nonchalant shrug. "Besides, I thought we could make a list of my stepchildren, in case the rest of them decide to pop in for a visit." She shot me a wicked smile. "You know they're all chomping at the bit to see me six feet under."

"Oh, that reminds me."

We both turned to face Brent, watching as he pulled a long white envelope from his pocket.

"That lady downstairs, the one who answers questions? She gave this to me and told me to give it to you right away." He smiled sheepishly as he handed it to Nora. "Guess I kinda forgot."

"Patsy Reilly," I murmured to myself, leaning over to see what it said on the envelope's front.

And stared in dismay at two words: *You're next.* Underneath them was drawn a crude skull and crossbones, almost cartoonish in style.

Nora and I looked at one another, eyes wide with shock.

"You'd better open it." My hands began to shake. "Or I can do it, if you don't want to."

"Want me to get it?" Brent thrust the wriggling puppy in my direction. "Here, you take her, Miss F."

"I told you I'm allergic to dogs." I waved the dog away. "And no, Mrs. Goldstein doesn't need you to open anything for her."

We watched silently as Nora slid a shaking finger underneath the gummed flap.

"Hold on!" I reached for the envelope. "Don't touch anything else, Nora. They can get DNA from saliva, where someone licked that."

"It's a press-n-seal." Her tone was dry, and I was glad to see she was recovering from the initial scare. "And who knows who's already handled this, including Ace Ventura over there." She nodded at Brent.

He grinned proudly at her words, petting the puppy's soft fur with a hand big enough to cover it in one swipe.

"That wasn't a compliment," Nora added, and I watched his face fall.

"It means you do a great job at taking care of animals." I spoke hurriedly, giving him a warm smile to counterbalance Nora's sarcasm.

"I know." He gave us both a vigorous nod. "Animals like me." He lifted the small dog and rubbed it against his cheek lovingly.

I wanted to sneeze just watching him.

"And it's a good thing they do. Don't forget you've got a four-hour pet sitting assignment at eleven." Nora slid a folded paper out of the envelope and smoothed it out on her lap.

This time her reaction was enough to make me jump. The puppy gave a small yelp as Brent squeezed it to him, his eyes wide as he stared from me to Nora.

"Nora? What does it say?" I tried to keep my voice even, not wanting to add to the tension.

Without a word she thrust it at me and then covered her face with trembling hands. I quickly scanned the paper, my heart starting to hammer as loudly as I read aloud what was written there.

"'Nora GOLD DIGGER. You took my money and I want it back. All of it.'" There was another drawing, a hangman's noose looped around her name in a tight embrace.

I turned to stare at my best friend. I'd been right. Someone wanted her dead.

Chapter 5

We sat staring at one another, Nora's face drained of all color while my own felt clammy from the cold sweat that had broken out. This was definitely not a joke, any more than Linda Fletcher's dead body had been.

"I thought your last name was Goldstein." Brent stood there watching us. "Sorry, Mrs. Gold digger."

"Brent!" We shouted his name in concert and he hurriedly backed toward the door.

"What did I say?"

The puppy reached out and licked his nose.

"I only said that I didn't…"

"Brent, go away. Just go, all right?" I pointed to the door, a sudden weariness causing my shoulders to sag. This retirement gig was taking more out of me than teaching a classroom full of teenagers ever did. "We'll call you when it's time for the next job, okay?"

"You don't need to yell at me." He edged through the doorway. "I only wanted to help." His eyes were round as he poked his head back inside.

"*Out. Now.*" I pointed to the hallway, using my loudest teacher voice.

He skedaddled without another peep.

Nora and I sat there in silence. I slid closer to her and put one arm around her shoulders. She was shaking, and it made me angry. How dare someone threaten my best friend like that? She was anything but a gold digger. In fact, she should've been awarded a purple heart for everything she'd put up with in her various marriages. All right, maybe she hadn't chosen wisely when it came to men. A lot of women didn't, right? Still, to call her a gold digger when all she'd done was take what was rightfully hers was absurd.

"Hey, girl." I said the words softly, giving her shoulders a small shake. "Let's have some more of that brandy, okay? Then we'll get the list made." And then we'll call the police, I added silently.

She didn't answer. Instead, she shook off my arm and slowly got to her feet, shuffling dejectedly toward her bedroom. "I'm going to lie down. Come and get me when the cleaning people get here."

"Oh, no, you don't." I jumped to my feet and went after her, firmly turning her around and guiding her back to the sofa. "You're *not* going to leave me to handle this on my own. No way, no how."

"There's nothing to handle." Nora dropped back down on the sofa, her limp form enough to make anyone worry.

Anyone but me, that was. This was one great acting job, in my opinion. I'd seen enough in my years as a high school teacher to know the signs. She'd either snap out of it or I'd snap it for her.

A sharp rap on the door made me jump. Giving Nora's floppy arm a non-too-gentle tug, I pulled her to her feet and pushed her toward the door.

"Answer it, Nora. It's probably the cleaning service."

It was. Karen, a tiny woman who was smaller even than the Timorous Twosome, smiled at us as she marched into the apartment. She carried a large metal bucket filled with cleaning supplies and had a plastic bag of rags hooked around her wrist. She looked from me to Nora and back, one thin eyebrow lifted in question. "You called about a deep kitchen clean?"

I almost laughed aloud. That was one way to put it. How Nora would explain the blood spatter and the fingerprint dust, I had no idea, but I could hardly wait to hear her try.

"Right this way, please. I guess I was expecting an entire crew, not just one person." Nora was still in her woe-is-me mode, her shoulders drooping as she walked to the kitchen, but I let her carry on.

Trust me, if she truly needed me, I'd be there in a heartbeat.

"Unfortunately, there was a slight accident in here yesterday. If you could get the stains off the floor, I'd sure appreciate it."

"What sort of stains?" Karen sounded suspicious, but she followed Nora into the kitchen anyway.

I silently counted to three, waiting for her reaction.

"Oh, my God! Is that *blood*?"

There was the sound of crashing metal and a loud screech as she dropped her cleaning bucket. I cautiously peeked around the corner and saw Nora hopping around like an angry stork, holding on to one foot and cursing up a blue streak. Karen was doing some sort of dance, both hands covering her eyes as the cleaning supplies rolled around the floor.

Nearly three hours later, the kitchen was spotless and Nora was settled back on the couch, her injured foot propped up on the cushions next to her. Karen had finally stopped spinning long enough for me to explain what had happened, and she'd gone to work, scrubbing the floor with a vigor that had threatened to take the design off the tile.

I'd convinced Nora to give her a little extra pay for the shock, assuring her it was worth it to keep Karen from running straight back out of the apartment.

"She should be paying me," Nora grumbled, reaching over to gingerly poke at her swollen big toe. "I tell you, Gwen, she's lucky I'm not suing the pants off her. Who uses a metal bucket anymore?"

I didn't bother answering. Instead, I brought her an ice pack, a notepad, and a pencil.

"What's this for?" She stared at the items, a truculent expression on her face.

"The ice pack is for your toe." I spoke with more patience than I was actually feeling. "The paper is for that list you still need to write. Or I can write it while you give me the names."

"Oh, fine." She gave an exaggerated sigh, crossing her arms over her chest in a petulant motion. "Get ready. Some of these names are doozies."

"Worse than Grace or Mercy?" I looked up from the notepad, grinning. To my relief, she smiled back. Crisis averted. "I must have married every man in Oregon who liked strange names. First up, Jebediah."

"Jedediah?" I was sure I'd heard incorrectly.

"Nope. Jebediah. With a B." She laughed at my befuddled expression. "Told you they were odd. My first husband's mother was a direct descendent from the Mayflower Biddles and boy, did he like reminding me of that little tidbit."

I stared at her for a moment, uncertain if this was a joke or not. I didn't see any mirth on her face. Instead, I thought I spotted a trace of sadness, a souvenir from a time she didn't really like to revisit.

"All right, Jeb-with-a-B it is."

Next was Verity, which was actually kind of cute, and then Charity, which smacked of all things Plymouth Rock and Puritan. By the time we'd completed what amounted to a roll call of obscure names from the offspring of husbands one to five, it was nearly three and I was starving. The breakfast casserole seemed long ago and far away, and I was ready for lunch. My stomach, always one step ahead, gave a loud grumble.

"Are you hungry?" Nora glanced up from her cell phone, a secret smile tucked in one corner of her mouth. She'd been texting someone in between names, and, judging by that smile, it was a M-A-N. Maybe I needed to ask her what *his* children were named.

"Ravenous. Should we go out or stay here?"

"I vote for out." Nora stood, testing her weight on the injured foot before dropping back down with a grimace on her face. "Or not. Maybe we'd better call out for something."

"Or I can walk to somewhere nearby." I glanced at the phone Nora had tossed aside. "Besides, Brent will be back soon and he'll be starving."

Nora gave a short laugh. "When isn't that kid hungry? Did you see how much he ate this morning? If I ate like that, I'd be a Two-Ton Tessie."

"It's his age." I lifted both arms and stretched, giving my lower back a twist at the same time. "That's better. I'm beginning to feel like a bump on a log with all this sitting."

"You could start walking the dogs." There was a mischievous glint in Nora's eyes. "Brent would probably be happy to let you take over that part of the business."

"Oh, hilarious." I was tempted to poke my tongue out at her grinning face. "Who'd stay here and keep the weird stepchildren away?"

"If they keep arriving like they have been, we've only got seven more to go." Nora held out one hand, using the other to tick off names. "Let's see. Phoebe's already made her appearance, no big surprise. Mercy and Grace as well, although I have no idea why, do you?"

I shook my head. "I don't recall them explaining why they showed up."

Nora smiled smugly. "I didn't give them a chance, did I? Had them on the run before you could say boo."

An idea was beginning to take shape in my hunger-addled brain. "Isn't that about the time you got the letter?"

Nora stared back at me, her expression blank as she worked on connecting my words to the white envelope.

"You're right." Her eyes held a hint of fear as she felt in her pocket for the letter. "Do you think *they* left it?"

I gave a one-shouldered shrug as I considered her question. "Maybe. They didn't get a chance to say their piece while they were here, and, quite honestly, they both looked one sandwich short of a picnic, if you know what I mean."

Nora shivered as if a sudden chill had come into the room. "Do I ever. When they were young, around seven or so, I caught them in the backyard trying to make one of the cats drink rubbing alcohol."

"Good grief." I stared at Nora, trying to get my head around something as crazy as that. "Did they get in trouble? And did the poor cat get away?"

"No and yes."

She laid her head back against the sofa's cushions, closing her eyes. I could see her scalp from where I was sitting, the poor frizzled hair just starting to grow back in. Thankfully, the hairpiece was still under the couch, since I didn't think it was doing her remaining hair much good.

"I managed to save the cat, which I gave to a neighbor, by the way, and marched those two menaces straight to my husband. And you know what that imbecile did?"

I shook my head.

"He laughed and said they were just 'high-spirited girls, trying to learn about their world.'"

I was dumbfounded. Who in their right mind would say something that ignorant? Ask any psychologist worth their salt and they'd say torturing animals is an indication of future bad behavior. I said as much.

Nora gave a snort and sat back up. "I can tell you I watched my own food and drink after that little escapade and got the heck out of Dodge. I made a killing off him for pain and suffering, or something like that. Of course, the lawyer got thirty percent of the takings, but it was still a hefty settlement."

"And now they want it back." I looked soberly at Nora. "And it looks like they want to make a killing as well."

We were sitting there in silence when the door opened. Brent stepped inside cautiously, poised to run again, the puppy now zipped into the front of his jacket.

"Hey, Miss F? Can I come in now?"

"Sure, boy wonder. Come in and take a load off."

Nora invited him inside, giving the furry carpet cannon a scratch behind the ears. I was certain it was already planning the next target on which to off-load.

I wasn't so naïve, though. "Brent, hold it right there."

He froze mid-step, one size-fifteen hovering above the floor, an expression on his face that gave it all away— to the active observer, that was. And Nora didn't seem to be observing anything at the moment, except the digital readout on her cell phone, with a dreamy expression.

Sighing resignedly, I lifted one hand and pointed to the kitchen. "If you must bring her with you, at least put her in the kitchen. She can't hurt the tile, and you can block her in there with a chair tipped on its side."

Nora didn't have anything like a baby safety gate in her apartment. But I knew how to jury-rig anything from nothing, thanks to my dad. He'd been the world's best at concocting a packed lunch from a single bread slice with mustard squeezed onto it in fancy patterns, or creating a baby jail from the nearest piece of furniture.

My five younger siblings had been constant inmates until the day they were caught trying to stage a jailbreak by tying my mother's prized hand-embroidered kitchen towels together so they could scale over the stack of barstools he'd used to pen them in that morning. With two sets of twins and a toddler, all under the age of four, it had been constant chaos in our house.

Not so in Nora's childhood home. As the only child of a self-made rocket scientist and a classical music teacher, she'd never been held captive in her own kitchen-slash-dining room to keep her out of the way. Maybe, I thought with sudden insight, this was why she liked men so much. Her first exposure to one of the breed had been a pleasant one, full of adventure and fun.

Recalling my experiences with my brothers, especially the older twins, sent a shudder through my body. If I hadn't known better, Grace and Mercy could have been their sidekicks in another life.

"Like this, Miss F?"

I gave myself a mental shake, staring at Brent for a moment while I attempted to drag myself back to the present predicament. He'd gotten one of Nora's hardwood and wrought iron kitchen chairs and sat it in front of the kitchen doorway. The puppy sat underneath it, watching the three humans with something akin to amusement, judging by the little pink tongue that lolled from the side of its mouth. Before I could answer, it trotted from under the furniture and headed straight toward me, the only allergic one in its vicinity. I could swear this thing had a sixth sense, one that could identify and latch onto the person whose reaction to pet dander made them look like they'd taken a dip in strawberry jam, seeds and all.

Already scratching the inside of my elbows, where a nasty-looking patch of small red bumps had appeared from nowhere, I leapt to my feet and began performing a jig down the hall toward the bathroom.

"Nora, could you please help him corral that dander machine in the kitchen? And Brent, obviously you don't have the sense God gave a goose." I paused mid-jig and made tipping motions with my hands, trying to show him how to gently lay the chair on its side in order to block the kitchen doorway.

"If you do it that way, the dog can't get out and I can stay in the living room, instead of having to shout at you two from the bathroom." I glared at my audience, including the small animal in my invective.

In response, it sniffed the carpet near my feet and silently let a stream of puppy pee hit the floor.

"Chaos" is a word that is sometimes misused. Having three dryer loads of clothes finish at once isn't chaos, but having a washing machine that refuses to drain the rinse water definitely is. And with Nora screeching at me to "do something" and Brent alternately scolding and caressing the small dog, it was definitely chaotic in that luxurious apartment. Ignoring both of them, I stomped back toward the kitchen, a nascent sneeze building in the back of my throat and my nose.

"Lay the chair on its side, like this." I put action to my words, letting the heavy chair hit the ceramic tile with more noise than was necessary. "Put the dog in the kitchen, Brent. And get that roll of paper towels, along with the clear spray bottle under the sink." I pointed to the cabinet next to the industrial-sized refrigerator. "Add water to it and then hand it to me. Can you do that?"

"Yes, Miss F. I'm not stupid, you know. I did graduate from high school." Brent's tone was sulky and he moved toward the kitchen with all the speed of a teenaged sloth who'd just rolled out of bed.

I took the paper towels and spray bottle from him without a word, keeping my gaze on the puppy. It had zeroed in on the area that had been scrubbed by Karen, its stubby tail held high like a signal flag on a ship.

"Can you look in the pantry and find the vinegar?"

I addressed the comment to Brent but kept watching the dog, curious to see how it would react to the place where the blood had been earlier. To my amazement, it sat down on top of the exact spot, lifted up its muzzle, and emitted a tiny howl.

Chapter 6

"Well, would you look at that." Nora had hobbled over to the kitchen door and stood just behind me, both hands on her hips.

I stepped farther into the kitchen, ignoring a moment of squeamishness, and knelt beside the wriggling ball of fur. Allergies or not, this deserved a closer look.

"Nora, I think we've got us a bloodhound." I inched closer to the puppy and held out one tentative finger, touching a soft ear. "Or at least part beagle. Did you see how she went directly to the—the spot?" I gestured to the floor as I stood back up, the puppy's dark eyes following my every move.

"Miss F, I thought you were allergic to dogs."

Brent moved around the center island and scooped up the squirming animal in one large hand. He held it close to his chest, leaning down to croon some baby nonsense in its ear. A tiny pink tongue crept out and licked Brent's cheek, making him laugh. I had to admit, it was cute. Full of pet dander, but cute.

"I think we should name her 'Agatha.'" I startled even myself. "And call her 'Aggie' for short. As in Agatha Christie."

Both Nora and Brent stared at me.

"She's a great little detective already."

"Agatha Christie wasn't a detective," objected Nora. "She just wrote about them."

"Same thing." I smiled at the little dog, wishing I could pick her up and cuddle her like a little baby. Maybe I'd pay a visit to my doctor and see about getting those allergy shots he'd mentioned on my last visit.

"But I already call her Nellie." Brent looked at me, frowning. "It's after my two greats Gramma Nell. She loved dogs like I do."

"Then make it 'Agatha Nellie.' It'll make her sound like a high-class purebred, which she might be, for all I know."

"She'll sound like a high-class something, all right," murmured Nora, and I gave her one of my frosty teacher stares. She gave me a sassy grin.

And Agatha Nellie gave Brent a little present, right down the front of his shirt.

When all of the puppy messes had been scrubbed up, the three of us went back to the living room, the puppy prancing at Brent's heels. It wasn't long before Aggie discovered the hairpiece that Nora had kicked under the sofa, dragging it out and giving it a fierce once-over, much to my amusement. Nora acted as if she hadn't seen anything.

"I'm still hungry," I announced as my stomach gave a mighty rumble. "If we aren't going to go get something, I can make some grilled cheese and tomato sandwiches. If you've got bread, tomatoes, and cheese, that is."

"I haven't been to a grocery store since I don't know when."

I sighed at Nora's words, visions of buttery, cheesy, tomato-y goodness vanishing into thin air.

"Why don't we try food delivery? We could have it delivered by Uber."

"I do that sometimes. All kinds of places have that now." Brent looked up from where he sat on the floor, dragging the hairpiece around for Aggie to chase.

"Indeed they do." Nora tapped her chin with one long fake nail, her eyes narrowing slightly. "I tell you what, Brent. I'll order the food and you can go get it for us, just like a regular Uber driver. How does that sound?"

"Sure, Mrs. G." He stopped suddenly, a look of consternation on his broad face. "I don't know if you can ask for me, though. Some places just send out their own drivers."

I had to hand it to Nora. She knew how to handle this kid.

"Then we won't call Uber. I'll place the order on my phone and you can go get it, just like a regular carryout. Sound good?"

I hid my amusement behind one hand as I watched Brent processing what she'd suggested.

Finally, something clicked behind his eyes and he smiled broadly, a bracket of soft lines forming on either side of his mouth. "That's a great idea. I'll even bring you extra napkins. I know people." Portlandians were famous for guarding their paper products like a miser and his gold.

"You do that." Nora smiled back at him, no trace of the usual sarcasm in her voice. She would have made a great high school counselor.

With our order finally placed ("Grandma's Kitchen—Family Food Done Right!") and Brent dispatched to fetch our late lunch or early dinner, I turned to face Nora, eyebrows lifted in question. "What? I can tell you've got something buzzing around in that noggin of yours. I could almost hear it from across the room."

Nora wiggled back against the sofa cushions, carefully resettling her injured foot on a throw pillow. Just when I couldn't stand it any longer, she stopped fiddling with her toe and looked at me, her face as sober as a judge. Notwithstanding the late Judge Sizemore, of course, whose car was discovered wrapped around a light pole the morning after his retirement shindig. Jerking my attention back to the present and away from judges, I waited to hear what she had to say.

"I've been thinking about Linda."

I wanted to roll my eyes. I'd been thinking about the woman as well, but I didn't want to talk about her. Least said, soonest mended, in my opinion. I kept my mouth firmly shut, though. There was no need to start an argument before I'd had a chance to eat.

Nora gave her foot another experimental wiggle. She didn't meet my gaze. "I think we need to hire a private investigator. You know, someone to help us figure out who killed that woman and why they killed her in my kitchen."

"I'm pretty sure that's what the Portland Police Department is doing." A tiny seed of distrust appeared in the back of my mind, blooming into full-fledged suspicion as I stared at her innocent expression. "Does this bright idea have anything to do with text messages? Or a man? Or text messages to a man?"

Nora flounced against the cushions, tossing her head as if she'd forgotten the fake ponytail was no longer there. "I have no idea what you're talking about. And I might have thought you'd support me in this. After all, I'm the one who had a dead body in her home, not you."

And you're going to have another one if you're not careful. I kept my murderous thoughts to myself. One dead body was a tragedy. Two would be downright disastrous, to paraphrase Oscar Wilde. And I had no desire to elevate myself from witness to suspect, thank you very much. Retirement behind bars sounded almost as grim as twenty more years in the classroom.

"All right. Tell me about this private eye. Number one, how'd you find him, and number two, what's his big plan? He's not going to camp out in the hallway, is he? That might give the game away."

Nora snorted. "I'm a little shrewder than that. No, he's not going to hang out in the hallway, smarty pants. He'll do detective things, follow people, look for clues. Solve the crime."

I tilted my head, tapping my chin with one finger. This was reminding me of a standoff with a particularly irritating parent, someone who thought she knew better than me how to handle thirty-eight students. Needless to say, I'd come out on top. Literally. When she'd dived at me, both hands reaching to grab my hair, I managed to trip her. Of course, I'd ended up tripping myself as well, landing with a thump on her back.

The school board hadn't been amused. The students had scored it a ten. The video had gotten over a thousand hits in the first half hour. I'd felt like a celebrity.

But I digress. Nora, it seemed, had found Another Man. Okay, he was a detective and probably didn't have a tenth of the bank account of her poorest ex-husband. And hopefully he didn't have any children named Ishmael or Ahab or Nemo. But he did have one of the most important criteria. He was still breathing. And apparently available for investigating duty. Sighing, I motioned for her to continue.

"What else is there to say?" Nora gave an exaggerated nonchalant shrug, a sure-tell sign she was feeling guilty. Probably for chasing this detective for something other than detection—of that, I was certain. "He'll be here at six."

"Oh, fine." I didn't bother trying to hide the irritation in my voice. "Nora, are you sure this what's-his-name isn't targeting you for your money? And by the way, you haven't told me his name yet." I stared at her through narrowed eyes, daring her to ignore my request.

"It's Marcus Avery," she mumbled, and I let out a squeal. She refused to meet my eyes and I had to admit she'd managed to blindside me good.

"Marcus 'I think I'm Sam Spade' Avery? The private eye with the roaming eye? The detective with the—"

Nora broke into my tirade, saving me from saying something I'd regret. "All right, all right. Calm down, Gwen. He's not as bad as you think."

I thought she was going to reach over and pat my hand or offer me a piece of candy as if I was a child who needed soothing. I glared at her, crossing my arms over my chest in my best Mercy slash Grace pose.

She looked at me for a long moment and then sighed. "I just thought it was for the best. Those hopeless officers I talked to didn't seem bright enough to fight their way out of a paper bag, much less find a killer. Marcus can help."

"The only help he'll give you is to help clean out your bank account if you're not careful. Honestly, Nora. Didn't that last story in the news prove what a sham he is?"

"Oh, that." She laughed off the scathing article as if it was the latest joke. "He'd been dating the journalist who wrote it and she got a little upset when she caught him canoodling a waitress over at the Sunny Side Up Café."

"Hmmph," was my only comment. What I really wanted to say was one of my father's favorite adages: There's no smoke without a fire. And Mr. Marcus Avery, Portland's answer to Philip Marlowe, a legend in his own mind, was an expert at conflagrations both great and small.

Aggie, who'd been sleeping peacefully next to Nora's feet, suddenly awoke and gave a sharp bark, her attention fixed on the front door. I heard something, or someone, shuffling around in the hallway, something too quiet to be Brent carrying bags of food. I quickly ran my mind over the list of stepchildren, wondering which of the darlings would be next to make an appearance.

When the knock came, I was on my feet in an instant. My nerves were really taking a beating lately, even more than usual. Or maybe I wasn't tolerating my daily coffee ingestion as I normally could. That in itself was a scary thought. Going caffeine-free in this city was almost worse than a death sentence.

"You might as well answer that since you're already standing." Nora glanced at the door as she reached over and picked up Aggie. "And besides, my toe is still killing me."

I shot her a suspicious glance, noting she'd stretched out a little farther on the sofa, managing to arrange herself in a more seductive pose. I opened the door, already knowing who I'd see on the other side.

In my family, there was that one annoying uncle the adults avoided like the plague and who always had a pocketful of Tootsie Rolls for us kids. He favored loud plaid jackets, tight polyester pants in shocking colors, and ties that could make your eyes water. Marcus Avery, detective extraordinaire, could have been his fashion twin.

"Well, if it isn't the Prince of Portland." I stared at the yellow-and-green striped shirt he wore above a pair of rather tight jeans. "Who let you out on such a fine day?"

"Gwen," Nora purred from the living room, "please let our guest inside."

"Good afternoon to you, too." He stepped past me. "My dearest Nora, it's so good to see you again." He reached down to take the hand she held out, holding it just under a ridiculously undersized mustache. He kissed it reverently as though she was the pope and he an acolyte.

Or she a millionaire and he a poor private eye with a bad wardrobe.

"Again?" I was almost too befuddled by the hand kissing to keep my thoughts to myself. "I wasn't aware you'd seen each other before, Nora."

"Why, yes." Nora spoke without looking at me. Her gaze was fastened firmly on Marcus's round face, that dreamy look from earlier back in her eyes. "Marcus and I have seen each other quite a bit lately."

I didn't care for the way she said the word "seen." It smacked of bridesmaid dresses and another ex-husband.

"Indeed." I didn't bother to hide the sarcasm underpinning my voice. This was heading downhill rapidly, and I hoped I'd get my share of the food before Nora decided to kick me out.

Aggie was still sitting on Nora's lap, and now Marcus Avery bent over and gave the puppy's furry ears an awkward pat. To my amusement—and satisfaction, if truth be told—Aggie nipped his fingers, causing him to snatch them back as if a crocodile had tried to eat them.

If he conducted surveillance the same way he approached a dog, it was no wonder he was the butt of every detective joke in the state. Sighing, I took a seat on the other end of the sofa. If I wasn't careful, I'd become as snarky as Nora. Two of us would be a recipe for disaster.

"Please, have a seat, Marcus." Nora indicated an armchair with a languid sweep of her arm that may or may not have been an attempt at elegance, a la Elizabeth Taylor in the role of Cleopatra.

I had to bite the inside of my mouth so I wouldn't smile. Marcus, on the other hand, seemed to fall all over himself as he sat down, his rather prominent blue eyes staring straight at Nora. I suddenly wished Brent was there. I'd have loved to see his reaction to the absurd scene playing out in Nora's living room.

As if I'd wished him into existence, the door flew open and Brent stepped in, large white bags dangling from both hands. Aggie gave a yelp and leapt off of Nora's lap, heading straight for Brent. Dropping to his knees, he leaned over and scooped the excited dog into his arms. It was enough to melt the layer of sarcasm that had started to form around my personality. What was better than a boy and his dog? I could almost forget the rash that had developed on my arms and around my ankles.

What I couldn't forget was the fact a murder had started this ball rolling, and the idea that Marcus Avery would be the one to play catch with it bothered me to no end. I was determined to get rid of the smarmy investigator once and for all.

"I'm glad we're all here." Nora smiled coyly, and I gave myself a mental shake and forced my wandering brain to focus. "Marcus and I have an announcement to make."

"You have a *what*?" I screeched, my temperature running from hot to cold and back again. It felt like a hot flash replay.

"An announcement, dear lady," intoned Marcus in his best manner, and I wanted to gag.

"I'm no one's 'dear lady.'" I gave him the gimlet stare of death. "And I'll thank you to remember that."

"And I can see why." Marcus's return salvo was delivered in the same smooth manner.

I redoubled my glare until he dropped his gaze, just in time to see Agatha Nellie take aim on his polished loafers. We really needed to get this dog some puppy piddle papers, or whatever those things were called.

Once that interruption had been taken care of, with Nora all but pouting as the attention moved from her to the puppy, I sat back and looked at her with renewed interest. Had she developed that rosy glow that some women did when they were in love? Or was it merely the result of elevated blood pressure? Either way, I was beginning to feel concerned about her health when it came to one Marcus Avery. Since the moment she'd first mentioned him, something had seemed slightly off-kilter.

"You be quiet, Aggie. We're going to listen to announcements, just like at school."

I had to stifle a laugh at his words. Brent was sitting on the floor, a wiggly Aggie in his arms and the food bags still on his wrists. I thought about mentioning that particular item when my stomach threatened to join in the conversation, but decided to hold back until Nora got her big announcement out of the way. Then nothing was going to keep me from getting at Grandma's fried chicken, biscuits, and berry cobbler—not even another wedding.

"Without further ado," Nora gave Aggie a stern look, "this is what Marcus and I have decided."

I let the words float through the air and into my brain, taking a moment to allow their full meaning to sink in.

"You—you're going to do what?"

"You heard me." Nora sat up straighter, holding out one hand to Marcus, who took it with a silly grin. "I'm going to turn private eye. And it's all thanks to this wonderful man right here."

"If you're going to start detecting, who's gonna run the pet sitting business?" Brent's broad forehead was wrinkled as he tried to make sense of Nora's news.

"You and Miss Franklin will, of course."

Of course. When we were children, Nora always made the plans and I was the one left to carry them out.

"Actually, Nora," I kept my voice even, "I think I'd like to give detecting a try as well. Won't that be fun? The *two* of us, just like the old days." *Old days as in this morning before a certain seedy detective appeared*, I wanted to add but didn't bother. The man had about as much sensitivity as a dead rat.

"And me," Marcus chimed in, his pointy nose almost quivering with anticipation. Or possibly with the idea of inching closer to Nora's money. "You've gotta have a license and I've got one. And we'll find out who killed that woman before the PPD even gets out of bed. No one gets ahead of Marcus Avery."

I wanted to laugh at his hammy display. Nora, on the other hand, seemed quite taken with him. I'd have to keep a close eye on this situation before she got taken for something else.

"Well, if you guys are going to play detective, I'm gonna do it too. Me and Aggie can be the K-9 unit. Won't that be cool, Aggie?" Brent planted a resounding kiss on top of the dog's head.

Aggie licked his nose in return.

"Oh, good grief!" Nora pushed Marcus's chubby hand away in exasperation. "We can't all be detectives, Brent. Someone has to take care of the dog walking and pet sitting jobs."

"I tell you what, my dear." Marcus sidled closer to Nora, catching the toe of his shoe in the ruined hairpiece and stumbling forward. "I'll take care of the investigating end of things and you little ladies handle the pets." Glancing down, he kicked at the fake hair, an expression of revulsion crossing his face. "And it looks like you need an exterminator, Nora. You've got mice. Big ones."

Chapter 7

With Marcus Avery finally dispatched to do whatever it was private eyes did, I took the bags of food into the kitchen and began filling plates for the three of us. Aggie was another matter. The little dog had trotted behind me, followed by her rather large shadow, and now sat at my feet waiting for me to drop a morsel of chicken.

"Brent, I think she's too little to eat any of this." I motioned to the containers of food sitting on the counter. "What have you been feeding her?"

Brent shrugged, his broad shoulders rippling underneath his shirt. "Whatever I'm eating, Miss F. Aggie here likes just about anything." He pointed to the berry cobbler, wrinkling his nose. "Except for fruit. I gave her some last night, and my mom got real mad when Aggie did a number two all over the kitchen floor."

"Thank you, Brent, for that visual." My stomach heaved slightly. I decided I might have to forego said berry cobbler until later. Much later. "Well, I'll let her have some of this crumbled biscuit and gravy, but I'm not sure she's got enough teeth to eat the chicken,"

With Aggie's dinner settled and the three of us seated around the kitchen table, it was time to figure out the next step. We couldn't let the pet sitting business fall to the side. It had only been two days, not enough time to see if it was going to be a success or not. And as Nora had pointed out earlier, we needed to keep bringing in jobs if Brent was going to work with us.

"Just think of it as doing Portland's drivers a favor," she'd said, and I agreed. Keeping Brent from behind a wheel was our contribution to society.

On the other hand, dog walking and the occasional pet sitting assignment wasn't going to cut it. We were going to have to get serious or find something else to do.

"But not detecting. That's not our job, Nora. Yes, I want to find out who killed Linda, and I really want to keep you from joining her in the Great Beyond, but let the experts handle it." I reached for the last biscuit, carefully tearing off another piece for Aggie. "And I'm not talking Marcus Avery here either. Speaking of," I scratched at the rash on my elbow, "when did you two start seeing one another? And how did I miss that?"

Nora gave a nonchalant shrug, popping a large bite of berry cobbler into her mouth. I waited until she'd swallowed it before nudging her arm. "You might as well tell me. I'll find out sooner or later."

"Fine." She heaved an exaggerated sigh. "I ran into him at the gas station last week. It's the one over by the mall."

I knew the one she meant. I'd used that one myself when I was still working. Since retiring, my car had sat in the unattached garage, collecting dust and saving me a ton of cash. "Was he getting gas as well?"

She suddenly grew interested in rearranging the food on her plate. I nudged her again.

"No, he wasn't getting gas. He was pumping gas." In Oregon, most gas stations were still a full-service business, with employees who pumped gas, took payments, and even cleaned windshields.

Nora glowered at me and I grinned at her. This was too perfect.

"I see. So, the detecting business must be a little slow lately."

"He didn't say, and I didn't ask. Really, Gwen." She stood with a flounce and headed for the sink. "You can be the biggest snob sometimes."

"I think it'd be cool to work at a gas station." Brent grabbed the last piece of chicken. "I like the smell of gas."

"I'll bet you do." I shook my head, wondering how much gas sniffing was responsible for his lack of common sense. "Brent, you probably need to take Aggie out for a potty break. Mrs. Goldstein and I will clean up the kitchen and then we'll have time to talk about tomorrow's jobs before I need to get home. Sound good?"

"Okay, Miss F." He stood, pushing back the chair with his knees and nearly overturning it.

I reached over and managed to upright the chair before it hit the floor.

Brent paused and gave me an admiring look. "You've sure got some strong arms there, Miss F. I bet you could take on The Rock."

I looked at him to see if he was joking. He wasn't. Brent's world was black and white—whatever he said, he meant, and whatever someone told him, he believed. A maternal feeling began growing in my spinster's heart—was it politically correct to still use that word?—and I wanted to keep this overgrown child safe.

And off the road.

"That's quite a compliment. I'd sure like to meet him sometime."

"So would I." Nora waggled her eyebrows in a suggestive manner,
I ignored her. Nora felt that way about most men, I'd noticed.

Brent and Aggie were back in just a few minutes, the little dog
scampering behind him. She came straight to me as I sat curled up on
one end of the sofa.

I gave her soft ears a quick pat. "All right, Aggie, that's enough. Brent,
can you get her, please?"

"She just wants to say hello, Miss F." He reached down for the puppy,
cuddling her close to his chest. "And maybe you're not allergic to her." He
buried his nose in her fur while a tickle built in my nose just watching him.

"It's not as bad as I thought, certainly." I leaned over to scratch the
rash on my ankles. "Nothing a little Benadryl can't fix. And as soon as
we get this show on the road, I can get home and take some. Nora, how
many jobs do we have tomorrow?"

We quickly went through them, assigning Brent the three dog walking
jobs and one pet sitting task with a pair of Siamese cats. I volunteered to
take on the two-hour assignment with a rather old parrot.

"It's got a sailor's vocabulary, the owner tells me," Nora cautioned.
"And it sounds like a fairly simple job, keeping an eye on it while he's out
running errands."

"Interesting." I lifted both of my eyebrows in question. I never could
master the one-eyebrow lift like Nora. "Any idea why someone needs to
watch a bird? I'm assuming he's in a cage, of course."

She looked up from her notes, a twinkle in her eyes. "Something
about the bird's propensity for getting out of said cage and trying to get
into the fridge. I kid you not." She spoke solemnly, holding up one hand.
"Scout's honor."

"So they couldn't just block the cage door or something?" Sometimes
the lack of resourcefulness of folks out there amazed me. It reminded
me of a fellow English teacher who'd constantly popped her head in my
classroom to ask for lesson plans. I wondered what she was doing now
that I wasn't there. Well, good luck to her. Maybe she'd learn to stand on
her own two educational feet. In the meantime, I had to deal with another
unimaginative person.

"It's not that easy, apparently." The twinkle was back and I was beginning
to feel slightly suspicious about this job. "The parrot has his own room
and knows how to pick the lock on the door."

I stared at her, my mouth hanging open. "You've got to be kidding me. A parrot with his own room."

"Right? A little crazy, granted, but it's folks like this that'll bring in the dough." Nora put a checkmark next to the name and smiled at me.

I didn't smile back. I was already thinking of ways to block the door to the room.

"Sounds like a lotta fun, Miss F. You want Aggie and me to come with you? She can get some practice with being a bird dog." Brent's expression was hopeful, and even Aggie's eyes looked brighter as if she understood the words.

I regretfully shook my head. I would've liked the company, true enough, but only because I had a long-seated phobia of birds—and bats—swooping down on me and getting tangled in my hair.

"No, you've got your own jobs to do. But thank you. Maybe you can do it next time, alright?"

"And we've got another busy day tomorrow." Nora stood, stretching her arms over her head. "While you two are out, I'll be detecting with Marcus."

"Oh, is that what they call it now? I tend to use another descriptor." My tone was just this side of sardonic. "And will this detecting take place here or elsewhere?"

"Wouldn't you like to know?" Nora held out a hand to me and I took it, letting her pull me to my feet. "Let's just say that if his tie is hanging on the doorknob, don't come in."

"Oh, that's just gross, Mrs. G." Brent's face was red, and Aggie gave a yelp as he hugged her tightly to him. "I thought old people didn't think about stuff like that."

"I guess that depends on your definition of 'old,' doesn't it?"

Brent looked truly horrified at the thought.

"Okay, you two, enough of this." I shook off her hand and walked to the door. "I'm leaving before this gets too deep and I need hip boots. Brent, I'm going to walk home and get some fresh air, so I'll see you in the morning."

"You want me to pick you up again?" Brent followed me into the hall, Aggie still clinging to his shirt. "It's no problem, Miss F."

I ignored Nora's amused expression as she closed the door behind us.

"It's fine." I reached over to give Aggie a little tickle. "I'll plan on walking back in the morning so you can come straight here, all right?"

"Well, if you say so." He stared at me, a tiny frown forming between his heavy eyebrows. "Hey, do you think Mrs. G. will pay me tomorrow?"

I stared at him for a second as I mentally switched gears. Sometimes Brent's conversational tangents were a bit difficult to keep up with, and, at this time of the evening, my brain was already thinking about bed.

"I'm sure she can if you ask her. Or I can ask her if you'd prefer." I smiled, noting the blush rising in his face. "Do you have a hot date tomorrow night?"

"Yeah. I met her at the dog park." He spoke proudly as if that had sealed the deal. "She's a dog walker too."

"Really? That's nice." I pushed the round button to call the elevator. "I'll make sure you get paid then. Don't worry about it, okay?"

"Sure thing, Miss F." He followed me into the elevator as the doors opened, his bulk filling most of the small space. "You know what? I really like working with you. You're kinda cool when you're not talking about reading and boring stuff like that."

And because I really liked working with him as well, I didn't say a word. Instead, I gave his arm a pat and Aggie a scratch between her ears. I'd have to remember to give his mom a call and tell her what a fine son she had.

My walk home was pleasant. The cloud cover from earlier in the day had burned off and the first stars were making their appearance, small points of light high above a city that was beginning to settle in for the night. As I neared my house, I was happy to see that most of my neighbors were already home. It made me feel secure somehow, knowing that if I needed them, they were only a few steps away.

Waving to the couple across the street as they helped a handful of children from their van, I opened my front door and stepped inside, kicking my new Birkenstocks off as I did. What I wanted was Benadryl and hot tea and a session with Netflix, preferably one with Jason Statham or Idris Elba.

What I got was something I hadn't planned for.

On my kitchen table was a white envelope, a twin to the one Nora had received, the same skull and crossbones sketched above my name. How it had gotten there bothered me less than the fact that I'd gotten it in the first place. I hadn't done anything except start a pet sitting business with my best friend.

Had I?

With a shiver, I reached out for the envelope and then stopped. Someone had placed it in my house, and unless they'd worn gloves, their prints would be all over it. Plus, I was beginning to feel spooked about how they'd gotten inside. I hadn't noticed anything amiss when I'd slipped my house key into the lock, and a quick survey of my front room and kitchen had shown that my windows were still intact.

As quietly as I could, in case they were still somewhere in the house, I tiptoed back to the door and grabbed my sandals as I ran outside to the safety of my small front yard. The family across the street had already gone inside, and the coziness I had felt upon arriving home was rapidly waning. Maybe I should have taken Brent up on his offer of a ride home. He was big enough to scare anyone away, and Aggie might have sniffed out the intruder. Shivering, I pulled out my cell phone and dialed 9-1-1.

Chapter 8

I was still shivering as I sat in the back seat of a police cruiser, waiting for the two responding officers to look through my house. Whoever had left the letter wanted me running scared, and they'd certainly done a good job of it.

"Miss Franklin? Are you all right?"

I jumped at the voice, turning to see a familiar face leaning in the open car door. Shelby Tucker had been a student of mine some years back, one of the many who had gone on to university with my blessing and a written recommendation. She'd graduated with a degree in journalism and a job at the *Portland Tribune*.

"Oh, Shelby." The quaver in my voice irritated me. "It's been quite an evening around here." I took in a deep breath, trying to calm my thumping heart. "You didn't happen to see someone skulking around my house today, did you?" I emitted a short laugh that sounded more like a noise Aggie would make.

"Miss Franklin, you always use the best words. No, there's been no skulking around here that I'm aware of." She reached over and gave me a quick hug. "We did have someone come through here earlier dropping off leaflets, but that was it." She fished in one pocket and pulled out a folded paper, quickly scanning the contents. "Something about a giveaway at this weekend's Farmer's Market." She held it up so I could see a garishly colored basket of apples splashed across the flyer.

"Really." I lifted my eyebrows, my interest caught. "Did you see who dropped it off?"

Shelby shook her head slowly, eyes narrowing in thought. "No, I don't think I did. I mean, I caught a glimpse of someone cutting through the front yard, but that was it." She grinned at me. "I finally got a day off after that huge political palaver over the weekend. These protests are going to be the death of me."

"Don't use the 'd' word." I shuddered. "There's already been one body too many around here for my liking."

"Yeah, I heard about that. Something about an old gal—sorry, Miss Franklin—found dead in those luxury apartments. It's not my beat." She gave a tiny shrug. "I get to cover politics, a full-time circus, in my humble opinion."

I stared at her for a moment, considering how much to say. It might be useful to have a direct contact in the news business, much more than that lame investigator dragged in by Nora and her over-active hormones.

"It's like this." I proceeded to tell her everything, from deciding to set up a new business to finding Linda Fletcher's very dead, very murdered body in Nora's kitchen.

Shelby listened intently, her journalistic nose on point. "Well, I'll be a son of a b—monkey's uncle." She stared at me, a stunned expression on her face. "You sure do know how to liven up retirement, Miss Franklin."

"Tell me about it." I laid my head back against the car seat, suddenly exhausted. "And right now, all I want to do is climb into bed and forget about everything."

Shelby straightened up as two officers approached the cruiser, their heavy duty flashlights shining like beacons.

"If it isn't the Bert and Ernie of the Portland Police Department. Long time no see." Shelby held out her hand to them in greeting. "Seems like just yesterday we were hanging out together, enjoying a riot or two."

I converted a laugh into a coughing fit. I could definitely see the resemblance between the television puppets and the two men standing by the car.

Bert groaned, flipping his flashlight in his hand like a baton, blinding me momentarily.

"And if it isn't the Annie Oakley of the *Trib*." They grinned at one another, friends joking in good-natured fun. "If that politician never shows her face here again, it'll be too soon for me. Who'd-a thunk it, Portland having a riot? I thought this was the most laid-back city in the U.S. of A."

"Right?" Shelby bobbed her head in agreement. "So, is it all kosher in Miss Franklin's house?"

"You two know each other?"

The two officers looked from me to Shelby, curiosity on their faces.

"She was a student of mine." I smiled at Shelby. "One of the best."

Ernie snorted. "Yeah, I'll bet she was a real pistol in class, too."

"You should see her in action." Bert nudged his partner, a wide grin on his even wider face. "I thought she was gonna tackle that protestor, the one who kept poking the bullhorn in her face."

"And I might've too, if he hadn't put it away. I swear, people get all het up about issues and lose their common sense."

"Indeed they do." I jumped into the conversation. "And I'm going to start protesting, myself, if I can't get back inside my house soon. Officers, I'm assuming you didn't find anyone in there?"

"Not a soul," Bert declared, a solemn expression on his face. "We've called for a crime scene team to come and take some prints and get that letter to the lab, but I think it's all right for you to go back inside." He peered at me through the car door. "You got anyone who can stay with you tonight? Or somewhere else to go?"

"She can stay with me." Shelby nodded at both officers. "If you want to, that is." She gave a quick look in my direction.

"That's really sweet of you, Shelby." I patted her hand and swung my legs out of the car, ignoring the twenty-one-gun salute coming from my knees. "I'd better stay here, though. You don't want an old teacher cluttering up your guest room."

"Oh, it's no bother, really." She smiled at me, but I detected the relief underpinning her words. I didn't blame her. At her age, I wouldn't want to entertain someone twice as old as me either, not to mention a former teacher.

"Besides, it looks like I won't be alone for long." I nodded at the white van that had just pulled alongside the curb. "Here come the troops."

With a promise she'd stop by in the morning before heading for the paper, Shelby said goodnight and headed back to her house, a duplex just half a block away. Bert and Ernie—Officers Fin Adams and Eddie Cluff—disappeared into my house, presumably to direct the crime scene investigators. The sooner they got it fingerprinted and photographed, the sooner I'd be able to crawl into bed with my nightly hot chocolate and my iPad. In the meantime, I stood quietly in the twilight, enjoying the muted sounds of the evening and the stars above.

"Hey, Miss Franklin." I turned around and saw Officer Cluff standing by the front door, one hand extended, an odd-looking object held on his open-gloved palm. "Have you seen this before?"

I pulled my sleeve down to cover my hand before taking the object and held it up to the porch light, an elongated "Z" in a lightweight metal. It looked like something my mother might have used in her crochet work, but I had never seen it before.

"No idea." I handed it back. "Where was it found?"

"Just inside the front door, under the edge of the rug." He dropped his head sheepishly. "One of the crime scene techs found it. Guess I must've missed it."

"You weren't here looking for anything except a possible intruder." I spoke mildly, stepping around him and into the house. "You did your job, Officer."

"Do you have any idea what it is?" He followed me, examining the object curiously. "I know I've seen something like this before, but..." He turned it over in his hand, eyebrows drawn together in thought.

"Kinda reminds me of a Slim Jim, just a lot smaller." Officer Adams peered at Officer Cluff's hand. "Remember? We took a bunch off that kid last summer, the one caught breaking in all those cars."

"Maybe," Cluff replied, looking at the little metal "Z" doubtfully. "I don't think this could pick a car lock, though. It's too skinny."

"No, but it might pick a simple door lock." I planted my hands on my hips, shaking my head in wonder. "Seems someone was able to get into my house using this thing."

"Hey, Bruno," he called over his shoulder. "I think Miss Franklin here has solved her own break-in."

"Not quite." I tipped my head modestly. "I only mentioned that this tool might have been used to pick my lock."

The white-suited tech called Bruno moved over to where the three of us stood, holding out his hand. Bert handed the object over, and I watched with interest as it was put into an evidence bag and sealed. This was almost like being in the middle of one of my mystery books. Not even Nora and her private eye could possibly be having this much fun.

Unless there was a tie hanging on the doorknob, of course.

I managed to sleep that night after the crime scene circus left, only waking one time when the wind began to pick up. Turning over in bed, I pulled the covers up to my chin, conscious of the chair I'd wedged under the bedroom door's knob. I wasn't even sure if that would help, but it made me feel safer. After all, if it worked for Miss Marple, it would work for me.

As I drifted off, it occurred to me that someone had taken great care to get into my house without breaking down the door or knocking out a window. That had struck me as an oddly caring touch, something that a friend or acquaintance might do. Tucking that thought to the back of my mind, I determinedly closed my eyes and went to sleep, the sound of wind chimes ringing a nighttime lullaby.

* * * *

The sun was shining with all its might when I set out for Nora's apartment the next morning. A brilliant blue sky, a gift from the winds of the night before, stretched out over Portland like a blanket, its edges held in by the Columbia River on one side and the rolling forests on the other. It was days such as this that made me glad to be a native Portlandian. Of course, I knew tomorrow might be the exact opposite, gray and gloomy and dripping with rain, but today was perfect.

Stepping off the elevator, I took a superstitious peek at Linda Fletcher's door and was startled to see it open. I listened for a moment, hearing someone moving about farther inside the apartment. Hesitating only a moment, I stepped inside.

A small woman stood at the kitchen sink, her back to me, with a pair of wireless earbuds stuck firmly in both ears. No wonder she hadn't heard me come in. Backing out of the room as quietly as I'd arrived, I made a big show of knocking on the open door and calling out, "Is anyone in there?"

I was making enough racket to wake the dead, Linda Fletcher notwithstanding. Hopefully. I gave a small shiver as I stepped back into the apartment. Cleaning crews I could handle. Ghosts? Absolutely not.

"Who's there?" The woman peered around the kitchen door, an anxious expression on her face and a slim cell phone poised in her hand.

Lifting both of mine, I gave her my best "welcome-to-a-new-school-year" smile, willing myself to appear completely innocuous. You know, like most teachers did on the first day of class, right before all hope was dashed at the sight of a twenty-page syllabus.

"Sorry for startling you." I stepped a bit closer. "Is it all right if I come in and peek around? I was a friend of Linda's." I mentally crossed my fingers at the white lie.

According to Kevin Bacon, I was a "one-degree friend," with Nora the link between us, although "friend" was a term I used loosely.

She smiled at me shyly. "Sorry. Not good English."

"I can come back later, all right?" I accompanied my words with wide gestures and an even wider smile, pointing from me to the door. Gestures were my default method of making myself understood whenever I'd had foreign exchange students or those whose English wasn't their first language. Often, I'd made them laugh with some of my de facto sign language, but I hadn't minded. Laughter, I'd found, was a great learning tool whenever a new situation created stress.

She just gave an apologetic shrug and turned back toward the kitchen. Suddenly, she paused and spun around to face me, one hand diving into the pocket of the smock she was wearing.

"Please. Take." She was holding out something small and shiny.

And instantly, a shiver began its unwanted trek up and down my spine. It was a twin to the metal object that had been found in my house the night before, the tiny tool that could be used to pick a lock.

Someone had definitely been in Linda's apartment as well. What on earth had they been looking for? A quick look around had shown nothing of value. In fact, "nothing" was exactly what I'd seen. All of Linda's belongings had already been removed, leaving it as empty as…I paused in mid-thought. Similes were my forte, or at least they had been. Now the only thing I could think of was "as empty as a refrigerator after Brent pays a visit." Not very elegant, to be sure, but very true.

Sighing, I headed for Nora's, my feet as heavy as if I'd been wearing concrete shoes. With a shaking hand, I knocked on the door. It was only when she opened it that I noticed there'd been no sign of a tie.

"Some friend you are. Why didn't you call me? You know you could've stayed here." Nora was clearly irritated, building up a fine head of righteous steam, both hands on her Lycra-encased hips as she glared at me.

I was sitting at her kitchen table, the mysterious metal object lying beside a fresh mug of coffee. Between it and Nora's huffing and puffing, it was getting downright humid in there.

"I didn't want to bother you." And I didn't want to sleep in the same apartment where someone had died, to be honest. I reached for the coffee and took a test sip. It was perfect, one of Portland Coffee Roasters' morning blends. "And how did you hear about it anyway?"

Nora gave a derisive snort over the rim of her mug. "I've got my ways, Sis. Good thing I told Shelby to look after you, isn't it?"

I stared at her, too astonished to speak. How in the world did Nora know my student? Come to think of it, why hadn't Shelby mentioned this little tidbit to me last night? I shook my head, taking another sip of coffee. Just another mystery to clear up, once we got this entire Linda Fletcher thing under wraps.

Until then, there was another more pressing matter. I slid the metal hook across the table toward her. "And now we've got something to go on besides anonymous letters. Do we know anyone who's been a locksmith? I'm pretty sure that this thing is some sort of a lock pick."

Momentarily distracted from her rant, Nora picked it up and examined it closely. "Are you sure that's what this is? I mean, look at it. It could be anything, from one of those wrenches that come with DIY furniture to, I don't know, a weird piece of jewelry."

I waved away her commentary with one hand. "No, I already thought of that. Number one, it's too flimsy to be used in building furniture. And two, the one found under my hall rug looked exactly like this. Swear on a stack of gradebooks."

We sat in silence for a moment, both of us staring at the mysterious object and sipping our coffee. If we were modeling for a painting, it could have been called "Contemplation of Life after Fifty." Or maybe "Two Old Gals Trying to Get Their Brains Moving in the Morning."

Finally, Nora set down her coffee mug and sighed, tapping both sets of neon pink acrylic nails on the tabletop. I stared at her suspiciously, waiting for an explanation. This, I felt sure, had nothing to do with my life and death experience of the night before.

With no enlightenment offered by my nail-tapping friend, I asked the question that had been hovering in the back of my mind since I'd knocked on her door. "So, no Marcus this morning?"

She gave a snort of disgust. "Nope. Not this morning and not any morning." She looked across the table at me, her cheeks flushed. "Do you know what that idiot had the nerve to ask me?"

Actually, I was pretty sure I did, but I let her say it anyway.

"He wanted me to foot the bill for an office for him and his two-bit outfit!"

No surprise there, but something she'd just said caught my attention. "You mean, he wanted you to upgrade the place he has now? Maybe move to better digs?"

"No. What I mean is this—the imbecile lost his office a few months back because he couldn't pay the rent. That's why he's been working at the gas station. Some men are complete idiots. No business sense whatsoever."

With that last damning statement, I could have shouted for joy. Nora was incensed. I was validated. I'd never liked the man from the moment his name had crossed her lips.

"Well, time to move on, pal." I stood, briskly rubbing my hands together as if ridding myself of the last of Marcus Avery's memory. "Would you like another cup of coffee?" I glanced at her and noticed her hands were trembling as they grasped the mug. "On second thought, I'm fixing you a nice cup of chamomile tea."

She gave a small shrug, staring at the table. Poor Nora. She went through men like I went through red pens. One of these days, I hoped she'd find one that made her happy. Until then, we had a murder to solve and a business to run.

Chapter 9

The idea of us solving a crime was a bit farfetched, even Agatha Christie-ish, but at that moment, it felt right. In my opinion, being exposed to a dead body, a pair of threatening letters, and two apparent break-ins constituted an invitation to an investigation, namely one that could find who might want Nora dead and why.

As I got ready for my encounter with the lock-picking parrot, we talked about who might know about opening doors without a key. My immediate suggestion was to ask Patsy, the concierge in Nora's luxury apartment building.

"She needs something to do besides hand out mints to old biddies all day long. Present company excepted, of course." I thumbed through my email account, trashing everything except a sale notification from my local Goodwill. That looked intriguing. "Besides, I think we owe her for tracking in dog doo all over her welcome mat."

"That was you, my dear." Nora glanced at me as she touched up her mascara for the umpteenth time. She was going to get those lashes so heavy with that gunk they'd soon break off like brittle tree branches in winter. It'd go well with her perm-shortened hair.

"Technically, yes. But I was out with *you,* passing out business cards, which was your idea."

Something was jumping up and down in the back of my mind, hand raised for attention. Try as hard as I might, though, I couldn't tell what it was. Something I'd just said about business cards? Or broken tree branches? Giving my head a little shake, I set my cell phone aside and waited for Nora to finish her grooming routine.

By ten, Brent had arrived, Aggie in tow, and had set out for the first of the dog walking jobs. Aggie was sporting a brand-new collar and leash in a hideously bright orange, and Nora eyed it with distaste. I had a feeling little Aggie would soon be the recipient of a rhinestoned monstrosity.

Seeing Brent had reminded me of what I'd promised him the night before. "Nora, when do you plan on paying the kid?"

And me, I wanted to add. I was positive that this whole Two Sisters thing had been started as a "paying hobby" for me to have something to do, not just another volunteer assignment in a long line of equally unpaid positions that had masqueraded under "and other duties as assigned" in my teaching contract.

"Today," she mumbled, blotting her bright red lips with a piece of tissue. "Why?"

"He mentioned something last night about having a date." I leaned forward and pointed. "You've got little white things all over your mouth, Nora. Makes it look like your lips were bleeding and you stuck toilet paper on it."

Out came the pocket-sized mirror once more and she scrubbed furiously at her lips, leaving a smear of red down one side of her chin. I decided to let well enough alone. If she couldn't see that for herself, she needed glasses.

"Well, I'd better be getting up to that parrot." I stood, stretching both arms over my head and giving my lower back a little twist. I was as stiff as if I'd slept with my worries, as my grandpa used to say. "Don't go bothering Patsy until I get back, all right?" I wanted to be there to both see her reaction and monitor Nora.

"Hang on a sec." She shoved the remnants of her beauty routine back into a clear makeup pouch. "I think I'll go with you. I'm curious to see a bird that can break out of a locked room."

"You mean you want to let it?" I stared at her, one hand already on the doorknob. "I thought the whole idea was to keep it from doing just that."

Nora shrugged, but there was an impish glint in her eyes. Or maybe that was only a side effect of wearing so much mascara.

"I want to see a stupid pet trick for myself, all right? Don't worry, you." She reached out to pat my arm. "It'll be fine. The parrot will be safe and sound in its room when the owner comes back."

Famous last words.

Making sure the door was firmly locked behind us, a typical "locking the barn door after the horses are out" response, we headed down one floor to an apartment that sat facing the east side of the building. This was where the much-touted walking path began, the one that meandered through a rose garden and then down toward the Willamette River. Idly wondering if the tenants paid extra for the view, I lifted my hand to knock on the door.

From inside came a loud squawk, followed by a string of words that could make a sailor blush. Before I could shush Nora's giggles, the door was opened by a short man with more hair on his face than on his head.

"I'm sorry about that." He gave us an apologetic half-smile. "Please come in. I'm so used to it that I don't even hear her sometimes. I'm Frederick Owen, by the way."

"That parrot's a *she?*" The comment tumbled out before I could stop it. Blushing, I started to explain myself, but Frederick just smiled.

"Indeed she is, and a rarity to be sure." He closed the door behind us and motioned for us to follow him into the kitchen. "In fact, I'll introduce you to her right now before I put her back in her room."

I let Nora go ahead of me. Visions of having to take cover under the kitchen table were lurking in the back of my mind, and it took a moment for me to close the door on such thoughts. This wasn't a Hitchcock movie. It was just a bird. With wings. And a beak. And those scary talons. At least Nora had worn her own talons, even if they were neon pink. Maybe she would keep me safe.

Before I could scare myself silly, I followed them into the kitchen and halted.

The bird—"She's a blue-fronted amazon," Frederick explained with pride—was sitting on the back of a kitchen chair, grooming its bright green feathers.

From where I stood behind Nora, I saw the patches of yellow and red on her breast, and I had to admit she was as breathtaking as her vocabulary. I could clearly see someone had painted the parrot's talons a lovely shade of rose.

"Her name's Pepper, and she's a great conversationalist." Frederick reached out one hand and gently stroked Pepper's feathers. "Who's a pretty girl?"

"I am, you numbskull."

I jumped as the words came out of the parrot's beak, its beady black eyes glancing at Frederick before returning to its grooming.

"Does she know what you're saying, like a real conversation, a back and forth type of thing?" Nora was edging closer to the chair as I edged closer to the door.

"I don't know, to be honest. I bought her from an older couple some twenty years ago, and she'd already acquired quite a vocabulary then, including the charming phrase she uses whenever someone knocks on the door." Frederick grinned, a wide smile that turned his cheeks into round apples. "I'm pretty sure her original owners didn't like company."

"I guessed as much," Nora laughed. "Can I touch her?"

"Sure, she won't mind. In fact," he held out one arm, "you can hold her if you'd like."

Without warning, the parrot opened her wings and flew onto Frederick's outstretched arm. I squealed and jumped backward, hitting my head against the edge of the doorframe. No way was I staying where the client could fly at me. No way, no how.

"Gwen! Are you okay?" Nora's face was tight with anxiety, with no trace of a smile there now. "You didn't whack your noggin again, did you?"

Hoping to forestall any hand waving in front of my face, which would have only made me dizzy, I made myself smile at her.

"I'm fine, just startled is all. I guess I've never been this close to a parrot before." I turned to look at Frederick. "She's really beautiful. And talented too."

"Yes, she is." With a pleased expression, he turned to look at the bird on his arm, running a gentle finger down her side. "She's somewhere around forty years old, maybe even close to fifty."

"You're kidding." Nora, her mouth hanging open, stared in awe at the parrot. "I had no idea birds lived that long."

"Not just any bird." Frederick was clearly proud of his pet. "This particular breed can live up to one hundred years."

"Now you're just pulling my leg." Nora stuck out one finger. "Can I touch her now?"

"Sure, and no, I'm not. In captivity, they might live to thirty-five or so, but in the wild it's a different story. Pepper is a rarity, like I said."

He adjusted his arm to bring Pepper closer to Nora, and I watched warily as she let her finger brush against the breast feathers. To my amusement, Pepper closed her eyes and squawked, "Do that again, baby."

I had to laugh, all panic and pain forgotten. This bird was a feathered version of my best friend, pink talons and all.

"Just ignore her. She can be…entertaining, to say the least." Frederick looked at the two of us and inclined his head toward the doorway. "Let's get her put away and then I need to get going. I'm meeting up with a couple of friends for our monthly backgammon challenge."

Nora's eyebrows went up slightly at his last words. I bit the inside of my cheeks to keep the smile off my face. Backgammon seemed like the perfect pastime for the owner of a sassy parrot.

By the time I'd listened to said sassy parrot scream obscenities from behind the locked and blocked door for thirty minutes, though, I wanted to turn it into a parrot fricassee. Nora sat there placidly on her phone, checking emails and reading her horoscope to me. Didn't Pepper the pesky parrot bother her?

"No, as a matter of fact." She looked up at my question, with a surprised expression. "My second husband had a mouth like a sewer, and I learned how to block it out, not even hear him when he got started on one of his rampages. Of course, that particular marriage was my shortest one. Only seven weeks and three days, to be exact. It took almost five times that long to get out of it and get my, shall we say, monetary compensation."

She winked at me and the spunky Nora was back.

"I've got an idea." I spoke slowly, tapping a finger on my chin. "Maybe if one of us goes in there with Pepper and talks to her, she won't be so upset. What do you think?"

Nora let out a bark of laughter. "As in, me in there with the parrot, you out here with the view?" She pointed toward the pair of French doors that stood open, leading to a small balcony and a view of the walkway.

I shrugged. "If you insist."

"Oh, hilarious. Listen, we can both go in there, communicate with the dumb bird or whatever it is Frederick does, and then get the heck out of there before he gets back."

"Sounds good to me."

I jumped as the frustrated bird gave the doorknob another rattle and let out a string of words that would have landed her straight in detention if she'd been one of my students. I heard the sound of scratching on the doorframe as the parrot used her strong beak to scrape at the wood. "Let's do it before she eats her way through the door."

Nora tucked her phone inside her blouse, a move I pretended not to see, and shoved the small bookcase aside. Inside the room it was suddenly quiet.

"What, no comment from the peanut gallery?" I cocked my head to the side as I listened intently, waiting for another profanity-filled observation.

To tell the truth, the silence bothered me more than all the cursing and obscene suggestions. What if the man's prized bird had just dropped dead? She was pretty old, after all. With a thumping heart, I cautiously turned the key in the lock and cracked open the door.

When they said your life flashed before your eyes in moments of deep stress, they weren't kidding. Of course, this particular stressful moment would only apply to me if I was a bird, because what flashed before *my* eyes was a face full of green feathers and beady black eyes.

Pepper had been waiting for us, the canny old bird. With a loud "See ya, sucker," and an unearthly squawk, Pepper flew straight for the French doors and freedom.

"Well, we can kiss this fee goodbye." Nora's tone was flat, defeated. She stood there with hands hanging at her sides as if they didn't know how to work any longer, and I could see a long tear on one sleeve where Pepper's claws had caught her upraised arm.

I couldn't reply. My mouth was open, but no sound came out. It had happened so quickly there hadn't been time to react. Never again would I call a bird "stupid." They most decidedly weren't.

It was beginning to feel as though Alfred Hitchcock had gotten it right after all.

I slumped into an easy chair that squatted next to a marble-topped table, facing the magnificent view from the balcony. Nora remained standing, as unaware of her torn sleeve as she seemed of me. This had hit her in the metaphorical gut, a symbol of failure. And Nora Goldstein didn't fail.

I wasn't sure how long I sat there, staring miserably outside at the bright day. If I was a caged parrot, I supposed I'd have taken off as well. Of course, the cage was actually a room, and the parrot was a two-bit, no-good lock picker. Like the person who'd come into my house, as well as Nora's. It was only too bad they weren't dressed in the same flamboyant colors as Pepper, easily spotted against a gray Portland background.

Suddenly, I sat straight up, my eyes fixed on the tree nearest to the balcony. I thought I'd seen—yes, there it was again, a flash of neon green among the darker green foliage. Scarcely daring to move my mouth, I murmured, "Nora. Don't make any sudden movement, but I think I've spotted that dang bird."

She cautiously turned her head in the direction I was staring.

"Wait, I think I see her—yes! There she is, near the top. Oh, Gwen, do you think we might be able to get her back inside?"

An idea hit me, something slightly crazy but still…

Inching my way to the edge of the chair, I slithered down onto the floor and crawled across the room to the open parrot room-slash-cage. If only my students could see me now, stretched out like a crazed contortionist. I'd have been a number one hit video on the internet.

Slipping inside Pepper's room, I struggled to my feet and stood still for a moment, letting myself catch my breath. It didn't smell as badly as I'd thought it would, thank goodness. Looking around, I saw the various items Frederick had gotten for Pepper: a handful of small chew toys, a large stick that looked as though it had been dipped in honey and rolled in birdseed, and—wait. I spotted the little stuffed animal behind a large tree branch that was presumably a parrot perch. I wasn't sure why it caught my eye as it did, but I was rolling on gut instinct at the moment. It reminded me of teaching, in a way. You could have the best lesson plan in the world, but if it didn't fit a specific class, it would crash faster than a teen coming off a sugar high. It took instinct to lead a class, and that was what I was counting on now.

Grabbing the animal, I slipped back to my hands and knees and made my way over to the French doors. This would be the big moment. I'd need to put this somewhere for Pepper to spot it, and somehow be able to lure her back inside once she'd flown over to investigate.

"Nora," I muttered from the corner of my mouth, "go in there and get that long seed stick, the one that's propped up against the wall. And get down so she won't see you moving."

"It's not like she can read our minds," she grumbled, but she did as I asked, her Lycra-covered backside swaying from side to side as she made her way across the floor. Could the woman ever do anything without turning on the come-hither charm? Maybe it was just a habit.

We'd just gotten the animal and seed stick in place when there was the sound of a key in the front door.

"We're dead." Nora groaned, dropping her head into her hands. "Dead, dead, dead."

"No, we're not," I snapped. "Linda's dead. We're just busted."

"Well, so sorry, Miss Wordsmith. I happen to think 'busted' and 'dead' are pretty much the same thing in this situation."

"No one's busted. Or dead."

My head whipped around fast enough to spin. Frederick Owen stood behind us, a wide grin on his face as he looked at the two gals crouched on the floor, trying to hide from a bird.

"I'm the one who should be sorry," he said nonchalantly, walking through the doors and onto the balcony. "I forgot to mention that Pepper likes to get out once in a while and enjoy the fresh air. I was just concerned about her snacking habits when I'm not around. She's on a strict diet until the vet says she's over her infection." We watched as he held out one arm and gave a shrill whistle. Instantly, there was a flash of green as Pepper, that ungrateful wretch, sailed out of the tree and toward her owner. "Who's a pretty girl?"

"Oh, my lord," I muttered as we headed back to Nora's apartment. "I feel like I need to be disinfected or something. He could've had the decency to tell us."

"You've got that right. Do you think we'll catch the bird flu or whatever it is?" Nora's face looked sick, and I wasn't feeling that well myself. I'd handled that idiot bird's chew toy, for goodness sake. It was enough to make my skin crawl.

Suddenly, Nora gave a snort of laughter that startled me. I looked at her sharply, wondering if this was the first sign of avian flu: hysteria, to be followed by gnashing of teeth and foaming at the mouth. Or maybe that was rabies.

"Are you all right?" I reached out a tentative hand, not willing to catch anything I didn't need to. "Should I, I don't know, call someone?"

Instead of answering, she began laughing even harder, leaning up against a wall and howling with mirth. I was looking at her, trying to decide what to do, when a familiar voice sounded behind us.

"Everything okay here?"

I turned to see Patsy, the building's concierge, standing there with a look of curiosity.

I just shook my head, pointing at my gasping friend. "I told her a joke and she thought it was the best she'd ever heard." I shrugged, trying to smile. "I was famous for my jokes at school."

"Oh, yeah?" Curiosity had been replaced with skepticism. "Let's hear it then."

I had to think fast. I was actually one of the worst joke tellers this side of the Pacific, and that covered a lot of territory. On the other hand, I *was* known for my quick, on-the-spot thinking.

"You wouldn't want to hear it," I said lightly. "It's one of those—*blue* jokes, you know what I mean?"

"Indeed I do." With a disapproving sniff, she turned around and began marching the other way, but not before I saw what she'd had in her hand.

Our prim and proper concierge had been holding a metal object exactly like the one I had in my pocket, like the one that was now on its way to some crime lab for testing. Patsy Reilly had the tool to pick open a locked door.

Chapter 10

Before I shared that last little tidbit of knowledge with Nora, I had her latest crack-up to deal with. All right, I'll admit she wasn't "cracking up" in the psychiatric sense of the words, but she was coming close. Laughter, in her case, didn't appear to be medicinal.

Hands on my hips, furious with her for forcing me, yes, *forcing* me to lie once more, I turned to face a flushed Nora. She was still leaning on the wall as if it was made to hold her upright, wiping tears of hilarity from raccoon-like eyes.

"Nora, you're a complete wreck. That goop you put on your eyelashes is now all over your face." It really wasn't, but I wasn't in the mood to be specific. Besides, I figured her vanity might snap her out of this silliness when nothing else would. "And what's with this tendency to cackle like a crazed chicken whenever something like that happens, anyway?" I gestured behind us, meaning both the Pepper incident and the run-in with Patsy. "You never did that when we were kids."

Nora finished wiping her eyes, using both hands to scrub at the skin beneath them. She'd only managed to create further chaos on her face, black smears that stretched from her eyelashes to her chin. Hopefully we wouldn't meet anyone else before we got to the safety of her apartment.

"Blame it on hubby *numero uno*, Sis. He was a real piece of work, let me tell you."

I reached out to pull her away from the wall, tucking one arm through hers and directing her down a mercifully empty corridor.

"So, this is the father of Verity, Charity, et cetera? That hubby?" I fished in a pocket and found a tattered bit of tissue. "Here. Use this."

"Thanks." She took it from me, tiny pieces of lint floating in the air between us like miniature fairies. It must have been through the wash cycle a couple of times—I really needed to start checking my pockets. "You'd think a man who named his kids after virtues would be a bit more saintly, wouldn't you?"

"So he was, what? Not saintly?" I hated to pry, but a quick sideways glance at her semi-scrubbed face hadn't spotted any hastily erected barriers. Nora could throw up a conversational stop sign faster than anyone else I knew, and she was an expert at compartmentalizing her life. To say I didn't know much about her various marriages wasn't as strange as it might seem. If she wanted you to know something, she'd tell you.

"He wasn't abusive in the traditional sense, if you get my drift. He was more, I don't know, *sly* about it. Cutting. Critical. And always in public, where I didn't dare react. Or maybe I didn't have the guts. At home, he ignored me, except when he wanted dinner and dessert, if you know what I mean."

I did.

"By the time I got out of there, it's a wonder I still felt like a human being."

I waited a moment, but when nothing more was forthcoming, I asked the question that had been dancing in the back of my mind for the past few minutes. "So, this hysteria is a reaction of sorts to something. Can you explain? I want to understand, Nora." I gave her arm a squeeze. "It's either that or I book us both into the nearest funny farm for a little r and r."

Nora took in a deep breath as if she was going to reveal the biggest secret of them all. Maybe she was. Maybe it wasn't as bad as she'd made it out to be. And then again, maybe it was worse.

"One day, when the put-downs were especially awful, and even the children were laughing at me, in public, mind you, I decided to shock them into silence. The only weapon I had was laughter. And trust me, Gwennie, I laughed like a loon. It was so bad, or good, depending on your point of view, that he marched all of us straight home." She gave a sad half-smile.

I wanted to find the self-righteous idiot and kick him and his offspring clear to Timbuktu and back.

"After that, whenever he even acted like he was going to start up again, I would look straight at him and start giggling. Nothing major, nothing too loud, but just enough to let him know I would put on a show so everyone would see he'd married a complete cuckoo. He hated looking stupid in public. He was on the board of deacons at our church as well as the city council."

It was such an unbelievable story that I had to believe it.

"So, now, whenever you have an experience that makes you feel crazy—not that I think you are," I amended hastily, regretting the earlier comment about the funny farm, "your reaction is to laugh. Is that right?"

She nodded, and this time there were real tears in her eyes. I stopped walking and gathered her into my arms, holding her tightly as she cried softly into my shoulder. I really hated that man, and I was glad Nora had taken him to the cleaners. Charity and Verity had better stay far, far away from her or they'd be dealing with me this time.

"Oh, there you two are."

I turned to see Brent standing behind us, Aggie sitting by his feet like the trained dog I knew she wasn't. Judging by his knowing grin, I could just about see the direction his little train of thought was chugging as he stared at us. I needed to derail that engine, quick. Nora didn't need another person of the male persuasion laughing at her.

"Mrs. Goldstein and I have just had a rather bad experience." I motioned for him to move ahead of us. "We'll tell you about it when we get back inside, all right?"

"Sure thing, Miss F. And me 'n' Aggie had something happen to us, too, didn't we, girl?" Brent leaned over to scoop the little dog into his arms.

She licked his chin, making him smile.

Once we were back inside Nora's apartment and I'd handed out mugs of strong coffee, it was time for a debriefing. As far as I knew, there was only one more pet sitting job left for the day, and Brent would be dealing with that at three. Since it was with two Siamese cats, I was certain little Miss Agatha Nellie would be spending the time with Nora and me.

I scratched at the bumpy rash on the inside of one elbow. "Well, I'm sure you had quite an adventure today, Brent. Why don't you go first, all right?"

I glanced over at Nora and saw her color had returned to normal, but she still sported a few black smudges under her eyes. She looked like a football player ready to tackle the opposing side. Maybe she was. Catching my eye, she dropped one eyelid and smiled. I let out a small sigh of relief and smiled back.

"Well, you remember I told you about that other dog walker, Miss F.? The one I, you know, kinda like? She's really cute and all that, yeah, but that's not why I wanted to, you know, take her out."

This was like pulling teeth. I gritted my own.

"And? Is there another reason?" Nora sounded much calmer than I was feeling.

He nodded vigorously, looking mighty pleased with himself. I wanted to reach out and shake the answer out of him.

"Her dad is one of those cops that was here, the ones checking on the oven the day that lady died. I figured I could kill two birds with one stone, you know, like get the down low and have a date at the same time. Cool, right?"

"Very cool," I agreed. "Which one?"

"Which one what?"

Wow. This kid's train of thought could jump the rails without warning.

"Which police officer is her dad?" I carefully formed each word, using my faux patient voice that materialized whenever I dealt with a particularly irritating student. "Was it Iro...Officer Taylor or Officer Reinhart?"

"Huh?" Brent looked truly flummoxed. Then his face cleared. "Oh, not those guys. Her dad's the main one, Detective Woodley. He's the cop who doesn't have to wear a uniform anymore. He's in charge of the case."

These last words sounded as if he was simply parroting back what he'd been told. It was certainly an interesting tidbit, though, and I told him so, making him glow with pride. That had always been my *modus operandi* in the classroom. Scold if necessary and praise as soon as possible. It worked as well now as it had then. By the time Nora started telling about our run-in with Pepper the Pesky Parrot, Brent was beaming at me in particular and the world in general.

Yes, ma'am, I still had it. Retirement hadn't dulled the edge of my people management skills one iota. What I didn't have was an explanation concerning why Patsy Reilly needed a lock pick tool. You'd think a concierge, a trusted member of staff, would have access to a master key if she needed to open a locked door. That was something I was determined to find out as soon as I could.

Once Nora had assured our little spy-slash-Romeo that yes, he would indeed be taking home some money that evening and he'd left for the last pet sitting job of the day, I turned to confront my best friend.

"So, just when were you going to tell me?"

Nora sat facing me, her feet tucked underneath her as she sat on the couch. Aggie, of course, sat on her lap, and I could swear she was scowling at me as well.

"Right now. As soon as I had a chance."

It was my turn to feel hurt. "Really, Nora. Between hauling you back here and listening to Bright Boy stutter out his plans for playing detective, it's a wonder I'm still in one piece."

All right, that last statement was a little dramatic. And probably just this side of untruthful. I'd dealt with much bigger issues at work, and it hadn't bothered me. But, to be honest, this entire hanging out together for most of the day was beginning to get to me—not to mention a dead body and a crazed parrot. I needed some solitude, but I also wanted to get to the bottom of this whole thing. And now Brent looked like he was going to get the goods—the info on Linda—and beat me to the punch.

No wonder I was feeling out of sorts. And sorry for myself. And very itchy. I glanced at my ankles. The tiny red bumps had begun to spread up my white legs. Fabulous. Now I'd look like a candy cane and it wasn't even Christmas.

To my surprise, I found I was crying. Nora hastily set Aggie on the floor and came over to sit by me, putting a comforting arm around my shoulders.

"It's just all gone wrong," I sobbed, using one foot to nudge the little allergen away. "First, you think I need a job, and then someone gets killed in your kitchen, and now everywhere I look, someone else has these things. I'll never feel safe in my house again." I dug into my pocket and pulled out the Z-shaped metal hook and waved it in the air like a weapon. "Plus, I had to sleep with a stupid chair wedged under my bedroom doorknob and it probably wouldn't have worked anyway."

And with that pronouncement, I cried even harder. Nora, bless her wise heart, let me. When the waterworks were finally over, I reached in my pocket for the tissue I'd left there, only to remember I'd given it to Nora. Well, there was more than one way to skin a cat. Lifting up the hem of my new-to-me T-shirt from the local Goodwill—they gave teachers a twenty percent discount, and I hadn't quite gotten around to telling them about my retirement—I wiped my nose with a gusto that left it feeling raw.

"This has certainly been a day for tears, hasn't it?" I laughed shakily, glad I didn't wear mascara. It would have been running down my face in black rivulets. Or in black splotches under my eyes like Nora's. "I suppose we need to get cleaned up a bit so we can pay a visit to little Miss Concierge."

"They say the eyes are the windows of the soul," said Nora, "and I think our windows got a pretty good scrubbing today."

"Indeed they did." I smiled at her comment. Words had always been able to create immediate pictures in my mind, and I liked the idea of having a sparkling clean soul. With everything that had occurred over the past few days, I'd been due for a good cleansing.

We were ready to rock in less than five minutes, to my amazement. Nora had given her face a quick scrubbing with a wet wash cloth while I splashed cold water on mine. I'd never been one for wearing makeup anyway; a swipe of powder and maybe a dash of lipstick was all I'd ever done. But for Nora to head out *sans* war paint? That was telling. She'd turned her attention to something else besides playing the role of man eater. Patsy Reilly should be on her guard.

Patsy was back behind her desk, frowning slightly as she flipped busily through a large appointment calendar that doubled as a blotter. I was pretty sure she heard us approaching—Birkenstocks made a telltale shuffling sound, after all—but only looked up once we were standing directly in front of her. Even Aggie, who'd ridden down in Nora's arms, was silent for once.

"Good afternoon, ladies." Her tone was formal, with the implied message that she'd already forgotten the scene in the upstairs hallway. "How can I help you?"

Instead of answering her, Nora turned to me.

"Gwen, show Patsy what you have in your pocket."

All right, then. We were going to go in with guns blazing, no warning shots beforehand, no pleasant exchanges. Nora was definitely locked and loaded. I gulped, reached into my pocket, and produced the metal tool.

Patsy leaned forward, examining it with nothing much more than polite interest. I thought I spotted a flicker of something, maybe caution, in her eyes before she turned her gaze on me.

"Very nice." She reached for the calendar once more. "Is that something you found and want to turn in?"

Nora sat Aggie on the desk and leaned in, her gaze fixed on Patsy's with an intensity that might have scared someone else. Patsy only managed to look amused, but she'd slid back in her chair just the slightest bit. Maybe she was allergic to dogs as well. More than likely, though, she was allergic to Nora and her attitude.

"Actually, we'd like for you to tell us exactly what it is." Nora leaned in even closer, and this time Patsy didn't bother hiding the fact she was more than uncomfortable with the personal space invasion. "And before you start hemming and hawing and acting like you have no idea on God's green earth what it is, there's something you ought to know. Gwen?"

Oh, fabulous. I'd always hated spotlights. This one was composed of two megawatt beams directed on me, shining beneath a pair of furrowed eyebrows. All pretense of amusement was gone from Patsy's face, and I was caught in the full force of a rather unfriendly glare. Even Aggie was staring at me, her dark eyes round in that pointy little face.

"Well," I began hesitantly. "Earlier on, when I...we...saw you upstairs, you were holding something that looked exactly like that." I glanced at the piece of metal that now lay on Patsy's desk. "So, I guess we decided to come ask you what it was." There. I'd managed to get something out without strangling on the words. With a tiny shrug, I looked at Nora.

"Oh, for goodness' sake, Gwen." Nora gave me a hard stare and then turned back to face Patsy. "We already know what it is, so you don't need to play coy with us. It's not becoming to someone your age anyway." Her tone was so sweet it made my teeth ache.

I looked at my feet to hide my smile. Nora was coming all cannons blazing. She knew right where to aim, too, and she'd scored a direct hit with that last remark.

A furious Patsy jumped to her feet, eyes mere slits in her face. "Just because you've got money to burn, Mrs. Goldstein, and can pay to keep your looks, it doesn't mean the rest of us can." She was practically steaming, and I reached out one hand and placed it on Nora's arm as a precaution. If there was going to be a brouhaha at the concierge desk, I was going to do my best to halt it. "Now, if there's nothing else, I'd appreciate it if you'd leave me alone. Some of us have to work for a living." She seemed like she wanted to say something else, but at that moment, the main lobby doors slid open with a sigh, letting in the sound of rain and the smell of damp pavement. Taking a deep breath, she steadied herself. "Welcome to Portland's only luxury apartments. How can I help you?"

I glanced over my shoulder and spotted the man who stood there, a flat cap on his graying hair and a rather showy salt-and-pepper mustache under his equally prominent nose. Leaning over and grabbing the metal tool, I slid it back into my pocket and gave Nora's arm a slight push. It was time to make our exit.

Or it would have been if the man hadn't taken one look at Nora and stopped in his tracks.

"Well, as I live and breathe. I believe that's my sweet little stepmother standing right in front of my very eyes. Nora, how are you?" With a rather theatrical sweep of his cap and a tiny bow, he held out one hand in greeting.

Nora froze in place, an expression of incredulity on her face. "Buddy? Buddy Levinsky? Is that you?"

Another bow and sweep of the cap. This time I could see exactly why he wore it. Where there once was hair, there was now a very large, very red bald patch. I should have guessed it anyway, judging by the size of the mustache. The ol' migration of hair could do damage to a man's easily bruised ego.

"I'm honored that you remember me. It was a long time ago, after all."

There was something in his tone that I didn't like. Nora didn't either, apparently.

She handed a yapping Aggie to me and planted both hands on her hips, a Fury in spandex and stilettos. "I recognize you because you're a spitting image of your skunk of a father. Now, unless you're prepared to make an appointment with my lawyers, I believe our little visit here is done."

Without a backward glance, Nora spun on her heels and stomped her way out of the lobby. I gave both Patsy and Buddy a little waggle of my fingers and followed my best friend, burning with curiosity. At the rate these errant stepchildren were showing up, we'd soon have the entire dysfunctional clan together.

"What was that all about?" I was shuffling as quickly as possible to keep up with Nora, curling my toes so my sandals wouldn't fly off my feet. For someone in a pair of three-inch heels, that woman could move.

"I don't want to talk about it right now," she snapped and then turned to look back at me, with a contrite expression. "Sorry, sis. It's not your monkey, not your circus." She reached out to press the "up" button for the elevator and took the little dog out of my arms. "I'm just glad I ran into him downstairs and was able to head him off at the pass. I have a gut feeling he was here to see me. Knowing Patsy, she would've been happy to direct him to my place."

The elevator doors opened with a muted hiss, and we stepped inside. I looked curiously at Nora, trying to remember where Buddy's skunky father fell in the lineup of husbands. Maybe match number three? Or four? I gave my arms an absentminded scratch as I thought about it.

It was a silent ride to Nora's floor. Slipping my hand into my pocket, I found the metal tool and pulled it out, examining it closely. I felt like I was playing the trombone, moving my hand in and out, trying to get the perfect focus. I'd never needed glasses before, and I wasn't crazy about getting them now. Maybe it was just an issue with the elevator lighting.

"If you can wait, I've got a magnifying glass in my desk."

I looked at Nora to see her wide grin.

"Or I think I've got an extra pair of readers lying around somewhere."

I wrinkled my nose at her. She could be so funny sometimes. Not.

"I just wanted to take a peek at it, smarty pants." I shoved it back in my pocket and crossed my arms over my chest. "Did you notice the way that Patsy reacted when she saw it?"

"I sure did."

The elevator stopped with a small jerk, the doors sliding open onto the empty hallway.

"Come to think of it," Nora continued, "she knows exactly what it is. What I want to know is why she does. I mean, it's not something the average Joe would have any idea about."

"That's what I was thinking as well." I smiled in agreement as we stepped into her apartment. Kicking off my Birkenstocks, I reached down to massage my toes. They were sore from curling against the shoes as I tried to keep up with Nora. "If you want me to, I can go back and ask her about it, just me." I straightened up and gave her a grin. "I'm thinking I might get more out of her if I'm by myself. It's the old 'sun and wind' story, you know?"

"Oh, whatever. Maybe I like being the storm." Nora held onto the end of the sofa and kicked off her heels with a groan. "Besides, that woman really rubs me the wrong way."

"Well, I'm pretty sure it's mutual." Sinking down on one end of the sofa, I let my head fall back against the cushions and closed my eyes. "I'm beat. I didn't sleep that well last night, knowing someone had been inside my house without my permission."

"I can imagine. Want me to make you a coffee?"

"No, that's all right. I probably need to cut out the caffeine so I can get some sleep tonight." Opening my eyes, I sat up, a yawn nearly splitting my face in two. "Actually, Nora, I think I'll buzz off home now. Don't forget to pay the kid, okay?"

"I'm sure he won't let me forget. By the way, did he happen to mention when he was going out with this cop's girl?" Nora sat watching as I stood up and began walking toward the door, my head feeling three times heavier than normal. "I want to go over some questions with him so he knows what to ask."

I dipped my head in agreement as I slipped my feet back into my sandals. "That's a great idea. You might even write them down, make a cue card for him to study." I opened the door. "At least that's the way I used to have my students acquire new concepts. Flash cards, talking points, whatever you call it. It's the best way for kids with visual learning preferences to learn new ideas. Just remind him not to read from it." I could just see Brent whipping out an index card and posing questions like a contestant on some silly dating show.

"I'm not sure Brent has a specific learning preference." Her tone was as dry as a well-made martini. "Maybe we can have Aggie do the talking instead."

"Or Pepper." I shook my head, smiling ruefully. "I have a feeling that bird could carry on a full-blown conversation if she wanted to."

"Isn't that the truth?" She walked over to the door with me, Aggie scampering at our heels, and gave me a quick hug. "You be careful out there, Sis. And text me when you get home."

"I will. And I'm probably going to bed early tonight, like before the sun goes down, so if you need me for anything, you'll have to wait until morning. I'm sure glad today's Friday. We need the weekend off to recover from this crazy week."

"Tell me about it." She dropped her arm and stood back, shaking her head. "And I swear that if I see any more of those ignoramus step kids of mine, I'm gonna spit nails. They're just like flies, buzzing around, trying to find the nastiest place to land."

Impulsively, I hugged her back. "If any of them come around tonight, you just march yourself over to my place."

"You're a sweetheart." She dabbed at her eyes. "And now get out of here before I start bawling again."

Later I would wish I'd been paying better attention to my surroundings as I left the apartment building. I might have given a certain mustachioed man more than just a passing glance as I headed home.

Chapter 11

True to my word, I was bathed and in bed before the sun had fully set, cuddled up with my favorite book, *Hickory Dickory Death*, and a mug of peppermint tea. Some folks might have seen that as eccentric behavior, but I liked the comfort and security of sitting in my bed. And, no, it wasn't the product of older age. I'd always fled to the safety of my room, book in hand, whenever life was too much or I couldn't stand the chaos of having five younger siblings. Living between the covers of a good novel was the way I handled stress.

I was just about ready to call it a night when I first heard a slight noise, almost like the brushing of pine branches against the side of the house. I listened briefly, heard nothing else, and decided that was exactly what it had been, a tree branch moving in the ever-present breeze.

When it came again, louder and more insistent, I was up and out of the bed before I even knew what was happening. Unless the pines around Portland had started knocking on doors, this was definitely not a tree.

Reaching for my cell phone, I held it to my rapidly beating heart and stood still for a moment, trying to decide the best course of action. Should I quickly get dressed and then dial 9-1-1, or should I try to sneak out to the living room and see if I could spot the intruder? Maybe it was a neighbor just stopping by to see if I was all right after last night's fiasco. Or maybe it was the person who'd come into my house and caused said fiasco.

"Now I lay me down to sleep," I began muttering under my breath as I dropped to my hands and knees, adding with feeling, "and please don't let it be a permanent sleep either." I really needed to learn another prayer. I began crawling across the room and into the short hallway that connected the back of the bungalow with the entryway and straight into the living room.

And found myself staring into another pair of eyes.

The legendary Seattle Seahawks fans had nothing on us. Between the shrieking and screaming, the two of us could have registered on the Richter scale for sheer noise level.

Finally, out of breath and exhausted from leaping about in the dark like a deranged frog, I fell onto my couch, eyes closed and chest heaving. I would have loved to have said "with my bosom heaving," but that part of my anatomy had begun a southern migration years ago. Still, it took a moment for me to calm down before I dealt with my best friend.

"Would you mind telling me just what you were doing in my house, crawling around on the floor like some geriatric baby? In heels, no less?" I gave her stiletto-shod feet a look of disgust, having nearly had my feet perforated by them as we'd jumped around the room.

Nora's eyes were shut, though, so the whole effect was lost on her. Instead, she was smiling, lips curled in what could only be called a smirk. I wanted to throw my Multnomah Falls souvenir pillow at her.

"Well, it worked, didn't it?"

"What worked? You nearly giving me a heart attack? What if I'd called the cops? You'd be on your way to jail right this moment, and, trust me, I'd be pretending I didn't know you."

"But it worked." She held up one hand and I could see the twin—or triplet—to the metal tool I'd been given by the cleaning gal. "Insert, twist, and voila! In like Flynn."

"You make it sound so sordid." I sat up and crossed my bare legs underneath me. "So, you came all the way over here to prove you can pick a locked door?"

"Maybe." She sat up and gave me the full Nora smile. "Actually, I wanted to leave this for you as well." She waved a piece of paper at me and winked. "Payment for services rendered, as promised."

"Oh, dear lord. You break into my house so you can pay me? You sound like a complete basket case, you know that?"

"I call it killing two birds with one stone, for your information. We wanted to know what this little doodad was for, and now we know. For sure." Again, the metal tool was held out for my inspection. "Aren't you curious about where I got it?"

I was, but I wasn't about to let on just how curious I felt. I let her stew for a moment. I needed coffee, a caffeine jolt to kick start my heart back to its normal rhythm.

Conscious of my bare legs hanging out beneath an old sleep shirt I'd snagged at the Goodwill, I stomped to the kitchen end of the room and began banging mugs around. I needed to take my frustration out on something, and coffee cups could be replaced. A best friend couldn't.

Behind me, Nora giggled and I turned around to make sure it wasn't a giggle of the other variety, the type she had used as a weapon against a ruthless ex-husband. It wasn't. She was pointing at my legs, her eyes crinkled with laughter.

"What? Is there a problem with the way I look?" I glared at her as I filled the coffeepot with water. "May I remind you that this is my house and I was in my bed, trying to get some much-needed rest. I didn't know I'd have my crazy friend joining me."

"They're just so white!" Another burst of laughter. "Don't you ever get any sun on those things?"

I didn't bother answering. Here in Portland, we were lucky to get three sunny days in a row. A tan was the least of my concerns. I glanced at her legs, but they were encased in a tight pair of black leggings, per usual, so I had no idea if she was tanned or not. Come to think of it, I'd rarely seen her out of what I thought of as her uniform: skin-tight top in whatever neon color had caught her eye and the perpetual black leggings. And stilettos, of course. The woman was a walking advertisement for Lycra and heels.

I carried a steaming mug of coffee over to her and sat back against the arm of the couch. It was time for some answers, and I didn't need a cue card.

"All right. Where'd you get that thingy, and how did you get here?" I indicated the silver tool that lay between us on the couch. "And why couldn't you wait until tomorrow to give me a check?"

Her expression became mischievous, her smile playful. This was Nora at her finest. Everything could be made better with a joke or two, as long as it wasn't on her.

I was getting a trifle impatient. My bed was calling, but after the coffee, it'd probably be a while before I got back to its comforting embrace. "Well? Spill it, girlfriend. And quick."

"I drove myself. And I took it out of Patsy's desk."

I stared at her for a moment, my coffee mug suspended in the air. "What in the world? I'm sure she wouldn't have left something like that lying around, Nora. And please don't tell me you somehow bypassed the security cameras and picked the lock on her desk. They'll kick you out of the building faster than you can say 'thief.'"

"All right, I won't." She grinned at me over the rim of her mug. "At least I didn't mess with the camera. Brent did that."

"He did *what*?" I had to set my coffee down before I ended up with a lap full. "And did someone see you two? Call the cops?"

Nora snorted. "Of course not, silly. I wouldn't be here otherwise, would I? No, he just sorta blocked the camera's view for me while I went through the desk. No big deal." She gave a nonchalant shrug. "By the way," she took another sip, "he said to say thank you for the card idea."

I groaned. My life, my orderly life, was fast becoming a farce. Not only was I friends—*best* friends—with a burglar in training, I was now mentor to a wannabe spy. Maybe another year or two in the classroom wasn't such a bad idea after all. It'd probably be better on my blood pressure. Sighing, I reached for my coffee.

With my cat burglar friend finally dispatched and the promise of a good night's sleep ahead of me, I slid my heaviest armchair in front of the door as a precaution. At least I'd have a better chance of catching someone if they had to deal with the oak monstrosity, a yard sale purchase from many years back. My back door was easier to block. I dragged the kitchen table in front of it and piled a few chairs on top for good measure. Not perfect, but better than nothing.

Whatever it was, either the jumping around or knowing my doors were fortified, I was able to sleep uninterrupted for seven glorious hours. A quick shower, a restorative cup of coffee, and I was out the door—after hauling the armchair out of the way, of course. In the morning light, it did seem slightly ridiculous. Most things did, including my reaction to Nora's nighttime visit. I had to admit the two of us must have been quite a sight.

Smiling, I began the walk to her apartment building, taking in deep breaths of the moist air that had blown in from the ocean overnight. Living next to both a major river and the Pacific Ocean had its advantages, not the least of which was lots of greenery. Of course, some of the green took the form of algae and mold, thanks to the cool, damp climate, but we did have more than our share of trees and flowering shrubs in Portland.

And they were perfect for hiding folks that didn't want to be seen. I'd already walked past a dwarf flowering strawberry tree before I noticed someone was walking behind me. Too close behind me. When I felt the hand on my shoulder, I let out a stifled scream and swung around, losing one Birkenstock as I did.

"Marcus Avery! What the heck are you doing? And I know you were following me, so don't act as though you weren't."

I was fuming, practically steaming, as I turned to face a rather sheepish looking Marcus. I'd already reached for my front pocket, where I'd stored the lock picker Nora had taken from Patsy's desk as well as the one given to me by the apartment cleaner. I wasn't sure how much of a weapon they'd be, but maybe I could get in a good eye jab or two. And if this goofball didn't have a good reason for scaring me halfway to death, I still might do it.

"Sorry, Miss...Miss..." He stuttered, probably waiting for me to supply my name.

I didn't. Instead, I simply crossed my arms and gave him my best glare.

Finally, he shrugged, thrusting both hands into his jeans pockets and stared at his feet. "Look, I know you're good friends—"

"*Best* friends," I corrected him.

"Okay, best friends with Nora." More shuffling and a quick glance up. "Can you tell me what it was I did wrong? I mean, I keep calling her and she doesn't answer me. I know she knows it's me, too." He looked straight at me, eyes blinking rapidly as though something was in them. Maybe there was.

I had to stare at him in amazement. *That's* what this was about? Marcus Avery, the Don Juan of Downtown, the Love 'em and Leave 'em Lothario, was asking about Nora? *What an idiot you are*, is what I wanted to say.

"Maybe she doesn't want to talk to anyone right now," is what I said instead. "She's got stepchildren coming out of her ears at the moment, probably because they all heard that she was dead, and she's starting to feel a little defensive, you know?"

He bobbed his head eagerly, almost like Aggie when she was waiting for a treat. "I know. And I told her I could help her with that, maybe dig up some dirt on them so they'd leave her alone."

He actually looked proud of the suggestion, as if dirt digging was an honorable pastime. I wanted to turn around and walk off in disgust. There was something in his eyes, though, that reminded me—God help me—of Nora herself. They were both lonely people. Maybe I could do something...

"Listen," I said briskly, looking around. "Do you have a car or something nearby?"

"Yes. It's actually right across the street." He pointed to an older Dodge Caravan, one of the original models that always seemed to be bright red or dull blue. His, of course, was a conspicuous metallic green.

I had to shake my head. Not a very slick choice for a private eye.

"All right, here's what you need to do." I quickly outlined my plan, shushing him occasionally as I gave him the specifics. "And make sure you do every last bit of that, Marcus. Take it from me. I know what Nora likes. And doesn't like."

He beamed at me, an almost fanatical light in his eyes. Maybe I shouldn't have encouraged him so much. "I will, absolutely, Miss—"

"Gwen. Call me Gwen."

I said goodbye to a reinvigorated Marcus Avery and continued walking toward the apartments, wondering what I had just done. If things didn't work the way I'd planned, then you could probably call me "Mud" instead of Gwen.

"Hey, Miss F."

The sound of hurried footsteps behind me made me swing around in mid-stride. Brent, his arms full of a grinning Aggie and a large canvas bag, came trotting up, a matching grin on his face.

"You'll never guess what I heard, Miss F. Not if I live to be as old as you and Mrs. G., I'll probably never hear something like this again." His eyes opened wide. "Cross my heart and hope to die."

"I hope not. Do you want to tell me right now or wait until we get to Mrs. Goldstein's?" I reached out one tentative finger and gave Aggie's chin a scratch. "How are you, girl?"

"You're really starting to be a dog lover, you know that?" Brent looked at his puppy and smiled proudly as if she was singlehandedly responsible for my conversion. "You'll be getting your own dog before you know it."

"That might not be a bad idea." I thought about the past few nights. Having a built-in alarm system would certainly be comforting. And maybe I could train him or her to dislike Lycra. "We'd better get inside before Nora wonders where we are."

Nora was more energetic than I thought she'd be after her foray into cat burglary. Today's wardrobe choice was the ubiquitous black stretch pants, these with tiny pink flowers embroidered near the ankles, and a top in a color that reminded me of Pepto-Bismol.

"Well, if it isn't the Dancing Queen herself." Nora leaned over and gave me a quick kiss on one cheek, dropping one eyelid in a roguish wink. "You've really got some moves, Sis."

"Poo to you." I had to smile. Anyone who might have spotted my jig in the dark would have put me down as either completely uninhibited or off my rocker. "You weren't so bad yourself."

"Did you guys go clubbing last night?" Brent looked from me to Nora, his eyebrows raised. "I sure would've liked to have seen that."

I started to explain what had happened, but Nora interrupted me, her tone casual. "It's a club for people over fifty, kid. You're too young."

"Oh. I guess that's kinda cool, old folks getting to have some fun. My grandma always said—"

"All right, Brent. We get it." I turned to Nora, rolling my eyes. "What's on the agenda today, old-timer?"

Nora poked her tongue out. I returned the gesture.

"There are three dog walking jobs and someone called to ask if we did any pet grooming."

I shook my head vehemently. "Absolutely not. Can you just see us trying to hold a squirming dog still enough to wash and clip it? No thank you."

"Keep your girdle on, Sis. I turned it down, all right?" Nora grinned and waved a piece of paper at me. "But I did take this one for later this afternoon. Round two with Pepper."

"Oh, heck no." I held up both hands, waving the idea off. "There is no way I'm going back there with that nutty bird."

"It'll be fine. Look, it's just for a while. The owner has some errands to run, that's all."

"So, Pepper's still infected, or whatever?" I shuddered, imagining the different things I could get from a sick parrot. Didn't people catch infections from ill animals, like mad cow disease? Maybe there was mad parrot disease as well.

"He says she's much better, but he's still watching what she eats." Nora shrugged. "You don't need to go, Sis. I can do this one by myself, all right?"

"We'll see." I was half listening for Marcus, wondering if he'd be able to follow through with my instructions. If he could, well, there might be hope for him.

"Um, if you ladies don't mind, I've got something to tell you."

I'd almost forgotten about Brent's date the night before with the cop's daughter.

"Let's go into the kitchen." Nora motioned for us to follow her. "A friend stopped by this morning and brought a dozen Voodoo Doughnuts along."

I saw a little smile lurking in the corner of her mouth, and I groaned silently. If there was another man in the picture, Marcus was really going to have his work cut out for him. At least I'd told him to bring flowers. Hopefully she'd like those as well as pastries.

When we were all seated, each with a fresh mug of coffee and a donut—I had a Bacon Maple Bar and Nora chose a Homer, its strawberry icing covered with candied sprinkles—I nodded at Brent.

"Okay, let's hear it. What did you learn last night?"

Brent took a big bite from his Grape Ape donut. "Well, she told me that—"

"Hold up there." Nora held up one hand. "Swallow the donut first, please. I really don't want to see a train wreck in a tunnel." She shook her head, half-smiling. "Just like a big kid. How'd you put up with that for twenty years, Gwen?"

"By not doing cafeteria duty. I chose bus duty instead. Much less stomach-turning."

"I'm sitting right here." Brent looked from me to Nora, his lower lip pushed out. "I can hear you, you know."

"And we're both glad you're here, Brent." I reached over to pat his arm. "Now, what did you learn from…what's her name?"

"It's Rachel, and she told me about the post thingy. You know, when they cut open dead bodies?"

Nora made a face and I swallowed a bite of bacon quickly.

"Post-mortem. So, what did they find?" I reached for my coffee.

"That she didn't die from being stabbed." He paused and looked at me accusingly. "You didn't tell me she was stabbed, Miss F."

"I guess I forgot about that part, Brent, what with the oven needing to be checked and all. Some things just slip my mind. Old brain, you know?" I smiled, pointing to my head.

"Yeah, sure." He gave me a skeptical look. "Well, what Rachel told me is the lady probably would have died anyway because she'd been poisoned."

"Poisoned?"

Nora and I looked at one another, our eyes as round as the donuts.

"With *what*?" My voice rose on the last word, a squawk that made me sound like a bad imitation of Pepper the parrot.

"And this part is kinda gross, so cover your ears if you don't want to hear." He took another bite of donut and made a big production of chewing and swallowing.

I almost thought he was going to open his mouth and show us that it was gone.

"They checked her stomach and saw she'd eaten some kind of dessert and it had been laced with like a ton of sleeping pills, all crushed up and sprinkled on like sugar."

It clicked suddenly. The Danish we'd had during our initial "Two Sisters" planning session. How sleepy and lethargic I'd gotten after just a few bites. Nora, not eating her slice, had been wide awake.

"Oh, my God, Nora." I stared at my best friend's pale face. "That means someone had already been in here. Linda Fletcher must've eaten some while we were passing out cards."

Nora glanced at the spot on the floor where the body had been lying, her lips a thin line. "The woman had absolutely no shame. And look where it got her."

"That's a bit harsh." I pushed away my unfinished donut. "She died, didn't she?"

She didn't answer at once, but I could tell something was spinning in her mind. Finally, she looked up and said in a slow voice, "So, why stab her? Why the overkill, if you'll pardon the pun."

"Maybe she wasn't supposed to be in your kitchen, Mrs. G.," offered a solemn Brent. He reached down and lifted an excited Aggie to his lap, hugging her tightly.

"Of course she wasn't supposed to be in here." Nora's frown creased her forehead. "I was supposed to be home. As far as anyone knew, I should've been sitting right here. Or out there." She nodded toward the living room.

"Maybe whoever the killer was decided to peek back in and see if you'd eaten any of the Danish. If you had, you'd be sleepy and drugged, unable to fight back, right? And then, just like that," I snapped my fingers, "they could finish the job."

"Only it wasn't me they found. It was Linda."

The three of us sat in silence for a moment. Aggie was busy finishing off Brent's donut, purple crumbs dotting her whiskers.

I couldn't eat another bite. The "what ifs" were too big to ignore. What if Nora hadn't met me for coffee? What if I'd eaten the rest of the Danish? What if we hadn't decided to pass out business cards?

And what if someone still wanted Nora permanently out of the picture?

Chapter 12

It was difficult to focus on the day's tasks after Brent's verbal bombshell. Nora appeared shaken as well, and I had to remind her several times to check her voicemail for additional clients.

"Sorry, Sis." She broke off staring into space and looked at me. Shadows were gathering under her eyes, a sure sign of an impending storm. "I just can't get my head around this whole debacle. Not that I don't think Linda's death wasn't a tragedy. It certainly was. But now I'm beginning to wonder which of my ex-steps wants me dead badly enough to poison me?"

"You weren't the one who was poisoned," I pointed out helpfully.

Nora glared in return. "You know exactly what I mean, smarty pants."

We fell into silence, each one wrapped in our own thoughts. Mine were beginning to smooth out somewhat, now that the first shock was over. Maybe it wouldn't be such a bad idea to get the keeper of the gate on our side, instead of antagonizing her.

"I think I'm going to run down and have a word with Patsy." I stood up and headed toward the door. "I'll be back in a few."

"Whatever floats your boat."

I looked over my shoulder and saw Nora give a slight shrug before turning her attention to her cell phone.

I paused, staring at her in concern. A halfhearted reply was definitely not her style. If anything, the very name "Patsy" should have been the proverbial red flag waving in front of the bull. Instead, Nora was acting like a reluctant matador who preferred to stay out of the ring.

With a little sigh, I left the apartment and headed downstairs. Patsy lived on the premises, one of the perks of dealing with the inmates of the building, and was usually the first to make an appearance in the reception area. I practiced my I-am-a-competent-woman face in the elevator, the one I used whenever I wanted to appear large and in charge. It usually worked, but, after the first glimpse of my target, I wasn't so sure.

Patsy stood behind her desk, talking rapidly into a cell phone and frowning at the floor. *Great.* Maybe this wasn't such a good idea after all. Before I could retreat, however, she raised her face and caught sight of me. I smiled tentatively, waggling my fingers at her in a hesitant greeting. She responded by turning her back.

Definitely not a good idea then. I was halfway back to the elevator when I heard rapid footsteps behind me. Turning, I saw Patsy was following me with such a determined expression on her face that I almost made a dash for the elevator's open door.

"Hang on a sec, all right?"

I stopped, mentally preparing myself for a confrontation. Nora should've been here with me, especially since she had been the one to fire the first volley across Patsy's bow.

Straightening my shoulders and willing my stomach to tuck itself toward my spine, I plastered a smile on my face and waited for the barrage of angry words.

"Look, Gwen, is it? I just wanted to tell you I'm really sorry we got off on the wrong foot the other day."

Patsy stood with both hands shoved into her front pockets, feet slightly apart. Completely non-confrontational body language. I let myself relax a bit and my midsection almost groaned with relief. It was quite the chore to hold all that table muscle rigid for more than a few minutes.

"I was actually headed down to tell you the same thing." I smiled at her and held out a hand. "Gwen Franklin. Retired."

"Must be nice." Her voice was hesitant, but her smile was genuine. "Nice to finally meet you." She motioned behind her. "I need to take care of something really quick. Would you mind coming back to my desk? I just made some coffee."

That was the magic word for most Portlandians. We probably consumed more coffee per capita than most places, and we liked ours hot, thank you very much. None of that iced business here. I smiled in agreement and we began the short stroll back to the lobby.

"Give me just a sec. You can have a seat there." She pointed to a comfortable armchair in front of her desk. "I've just gotta get this email answered and then we can talk." She reached up and rubbed her eyes, and I noticed that the bags underneath them were big enough to carry a change of clothes. "I don't sleep well most of the time, and last night was worse than usual." She shrugged and gave a short laugh. "So, I drink coffee to balance it out, right?"

I didn't reply. Caffeine, the drug of choice for insomniacs. And high school students who either stayed up too late working or texting, as well as Nervous Nellies like me who were afraid of things that went bump in the night.

I waited in silence while Patsy sat tapping at a keyboard that could be cleverly tucked away out of sight when it wasn't needed. Like everything else about this building, the desk was constructed for efficiency of line and use. Quite unlike my house, where things were chosen for cost effectiveness and comfort. Still, I supposed this was how the rich spent their money, Nora aside. She preferred quality over everything, and quality could be very comfortable indeed.

"There. That's finished." Patsy gave a final tap on the keyboard and pushed the entire thing back under the desktop. "I had to confirm the guest speaker for our next coffee klatch." She grinned at me, and the pleasant crinkles at the corners of very blue eyes stood out. "You ought to come, Gwen. This month's guest will be talking about gravestone rubbings."

"Gravestone rubbings?" I lifted my eyebrows. "And what's that, if you don't mind me asking?"

"Just what it sounds like, unfortunately. Or I guess if you're into stuff like that, it can be fun." She grimaced, wrinkling her nose as if she'd caught a whiff of something unpleasant. "I prefer to stay out of cemeteries, but maybe that's just me. I had enough of that when I was a kid."

"Lots of funerals?" I asked sympathetically, recalling a few times in my own childhood when I'd lost a distant relative or two.

"No, nothing that normal." She stood, motioning to the coffee machine that sat on its own table, a monstrosity with two spouts and several blinking buttons. "Would you like a regular cup of joe or something a little more fancy? I can do either."

"Just regular." I was still curious about her last comment. "So, why did you hang around cemeteries?"

"My mom was into genealogy, that sort of thing. I guess my dad's ancestors came over on the Mayflower or something, and she thought it would be cool for me to have a record of stuff like that. To be honest," she said as she carried a brimming mug over to me, "I couldn't care less. But it meant a lot to her."

I nodded, taking the coffee cup and carefully setting it down on the edge of her desk. It was thicker than normal—my kind of mug—and decorated with the building's logo.

"Is your dad still around?"

She shook her head, leaning down to sip at her own coffee. "He split when I was still a baby. I've actually never met him, and with my mom dying a few years back, I don't have anyone to ask."

"I see."

What a trivial comment. I didn't "see" anything except a young woman—young to me, that was—who worked long hours and who probably didn't deserve to clash with Nora or anyone else. Like most folks on the front lines, Patsy absorbed a lot of nonsense.

"So, what was it you needed to see me about?" Patsy looked at me over the rim of her cup, her eyes as bright as the morning sun that had crept out from behind the clouds.

I stared at her in confusion for a moment before I recalled exactly why I'd come downstairs to begin with. My face warmed. "Only to apologize, which I hope you've accepted."

Patsy waved a hand at me, with a half-smile. "Don't even let it bother you. Believe me, I've heard worse."

"But you shouldn't have to, so that's why I'm here." I reached into my pocket, where I'd hidden the lock pick, and handed it to Patsy on the palm of my hand. "And I believe this is yours."

She said nothing, both eyebrows lifting as she reached out to take it.

"And sorry that we thought we needed to take it to begin with," I added somewhat awkwardly. How did one apologize for burglarizing the concierge, anyway?

"Actually, it doesn't belong to me." She opened a side drawer on her desk and dropped the metal tool inside with a clink. "Mrs. Goldstein's friend, the one who's a private investigator? It's his. He dropped it the other day and asked me to find it and hold it for him until he could pick it up." She smiled at me but there was a slight wariness in her eyes. "My late husband was a locksmith, so I knew what I was looking for. Reilly's Locksmith of Portland. That was us until he passed away." She paused a moment. "It's certainly not something I'd keep on me, though. Too many chances for it to get into the wrong hands."

Marcus Avery? My mind was racing, and my mouth hung open like a fish gasping for air. I closed it with a snap, reaching for my coffee to cover my reaction. That man had a few questions to answer the next time I saw him.

Which, as fate and the universe would have it, was just then.

Marcus, a bouquet of flowers in one hand and a container of Nora's favorite coffee in the other, practically bounced inside the lobby's doors. A geriatric Tigger, goofy smile and all.

Which I fully intended to wipe off his face at the first possible moment.

"Marcus. Long time no see." My tone was as dry as the Arizona desert.

"What?" He appeared momentarily puzzled and then chuckled. "Oh, yeah. I get it. A real long time, right?" He winked at me, then nodded at the bouquet. "So, whaddaya think? Think she'll go for it?"

"Oh, I'm sure she will." I looked at Patsy. "Why don't you return his property while he's standing here?"

"My property?" Marcus's expression changed from jovial to one of confusion in less than a second. "What property?"

The man was either a top-notch actor or he really had no clue. I was betting on the former.

"Coyness does *not* become you." My patience, what was left of it after a string of interrupted nights, was wearing dangerously thin. "*That* property." I pointed at the lock picking tool in dramatic fashion as it lay in Patsy's outstretched hand. "That's yours, I believe."

"*That* thing?" He was jumping up and down on my last nerve, and I wanted to reach over and rip the flowers out of his pudgy hand. The coffee I'd keep for my own use. Call it a finder's fee.

"Yes, Marcus. *That* thing."

He slid a hurt glance at me and then bent over to stare at the tool, as if he'd never seen it before. It was a performance, all right, but I was beginning to feel just this side of uncomfortable as I watched him. Maybe it wasn't his after all.

Straightening, he looked me straight in the eyes. "Gwen, I have never ever seen anything like it. It's not mine now, and it wasn't mine yesterday. It's. Not. Mine. Period."

And with a grand gesture that nearly beheaded the bouquet, he turned on his heels and swept toward the elevator, his back as stiff as a board. No more bouncing Tigger.

I slumped back in my chair, staring at Patsy in bafflement. Marcus was the only investigator friend I knew of. Just how many men was Nora seeing?

"Sorry about that." Patsy replaced the tool and closed the drawer. "Not sure why he felt he had to deny it, you know?"

I shook my head. "No, actually I don't." I took one last sip of coffee and regretfully set the mug down. It was a surprisingly smooth blend, the kind that lingered just long enough in your mouth for you to taste it. "I guess I'd better go after him and apologize." I laughed, trying to regain my emotional equilibrium. I felt as though I'd just been clobbered upside the head with a baseball bat, to be honest. And maybe Patsy was confused.

Anything was possible in this building. "I guess this is just my day for saying I'm sorry to folks."

"Well, anytime you're here, feel free to join me for a chat. It gets a bit lonely, sitting here making small talk with the squirrels." She smiled at me and again I saw how tired she looked. If I was her, I would have been grateful for boring and lonely. It would've meant more time with Agatha Christie and her cast of characters.

"I will." I waved and headed for the elevator and Nora's apartment.

Marcus was sitting next to Nora on the sofa nearest the large picture window, one arm curved protectively around her shoulders, as she admired the flowers he'd brought. The look he gave me when I came in, however, reminded me of a student I'd taught many years ago. Whenever she'd done something to cause trouble, it was always the fault of someone else. I wasn't sad when her family picked up and moved halfway through that school year. I'd probably feel the same if Marcus left the state.

Still, if my best friend and business partner liked him, I'd need to meet him partway. Smiling widely like the Cheshire Cat, I plopped down on the nearest armchair.

"Those are absolutely gorgeous." I divided my smile between the two of them. "Good choice, Marcus."

"Aren't they, though?" Nora gave the bouquet another rapturous sniff and turned to smile at Marcus. "Looks like I've got myself a new beau."

"It's called a "boo," Mrs. G." Brent spoke up from his seat on the floor. "You'd think someone your age would know these things."

Aggie, tail wagging and furry rump in the air, jumped at the ribbon he was waving in front of her.

Nora laughed, but Marcus looked curiously like a tea kettle about to let off steam.

Determined to keep things peaceful, I leaned toward Brent. "How's Rachel? Did you see her over at the park this morning?"

Brent looked at me and color rose in his face. The boy was in love, I thought with amusement. I was surrounded with it. Thank goodness one of us still had some common sense.

He shook his head almost shyly. "Nah. She goes to the junior college in the mornings. I'll see her this afternoon. Speaking of that, Mrs. G.," he turned to look at Nora, "are there any pet walking jobs after, say, one?" Before she could reply, he spoke in a rush, nearly falling over his words in his haste to get them out. "It's just that I thought I could meet Rachel for lunch and then take care of the dog stuff later."

"As a matter of fact, Brent, there *are* two jobs at three thirty, and you could do both at the same time. The owners want the dogs taken to the park for thirty minutes. That'll give you and Rachel at least two hours. That should be enough for lunch."

Nora smiled as Brent flushed happily, waggling her fingers at Aggie. The puppy immediately pounced, a fluffy ball of brown and white fur.

"It looks like Miss Aggie's learned to do her business outside. Good job, kid."

"Yeah, my mom helped me. She said she was tired of having to raise another baby." Brent's expression was now indignant, and I hid a smile behind a cough. "She's not even any problem either, not like my little brother. He's always leaving empty chip bags and stuff around. Aggie's much better behaved, aren't you, girl?" He reached out for her and she bounded over to him, licking his outstretched hand enthusiastically.

I reached down almost absentmindedly to scratch my ankles and noticed that the rash wasn't nearly as bad as it had been. Maybe I was building a resistance to Aggie's dander. I sure hoped it was the case. I hated to admit it, but I was really beginning to like that little dog.

"Well, I should get these flowers in some water. I think I've got a vase in the cabinet above the fridge." Nora stood up, bouquet in hand.

Marcus started to stand as well, but she waved him back.

"Brent can reach it for me. He's tall for a reason, aren't you, kid." She smiled at him, and I could tell he'd grown on her just like Aggie had on me.

Brent and Nora's voices came from the kitchen, emphasizing the silence that had grown between Marcus and me. He wasn't going to budge from his perch on the Pouting Tree.

I'd have to make the first move. Good thing I had over two decades of dealing with attitudes. "I might have been a little hasty downstairs."

Marcus, the spoiled brat, didn't even look at me. I sighed loudly. This was going to be like pulling teeth. If he insisted on staying incommunicado, I just might have to resort to that. To my relief, since I wasn't sure I could actually dig out a molar, he turned and met my gaze.

"I'll say."

I saw the beginning of a smile.

"Friends?" He held out one chubby hand.

I leaned over and took it. We shook, and I returned his smile.

"Friends," I agreed.

"Well, I'm glad that's settled."

We both turned to see Nora standing in the doorway to the kitchen, the bouquet almost hiding her face. Brent towered behind her, Aggie riding on his shoulders, her tongue hanging out in delight. Maybe she was part Siamese cat, partial to heights. She looked comfortable up there, one paw resting on the top of Brent's head. I had to smile at the picture they made, a boy and his dog. Like it or not, I was definitely getting soft about animals.

Hopefully, though, I wasn't getting soft about where the murder investigation was heading. No matter who the suspect was, I wanted them caught. And if the lock picking tool had something to do with it, I wanted to find out. Someone had brought it into this building. Someone who'd already used one on Linda Fletcher's empty apartment, not to mention the one found in my house.

Maybe Patsy could help us with this angle. After all, her husband had been a locksmith, right? I grinned at Nora, giving her a thumbs-up.

"He's not such a bad egg." I gave Marcus a playful nudge, nearly knocking him off balance. "Anyone who brings coffee and flowers can't be so bad."

"Isn't that the tru—hey, wait a sec." Nora peered at me around the flowers, her eyes narrowed. "How did you know about the coffee? I'd already put it away before you got here. Are you getting psychic on me or something?"

Marcus gave a low groan. This was what trying to play peacemaker did. It only got me into more trouble. Well, in for a penny, in for a pound, and all that other jazz. Lifting one shoulder in a nonchalant shrug, I looked from a red-faced Marcus to Nora, suspicion written all over her face.

"Well, the cat's out of the bag, so to speak, so you might as well know." I pointed at the flinching investigator, gesturing dramatically as I spoke. "Here you have a man who's so infatuated with you that he actually planned this out, Nora. Sought my opinion. Made sure he only got the things you liked. I don't know about you, but I'd feel mighty special." I beamed at Marcus. "And I think he did a great job, don't you?"

I was beginning to feel like a character out of *Hello, Dolly!* or *Fiddler on the Roof.* I fully expected to hear the strains of "Matchmaker, Matchmaker" coming from somewhere in the background. I'd morphed from teacher to business partner, burgeoning animal lover, and now couples' counselor. No one had told me retirement could be so busy. I almost needed a nap just thinking about it.

Before that could happen, though, I needed a straight answer from Marcus about the lock picking tool. His reaction downstairs still bugged me, almost as though it was overplayed. Granted, he could have been telling the truth, but...

Taking in a deep breath to steady myself, I dropped the bonhomie from my voice and turned to stare straight into his eyes. "Marcus, what do you have to say about *this*?" And from my pocket, I withdrew the tool the cleaner had given me.

"I don't know what you're talking about. I really don't."

Marcus's expression was definitely not friendly now, and Nora looked at me as though I'd lost what few marbles I had left. I was beginning to wonder myself, but I pressed on, unconsciously straightening my shoulders as I stared at him.

"Look, I'm not saying this is yours." I was beginning to waffle, trying to placate my best friend and still uncover whether or not her new love interest was a killer. She'd thank me later if it turned out that he had something—just what it could be was still nebulous—to do with the whole sordid mess. "But have you ever *seen* something like this? Or used something like this?"

Eyes narrowed, he reluctantly held out one hand for the tool. I dropped it on his palm, careful to keep my fingers from touching him. Some atavistic instinct, probably—not wanting to make contact with potential evil. Plus, I could tell he hadn't washed his hands after handling the damp newspaper that had been wrapped around the bouquet's stems. Hopefully Nora would be able to up his hygiene game.

If he was still around after this little event.

Brent and Nora watched in silence as Marcus turned the tool over in his hands, inspecting it from every angle. My heart began to thump a bit faster as I watched him. I'd gotten fairly good at reading faces over the years. Students who swore they'd done the work and turned it in but really hadn't always had a distinctly different reaction from those who'd truly completed their assignments. Marcus was beginning to look like the latter to me.

"I know I've seen things like this, or almost like this. I'm an investigator, after all, so I've probably even *used* things like this. But, no, I do not recognize what this is exactly. And it sure isn't mine. As already stated earlier."

He looked right at me. Heat rose in my cheeks at Nora's sudden glance in my direction. I'd have to explain myself in the very near future, of that I was sure.

"Ah." Not the most elegant of replies, but that was all I could manage at the moment.

Aggie, bless her furry little heart, began barking, and we all turned to look when she trotted over to the door and sat down in front of it, her pointed black nose lifted in the air.

"I'll get that." Marcus was in full protective man mode, and when he strode to the door, his chest puffed out like the prow of a ship heading into battle.

I had to hide my smile. Nora beamed with pride as she watched him, and Brent was occupied with keeping Aggie from nipping at the feet of our visitor. On second glance, I wished he'd let her take a chunk out of those ankles.

Without a word, in walked Buddy, arms held wide in greeting and a broad smile plastered on his tanned face. I thought Nora was going to split a gizzard. Between holding her back and keeping Aggie from tearing a new ventilation hole in Buddy's pant leg, Brent and I had our hands full. Marcus, his true colors waving high above the deck of his declared manhood, had retreated behind the sofa.

"Well, isn't this just the coziest?"

Phoebe Hayward, step-creature from the black lagoon, pushed her way past Buddy and posed just inside the doorway. This was going to be one reunion for the books.

Chapter 13

"Phoebe, you can get your shiny hiney out of my apartment right now!" Nora wrinkled her nose, giving her visitor a hefty sniff. "And you stink to high heaven of booze, woman. Good thing none of us are smokers in here. You're potent enough to give a whole new meaning to the phrase 'light it up.'"

Phoebe, dressed in a slinky gown that was more appropriate on the streets in another less salubrious part of Portland, stood there and grinned as if Nora had just said the funniest thing. But I thought I could see something jittery just under the surface of her lopsided smile, something not very nice.

Besides, I was pretty sure Nora had slapped a restraining order on this drunk bimbo. Directing my best friend over to the sofa and pushing her down on the cushions, I murmured in her ear, "Want me to give the Portland PD a call?"

"You betcha." Her face was still stiff with annoyance, but her breathing was dropping to a more normal level. That was good, especially since I didn't want to deal with hyperventilation on top of everything else.

Marcus, the brave he-man, reached over and laid a tentative hand on Nora's shoulder. "Would you like me to get rid of—of anyone for you, dearest?"

I missed her response because I was heading for the kitchen to make my phone call in semi-peace. Judging by the strangled noise I heard him give, though, she'd either slapped his hand away or given him the ultimate stink eye. If they ever had a stink eye competition in the Olympics, Nora would win gold every time, hands down.

My pal, the stink eye gold medalist.

Still smiling to myself, I reported the gate crasher to the local dispatcher and was assured officers were on the way. I thanked her and hung up, slipping my cell phone back into my pocket. I'd been on that thing more in the past week than I'd ever used it before. Maybe that was what hanging out with Nora did to a person. It forced you to keep an open line to the world around you, which wasn't all that bad. With a brief feeling of regret for the pile of cozies waiting for me at home, I headed back into the fray.

Phoebe was decidedly off whatever rocker it was she normally used. The exaggerated movements, the faintly disheveled appearance, and the smudged makeup hinted at a wild night that hadn't ended yet. And when she opened her mouth to speak, I was glad I'd called the boys in blue.

"So, I've been thinking, schtepmama," she drawled, slurring the last word. "How 'bout you and me form a partnership, make sure none of these lowlifes get their hands on the money?" She winked, pausing momentarily to get her false lashes unstuck from one another. "Like that cowboy over there, for example."

She pointed across the room, her finger wavering like a faulty arrow looking for its target. Buddy's face began to take on a rather muddy color, matching his balding pate's reddish hue.

Brent, I noticed, was watching her in fascination. It might have had something to do with the way her neckline had begun a downward trend, exposing what seemed like acres of freckled flesh. If she kept squirming around like that, we'd all be getting an up close and personal view of her nether region.

Nora, however, seemed neither amused nor fascinated. I saw, with growing apprehension, that her color was beginning to creep back into the danger category. Not a good sign. Before she could respond, though, all hell broke loose.

An annoyed Buddy, who'd stepped neatly aside when Phoebe had made her big entrance, suddenly lunged across the room toward her, meaty hands reaching out for her scrawny neck. She began to squawk in alarm, her skinny arms flapping in the air like a pair of plucked chicken wings. It was like having Pepper in the room, only not as pretty.

When the police arrived, they managed to pull Buddy off of Phoebe, who was screeching something about being "strangled against her will," or some other such nonsense. Even a half-blind gal like me could clearly see he wasn't strangling her. He was holding her in place by her neck. That was what I put in my eyewitness statement, at least.

Besides, if he hadn't held her like that, she would've been able to reach his, uh, tender area with her strappy high heels. I couldn't say I blamed him. I was pretty sure the cops didn't either. However, they took both step-monsters away at Nora's request, leaving the rest of us to collapse in the sudden silence.

Marcus had quickly scooted away from the fracas and was still hovering behind the Japanese screen that surrounded Nora's desk, his face as white as rice paper. Aggie was huddled inside the protective circle of Brent's arms as he sat on the edge of one armchair, his eyes as big as saucers. Nora and I sat side by side on the sofa, hands clasped as though we were five again and afraid to go to school.

If anyone else had stopped by at the moment, they would have thought we were auditioning for a horror movie.

"Coffee." Nora spoke abruptly, breaking the silence. "We need coffee." She turned to look at Marcus and waved him back to our end of the room. "Get over here, you big chicken. They're gone."

"I'm not scared." He eased out from behind the screen. "I just didn't want to, you know, get involved. Too many lawsuits when you try to interfere in someone else's business."

"I'm pretty sure you were just scared." I stood. "Okay, I'll get the coffee going. Brent, bring your shadow and give me a hand."

"Miss F., there's not enough light in here for me to have a shadow."

The kid could be so literal at times. In fact, he was literal most of the time. I motioned for him to get off his backside and follow me into the kitchen. Nora and Marcus needed some alone time, and I didn't want him to be there when it got started. His impressionable mind had already seen enough in the past few minutes, thanks to Phoebe and her choice of dress. Or undress, if you would.

The coffee Marcus had brought with him was one of the better blends found in and around Portland coffee shops, an Ethiopian light roast called Yirgacheffe. I usually just called it "yirga" for short since I felt a touch foolish trying to say the exotic name in my flat northwestern intonation.

"Brent, put Aggie down for a moment and reach those coffee mugs for me, please."

I pointed with my chin to a shelf above me. Nora's housekeeper had been in earlier and had moved them up higher, well out of my reach and nearly out of Nora's. It seemed to be her not-so-subtle way of letting us know we drank too much coffee. Of course, she was from somewhere in Arizona and probably thought we needed to switch to iced tea or something equally ghastly.

I waited for the coffee to brew and watched Aggie as she began sniffing her way around the kitchen, stopping to inspect an interesting spot or two as she made her rounds. I was curious what she'd do when she got to the place where Linda's body had been. The floor had been mopped numerous times since and there was no visible trace left behind.

I wasn't surprised, though, to see the little dog alert on the exact spot as before. She was definitely homing in on the scent, despite the many applications of floor cleaner. Wouldn't it be something if she could find out who was responsible for breaking into my house as well as Linda's apartment?

"Where do you want these, Miss F.?"

Brent was standing by the sink, two mugs clutched in each hand. He was a big fellow, no doubt about that, and I thought about the football coach's assessment of him. "Ferdinand," he'd called him, just like the flower-loving bull in the children's story.

I smiled at the idea and pointed to the table. "Put them there, please, and then go call those two out there to come join us."

I'd just filled the first mug when I heard Brent let out a squeal as though he'd stepped on a snake. Carefully setting the pot back on the warmer, I hurried out to see what had happened. Aggie was right behind me, ears pointing skyward, not wanting to be left out of the excitement.

Marcus and Nora must've been in some kind of lip lock before Brent had walked in on them. Nora's pink lipstick was all over Marcus's mouth and face, although it was difficult to distinguish it from the bright red spreading up from his neck.

Brent was still standing as though frozen. I gave him a little shove toward the kitchen, making sure he'd gone back in there before I addressed the geriatric Romeo now sitting a good two feet away from Nora, his hands clasped together in his lap.

"Listen, Marcus. And you as well." I turned my glare on Nora. "We all know you two like to canoodle, but could you please remember we've got a kid in here? Not to mention he was a student of mine, and his mother wouldn't appreciate him being exposed to this kind of nonsense."

Nora, her cheeks flushed pink, tossed her manufactured curls. Since giving up on the faux hairpiece, she'd begun playing up the perm angle, letting her hair twist itself silly all over her head. She was beginning to remind me of an unhinged Bo Peep. All she needed was the bonnet and a shepherd's crook.

Maybe she had the crook already, sitting there with Pink Passion lipstick all over his round face.

"I'll thank you to remember this is my apartment, Gwen. My house, my rules."

"Blah blah blah." I spoke indifferently, waving one hand at her. "Kind of like it was my place that you broke into the other night, nearly scaring me to death?"

Marcus's expression sharpened, his gaze shifting between Nora and me. Did I detect a sudden interest there that was more than mere curiosity? I didn't have time to dwell on that thought, however.

Aggie, over-excited by the noise and underwhelmed at all this human drama, decided to mark her territory right in front of my foot.

* * * *

I was glad to accept a ride home from Brent. I was physically weary, certainly, but more than that I was worn out emotionally. Trust Nora to come up with a "paying hobby" that came with its own dead body and death threats. I'd take teaching zero-hour classes for five years straight over this baloney, *and* a turn at cafeteria duty. That sounded much tamer than trying to find out who'd killed Linda and who wanted Nora dead as well.

I was so caught up in my own miasmic thoughts that I hardly noticed the several narrow escapes we had on the ride to my house. I'd almost gotten used to seeing a logging truck's front grill feet away from my face, and even Aggie was somewhat subdued as she lay cuddled between Brent and me.

"Okay, Miss F." Brent grinned at me as we screeched to a halt in front of my house, narrowly missing a row of mailboxes that stood guard at the edge of the road. "Guess I'll see you in the morning."

"Sounds good." I slid out of the front seat. "Be safe on the ride home, alright?" I reached over and gave Aggie's soft ears a tweak. "And you stop making messes everywhere, young lady."

I stepped away from the car and shut the door, waving as Brent turned the car in a wide circle without looking left or right. Hopefully his guardian angels were still on duty, although I imagined they probably needed to take it in shifts.

Smiling at that thought, I walked up the short path that divided my pitifully small front yard into two patches of weedy grass. I really needed to stay home long enough to do some work outside, but I'd become a sort of full-time resident at Nora's apartment lately. Maybe we could take it in turns: one week at her place, the next at mine.

I was finally drifting off toward sleep, my trusty armchair wedged under the doorknob of my bedroom, when it occurred to me we hadn't gotten a clear answer from Marcus concerning the odd little tool. Knowing how

Nora was beginning to feel about him, it was going to be an extraction job that would impress even the best dentist.

* * * *

The skies were overcast the next morning, thick with the promise of rain. I quickly showered and dressed and was debating on whether to call Brent or not when the clouds opened, drenching everyone unlucky enough to be caught outside.

"Well, guess I'll have to call the king of the road," I muttered to myself as I dug my cell phone from my jacket pocket. "Nothing like playing chicken in morning traffic to get the old heart pumping." Sighing deeply, I dialed Brent's number.

"Hello?" croaked a voice on the other end of the line and I nearly dropped the phone. Had I misdialed and gotten connected with the local mortuary instead? Whoever had answered sounded as though they barely had one toe in the land of the living.

"Brent? Is that you?" I listened cautiously, poised to hang up the second I heard any more creepy sounds coming from the other end. I could hear the sound of something rustling. Bed sheets? Body bags? I sighed in relief when he replied, this time sounding more alive.

"Yeah, it's me, Miss F." More sounds of movement and a short, irritated bark. Aggie. "Listen, I'm really sick this morning. I don't think I'm gonna work today, okay?" This was followed by an enormous sneeze and another excited Aggie yip.

"Not a problem." I didn't want to be exposed to whatever germ he'd picked up. "You stay right where you are and don't worry about a thing. Mrs. Goldstein and I will handle it."

"Even the poop scooping?" He sounded a little more alert now, and I shuddered at his question.

I'd completely forgotten about that end of the business, so to speak.

"It gets a little messier when it's raining, you know."

"Thanks for the tip, Brent." I was already trying to think of who we could rope into dog walking duties. "You get better. And make sure you eat and get washed up sometime today. You'll feel much more human if you do."

"I feel plenty human already, Miss F. I think that's part of the problem."

I smiled. Such a typical Brent comment. We'd miss him and his furry shadow today. Assuring him I'd check in with him later, I hung up.

My Uber driver was eighty if she was a day, and took almost double the time to drive me from my bungalow to Nora's building. At least I had time to admire the view. Who knew Portland needed so many cell phone and check cashing stores?

Nora looked as poorly as Brent had sounded. Still dressed for bed, a frilly robe of some unsubstantial material pulled tightly around her, she sat curled up in one armchair. With an economy-sized box of tissues on her lap and a bright red nose, she was the very picture of misery. I wished I'd brought an allergy mask with me.

"What's the matter?" I shut the door behind me, making sure the security bolt was firmly in place. "First Brent sounds like he's at death's door and now you."

I sat on the sofa farthest away from her chair, tucking both hands in my pockets for safety. You never knew what germs could be lurking about, and after surviving more years of sick students than I cared to recall, I wasn't playing with my health.

She shot me a look that was probably meant to be scathing, but the effect was lost as she suddenly scrambled for a tissue to cover a sneeze. That did it. I was going to call and cancel every last one of our jobs today and go hide inside my nice, germ-free house.

"Whaddabout me?" Nora blew her nose with vigor and then winced. When she dropped the tissue into the trash basket sitting on the floor beside her chair, I could see why. Her nose looked raw and faintly swollen, as if she'd been blowing it for hours.

"You look like he sounds." I wanted to cover my own nose with a tissue. I knew from experience just how far a sneeze could travel, covered or not, and I hadn't had my annual flu shot yet. Maybe I still had some Echinacea or golden seal in my teaching supplies.

"Oh, thanks, Sis." Nora let her head fall back against the chair's cushions and groaned. "I really do think I'm dying, though. It just came on all of a sudden last night, and I don't think I slept for more than two hours."

"I'm sure it's just a cold."

I'd dealt with more levels of illness than an emergency room doctor and could diagnose a kid from fifty paces. No one got out of taking a test in my class unless they met the Miss Franklin Standard of Sickness.

"Who's going to walk the dogs today?" Nora lifted her head briefly before collapsing again. "Brent's not here, I can't move, and I don't think you want to do it. Do you?" She opened one eye and looked at me.

I shook my head vigorously. "Not on your tintype, old lady. In fact, I'm going to call every client and let them know we're shutting down today due to quarantine issues."

She shot straight up in the chair, eyes wide. "You can't say that! That'll get us shut down permanently, especially if someone lets that tidbit fall where it shouldn't, as in social media." She snorted in disgust and then gingerly touched her nose. "Just let me get a shower and eat something first, then we can both go. All right?"

I shrugged, smiling inwardly. Just as I'd suspected, a mere cold. Dr. Franklin struck again.

"Sure, no problem. In fact, I'll make some hot tea as well. You look like you could use a good dose of sugar."

I waited until she'd dragged herself from the chair and had started down the hall before I made my way to the kitchen. It seemed oddly empty without Brent and Aggie. Could dogs catch a human's cold germs? I certainly hoped not. Aggie was too little, in my opinion, to get sick.

Wearing her typical black stretchy garb but foregoing a few layers of makeup, Nora was quickly ready to go.

"We've got three dog walking jobs today, but I'm going to call and see if they can all be done at the same time."

We were sitting in her living room, jackets on and to-go cups of hot tea in our hands. I waited for her to make the calls and listened to her assuring the clients that Brent would be back the next day and yes, wasn't he just the sweetest? That last comment had both Nora and me rolling our eyes in tandem, but it was the typical reaction to Brent. He was a huge teddy bear who loved animals and they, as well as their owners, loved him in return.

"Ready?" Nora slipped her phone into her jacket pocket—at least she hadn't stuck it in her top this time—and we headed out to get the first of the animals. "I thought we'd go by and grab Pookie first, then Max, then Buster."

"Pookie? Who in the world calls their dog Pookie?"

Nora shrugged. "No idea. Guess we'll find out. It's one of the clients Brent rounded up when he was at the dog park."

I'd heard it said that stereotypes were there for a reason. Someone always fit the mold. When the door was opened by a bearded tattooed man, his biceps bulging from under a leather vest, I almost laughed out loud. I didn't, though. I valued my life more than a quick snigger or two.

Besides, I also valued my limbs, which this giant of a man could have easily torn from their sockets without breaking a sweat. One look at him convinced me he'd probably done just that in the past.

He handed the rhinestone-encrusted leash over to Nora, who'd recovered nicely and even managed a spandex-enhanced wiggle or two. Smiling at him from underneath her oddly naked eyelashes, she promised to have Pookie, a petulant-looking white poodle, back in thirty minutes.

"And not a second more, I promise," she added with another flirtatious smile, while I groaned to myself.

What were the odds he'd probably set a timer and hold us to that promise? Fairly high, I reckoned. I started composing my last will and testament in my head, wondering if Shelby would want my collection of Agatha Christie books.

Max and Buster were both docile, decidedly on the elderly side, and Nora let me hold their leashes.

"Buster's owner said you need to watch your feet since he's got a leaky problem."

I looked at her, eyebrows lifted. "Who does? The dog or the owner?"

Nora snorted with laughter. With her cold giving her a husky rasp, she sounded like a Marlene Dietrich wannabe. It figured. Her colds made her sexier. Mine only turned me into a Shrek clone.

We'd almost completed the thirty-minute circuit when I caught something from the corner of one eye that made me pause. I'd just made my last poopy bag deposit when I glanced over and saw two folks who really shouldn't have been together, especially not in the same car. And certainly not smiling. It was almost creepy.

Walking casually back to where Nora waited with the three tired dogs, I said, "Don't look now, but I think that's Marcus and Buddy in that car across the street."

"Where?" Nora half rose, and I pushed her back down.

"Don't you ever listen?" I leaned down to pet Max, holding my feet carefully out of Buster's range. My ankles were already wet, and I didn't need another layer. "It's Marcus and that numbskull stepson of yours. Together. Looking like best pals or something."

"I don't recognize the car." Nora craned her neck to see around me. "Nope, it's definitely not Marcus's old junker. That must be Buddy's."

"Bravo, Einstein. How'd you arrive at that conclusion? The fact that he's in the driver's seat?"

"No." She spoke defensively, giving me that sideways glance that could melt Marcus's heart. My heart, on the other hand, was as small and cold as the Grinch's. "It just doesn't look like something Marcus would drive."

I rolled my eyes. There was no arguing with that level of logic. Besides, Pookie's very large, very muscly owner was waiting for his precious pup to come back in one piece, preferably on the dot of thirty minutes.

By the time we'd crossed the street and headed for the first drop off, the car was gone. Marcus was nowhere in sight, so he'd either parked somewhere nearby or had quickly hoofed it out of there.

We deposited all three dogs safely back with their doting owners.

"Did my widdle Pookie wike her walkies?"

"I'm sorry about Buster's bladder control issues. It's tough getting older, know what I mean?"

After that was done, we headed back to the apartment. I glanced at Nora. She was frowning, her normally Botox-smooth forehead wrinkled. Probably wondering about Marcus, that rat. If she found out he was in cahoots with Buddy, it would break her heart.

Better a broken heart than a broken bank account, in my opinion.

Chapter 14

The lobby of the luxury apartment building was appropriately quiet, soft music coming from hidden speakers and a hint of…coconut? I sniffed the air as we crossed the tiled floor. It reminded me of something vaguely summery, the smell from poolside or at the park.

We'd almost made it to the elevator when I heard someone call my name. Turning, I spotted Patsy as she left the private manager's office, carefully closing the door behind her.

"Great," Nora muttered. "Just what I need to make my cold feel better. Not." She kept walking, adding over her shoulder, "I'll see you upstairs, Gwen. I suddenly feel the need for a drink."

I wanted to giggle at the horrified expression on Patsy's face.

"Poor thing," I sighed, letting my mouth and eyes droop mournfully as I watched Nora walk away. "I keep trying to get her into rehab, but she just refuses to go."

"Thank goodness for that." Patsy put one hand on her rather concave chest and attempted a smile in my direction. "We all could use a friend like you." The scent of coconut was stronger now, and I couldn't resist another sniff.

"I heard that," Nora called out as the elevator doors slowly slid shut.

I just shrugged. Maybe if I let Patsy think I had some sort of struggle in my life, I'd get her to confide in me a bit more. Just what it was I wanted to learn, I wasn't sure, but if anyone could tell me things about the inmates in the building, it would be the concierge.

"She's not herself this morning." I smiled at Patsy, leaning in slightly. I was working the body language, doing what a certain teacher used to call "camping in their personal space." Hopefully it looked friendly and not threatening. "She's got the beginnings of a bad cold and that tends to make her grumpy." I smiled even wider, hoping it looked friendly and not like I was about to lose my marbles. "By the way, I can't help but noticing that lovely scent. Very tropical."

She flushed faintly but a pleased look crept into her eyes. "Thanks. It's a new hand lotion called Hawaiian Dreams." She lifted a hand to her nose and breathed in deeply. "It's my way of keeping my sanity when the weather isn't cooperating."

I completely understood. Here in Portland, there must have been hundreds, if not thousands, of folks that liked to dream of tropical beaches and bright sunshine.

And a pool boy or two. I always liked to add that little detail in there for good measure. My pool boy would have a head full of thick blond hair, rippling muscles under a golden tan, and…I broke off that train of thought before my caboose jumped the track.

"Well, they say positive thoughts help to keep the body and soul healthy. Hopefully we won't catch this latest batch of sniffles."

"It's going around." Patsy reached over and squirted a handful of antibacterial gel from a wall-mounted pump into her hand. "Can't be too careful now, can we?"

"No, indeed." I mirrored her actions. "We can never be too careful."

We stood there in silence for a moment, rubbing in the hand sanitizer. Patsy didn't seem inclined to tell me why she'd stopped me, and I was getting impatient to get upstairs with Nora. I was positive she'd only been kidding about needing that drink, but this was Nora. Anything and everything were possible with this gal.

"So, did you want something in particular?" I motioned vaguely at the elevator. "Only I should probably get upstairs ASAP and make sure she's all right."

Patsy nodded wisely. "It's always good to keep an eye on those with a problem."

She glanced down for a moment, as if her comment had landed somewhere near her feet. I waited patiently, not saying a word. I'd seen all the cop shows and read the books, and I knew that someone who has something to say will rush in to fill the vacuum of silence. I didn't have to wait long.

"I'm not sure if you're aware of this or not, but Mrs. Goldstein's, uh, boyfriend, is keeping company with someone else right now."

Keeping company? Who even said that anymore?

"Oh, do you mean Marcus?" I gave what I hoped was a merry little laugh. It sounded like the spray from a machine gun instead.

Patsy took a step away from me, eyes widening. Maybe she thought I was the one who needed rehab.

"I'm sure he has a lot of contacts, being in the detective business and such."

I could almost see the awkward teen hiding somewhere inside the grown woman as she dug the toe of one shoe into the floor. "Well, what I actually mean is he—Mr. Avery, that is—is spending a great deal of time with Mrs. Goldstein's stepson." She said these last words with a hint of smugness underneath, as if having a stepchild equaled something polite people didn't talk about in public.

I stared at her for a long moment, my mind racing through the names on the list Nora and I had compiled. Who did she mean by "her stepson"? There was more than one to choose from, if I remembered correctly.

"I'm talking about Mr. Levinsky, of course." When I still didn't respond, she said helpfully, "Buddy Levinsky? Kind of bald, large mustache, ridiculous hat?"

"Oh, *that* Mr. Levinsky." I sounded as though I met one nearly every day. "Is there a problem? Something I need to tell Mrs. Goldstein about?" My heart began to pick up the pace. Maybe this was the break we'd been looking for.

Patsy stared at me for a long moment and then gave a small shrug. "I just thought she ought to know, considering her reaction when he was here the other day. We do try our best to keep our residents comfortable." Another shrug. "Personally, I think Mr. Levinsky has more to fear from Mrs. Goldstein than the other way around. Just my opinion."

My eyes narrowed.

"She can be rather…difficult at times. Take Linda Fletcher for example."

Indeed. This was getting interesting.

"Let's." I gestured for her to continue. "I'd love to hear about the connection between the three of them."

"Connection? Who said there was a connection?"

She looked genuinely stumped, but I wasn't feeling the need to help her out at the moment. After all, Nora wasn't only my *best* friend, she was my *oldest* friend, close enough to be a sister. I stared steadily at Patsy, waiting for her to explain. Instead, she dropped her gaze, making a big show of checking her watch.

"We'll have to continue this another time, I'm afraid. Gotta take care of a few things for the boss." She looked at the manager's office and raised one hand in an awkward wave. "I'm sure I'll see you around, Gwen."

I didn't bother answering. Instead, I stood watching, as she scurried through a door marked "staff only," shaking my head and wondering what had just happened. With a glance at the security camera mounted above the reception desk, I turned and made my way to the elevator. I was sure she was watching me.

Nora, bless her heart, was lying on one of the sofas, her legs curled beneath her and mouth hanging slightly open as she slept. Tiptoeing past her, I headed for the kitchen to make coffee.

"Make one for me."

I jumped, nearly tripping myself on one edge of the Japanese silk screen.

"Good grief, Nora. That's a mighty good way to lose a friend, you know." I turned around to glare at her, one hand on my chest. "You're as bad as Brent behind the wheel."

"Glad to know I've still got it." She gave a sassy grin. "What did the ol' sourpuss want?"

"Hang on a sec," I called over my shoulder. "You're going to need coffee for this one. By the way, I'm glad to see you haven't hit the bottle."

"Oh, hilarious, pal. Just for that, you can add a dash of something to my coffee."

When we were settled on opposite ends of the sofa, each with a mug of fragrant Irish coffee, I told her about Patsy's concern.

"She seems to think Marcus and Buddy are cooking up something that might not be beneficial for your relationship. With Marcus." I took a small sip of coffee. "This is really good stuff. Makes me wish I would've had some in my desk at school. Probably would've taken the edge off a few department meetings."

Nora snorted. "I'd have paid money to see that, Sis. Can you imagine a roomful of happy teachers?"

I tilted my head, thinking about that for a moment. "It'd take more than a slug of Bailey's to liven up some of them. Nothing made them happy, not even using a Scantron for grading tests."

"So, why'd you stay so long? You always said the pay was bad, right? Maybe it was that cute science teacher you mentioned before." She gave me a sassy wink.

It was my turn to snort. "Right. If they were cute when they started teaching, the job quickly beat it out of them."

I paused a moment, thinking about my career. Why *had* I stayed? That was actually an easy question to answer.

"I loved it. I really loved the teaching, the atmosphere, even the students. Of course," I laughed, "there was always the classroom stinker, but I usually let the other students shut them down. Kids can be better at that than adults."

We sat there in silence for a few minutes, sipping coffee, engaged with our own thoughts. Finally, Nora stirred, placing her coffee cup on a convenient end table and reaching for the tissue box.

"So, Patsy thinks Marcus and Buddy are in cahoots against me." She swiped at her nose and let the used tissue drop into the nearly full trash can. "I'd say it's probably just Marcus trying to make peace, keep the step-monster away from me. He's like that."

Part of me didn't buy that explanation for one minute, but then again, I really didn't know either one of these men. She could be right. Smiling across at her, I lifted my mug in a mock toast. "Well, here's to getting well and making peace."

"I'll drink to that." She lifted her own mug and we smiled, two longtime pals enjoying each other's company.

It wasn't until later that I'd find out just how wrong both of us were.

Nora needed to rest, and I really didn't want to catch her germs, so I left for home shortly after three. It was pleasantly cool outside, and I enjoyed the walk back to my bungalow. The rain had moved out, leaving behind a layer of white, fluffy clouds that filled the skies over Portland. The city took advantage of days like these, and the streets were jam-packed with people out enjoying the day.

Shelby Tucker was waiting for me when I arrived home. She'd parked her car in front of my house and was leaning against its side, her cell phone clamped to her ear, one hand gesticulating energetically as she talked.

I waggled a few fingers at her as I approached, pointing at my house. She glanced over at me, holding up one finger. I gave her a thumbs-up and went inside, leaving the door standing open.

I'd just slipped off my sandals and turned on my electric kettle when she stuck her head around the door. "Miss Franklin? Okay to come in?"

"Yep. Want some hot tea? I need some after my walk home,"

Shelby slipped onto a kitchen chair, staring curiously around the room. "Interesting place for a table. Don't use your back door much?"

I'd left the kitchen table across the back door, effectively barring the way for anyone who had no business being inside my house. I tossed a grin in her direction. "It's a new feng shui thing, Shelby. You know, blocking the negative energy and making more room to dance."

"Feng shui? I had no idea you were into that, Miss Franklin." She gazed around the room, eyebrows lifted in question.

I laughed at her expression. "Just kidding. Can you imagine me dancing? And don't answer that." I playfully shook my finger and she gave a half-smile in return as if she was unsure of the joke. "It's a safety thing, at least until they get the person who broke into my house." I paused, holding up two mugs. "Sugar?"

"No thanks, just black."

She gave the kitchen another cursory glance. I wasn't sure what she expected to see in a teacher's house, but this was vintage Goodwill-slash-yard sale at its finest.

I sat down and carefully slid the full mug across the table to her.

"So, what's new at the paper? Anything you can share?" I sipped the hot tea, watching her over the rim of the mug.

Shelby wasn't in the habit of just stopping by for a casual visit. "Actually," she took a cautious drink from her cup, "I just got a call from the guy who covers the crime beat."

"And? Anything about my break-in?"

"No, it's a little bit more serious than that, to be honest, Miss Franklin." She set the tea back down and folded her hands on the table, staring at me with a sober expression. "He was listening to the scanner and heard a call out about a body being found down near the pier."

She paused a moment and my heart began to beat faster. Her manner and words were beginning to spook me good.

"Is it someone we know?" My voice quavered and I quickly took a drink, letting the warm liquid relax my throat. "Someone from school?"

"School?" She sounded confused for a moment and then gave a half-smile. "No, not there. Miss Franklin, do you know someone named Lazarus Levinsky?"

I stared at her, my eyebrows drawn together as I turned the name over in my mind. Something about the name was familiar, but...

"No, I don't think so, Shelby. Maybe I've heard it before, but no, it's no one I know." Thank goodness. I couldn't have handled any more bad news.

"That's okay then." She smiled at me, anxiety gone from her face. "For some reason, I thought you knew him."

"Wait a sec," I said slowly, unease beginning to tighten the muscles across my back. "Do you know what he looks like, this Lazarus Levinsky?"

Shelby shook her head. "I don't, but I can give my contact a call if you want."

"Would you please? It'd make me feel better." I tried to smile, but it came out slightly crooked, as if I already knew the outcome wouldn't be pleasant.

"No worries. I'll be right back." She gave me an encouraging smile. "Just hang tight. It might take me a few minutes to get through to him, all right?"

I nodded. "Of course. Thanks for checking, Shelby."

She went back outside, her cell phone already up to her ear. What would Miss Marple do in a situation like this? I almost chuckled at the thought, wondering how she'd view all the technology we took for granted. She'd probably love it. And she'd offer something sweet—for shock, of course. Anyone who read old mysteries knew sugar was medicinal and chocolate was a lifesaver.

I was putting a few oatmeal raisin cookies on a plate when Shelby came back inside, her forehead creased with concern.

"Everything all right?" I set the plate on the table, watching as she walked back to the table.

"Brian, the crime reporter, just told me police are at that apartment building your friend lives in, the one down close to where they found the body."

I froze, one hand hovering above the cookies. Why on earth would the police be at Nora's?

"It's a death notification, he said." Shelby's expression seemed troubled and she reached out to put a hand on my shoulder. "Miss Franklin, Brian said the name he heard is Nora Goldstein. Isn't that—"

I didn't give her a chance to finish the thought. Jumping up so fast that my chair turned over with a loud thump, I ran for the front door.

"Miss Franklin, wait! I can drive you over there, okay?"

I couldn't imagine Miss Marple ever feeling this helpless. But Miss Marple never had a best friend like Nora Goldstein either. I nodded gratefully, slipping my feet into my discarded sandals.

Chapter 15

I didn't bother knocking. With Shelby close behind, we burst into Nora's apartment. I probably looked somewhat deranged, but I didn't care. When it came to my best friend, I was all pitbull.

"Nora, is everything all right?"

Nora was sitting in one of her armchairs, looking as cool as a cucumber. The two officers who sat across from her, though, looked anything but cool. In fact, despite the chilly weather outside, both were sweating.

"I'm fine, Sis. It's these two nutcases that have things ass-backward." She wrinkled her nose, but I could hear the humor beneath the words. Nora was enjoying this encounter.

I breathed out heavily, trying to slow down my heart rate. Having a friend like Nora was almost like living on a treadmill. The emotional reactions could go from zero to sixty and back within the span of a few minutes.

"Shelby said—this is Shelby Tucker, one of my students, by the way— Shelby said she heard about a death notification from one of her colleagues. Since he also mentioned your name, Nora, I wanted to be here to help support you. Not that you look like you need supporting," I added hastily.

"If you wouldn't mind giving us your name, please?"

I looked over at the officers. One of them had pulled a small notepad from her shirt pocket, ready to take down my information.

"This is my friend and business partner, Gwen Franklin." Nora uncrossed her Lycra-covered legs slowly and all but oozed out of the chair, carefully pointing her high heels as though she were on a catwalk. And judging by the way both officers were staring at her, she might as well have been.

"I'm going to make coffee. Gwennie, just tell the nice folks what they need to know so they can get about their business."

I nudged a gawking Shelby in the ribs to get her attention. "Why don't you go and help Mrs. Goldstein, okay?"

Shelby followed Nora into the kitchen, her eyes wide. I sighed. Had these people never seen a woman walking in heels before? Of course, the heels were the exclamation points to a pair of shapely legs, showcased for all they were worth in Nora's signature tight black pants. I sighed again, casting a quick glance at my faded baggy jeans and newer Birkenstocks. I'd probably never have folks staring at *me* like that.

Clearing my throat, I snapped out, "If there's nothing else, Officers, I'll show you to the door."

Automatically, they rose and I had to hide a smile. I still had it.

Once they were gone and the door was firmly closed and locked behind them, I rushed to the kitchen as fast as my sandaled feet could move. *Nora had better be serving information along with that cup of coffee.*

"Oh, Miss Franklin." Shelby held one hand aloft, her cell phone glinting under the kitchen lights. "I heard back from my contact. He gave me a fairly detailed description of the—the body." She shot a quick glance at Nora, who sat across from her, calmly sipping from a hand-thrown ceramic mug. "Want me to give it to you now or later?"

I looked at Nora as well. If it was someone she actually knew, I didn't want to send her into shock.

"Oh, get on with it." Nora set the mug down on the table and sighed. "I already know who it is, you two. It's just the comedy of being notified when I haven't been in his life for the last thirty years." She shook her head. "I haven't seen Buddy Levinsky in years and now he turns up dead practically on my doorstep."

"It was Buddy? I thought they said his name was Lazarus something or other." I looked from Nora to Shelby, a tiny frown forming between my eyebrows.

"And that's exactly why we called him Buddy," Nora replied promptly. "His dad was called 'Bud.' *His* name was almost as bad. So, we just went with it. Kind of like a junior, only he wasn't, if you know what I mean."

"I suppose." I hesitated a moment and then looked at Shelby. "Go ahead. Just leave out any gruesome descriptions, all right?"

"I wouldn't do that to you." She leaned forward with an earnest expression on her face. "Although you did go on and on about descriptive writing when I was in your class, Miss Franklin. It's a good thing I didn't listen to you, especially since journalism is the opposite side of the coin." She grinned at me and reached out to give my arm a pat.

"Gotcha on that one, Sis." Nora laughed, and the mood lightened. She nodded at Shelby. "Did they mention how Buddy was killed?"

"Not directly, no. But based on the way he looked when he was found, I'd guess he was hit with something fairly heavy." She gave a small shudder. "The back of his head was pretty much gone."

We sat there quietly for a moment, letting Shelby's words mingle with the aroma from the coffee. I didn't need to see any pictures, thank you very much. I could make my own. Goosebumps were growing on my arms, and I took a long drink from my mug. I hadn't taken to the man, but I wouldn't have wished that on anyone.

Nora finally broke the silence. "How did they know how to contact me? Like I said, I haven't been in that kid's life for at least three decades. His dad made sure of that, even if I had wanted to be Buddy's stepmom."

I looked at her curiously. "Was there a reason you didn't want to be involved with him?" I thought about her comments concerning Mercy and Grace. Maybe he'd been the sort of child who enjoyed pulling the wings off of insects.

Nora shook her head pensively, her gaze fixed on her coffee cup. "No, not really. I guess I didn't want to keep playing mom." She looked up abruptly. "Some of us aren't cut out to be mothers, you know."

"I never had the chance." I spoke without thinking, and, to my embarrassment, tears filled my eyes. I swiped the back of one hand across my face, blinking hard to hold the tears at bay. Mouth pinched into a thin line, I abruptly shoved my chair back. "I think I need some of that coffee."

"You had a lot of children, Miss Franklin." Shelby put her hand on mine and smiled. "And I was just teasing about the writing. If you hadn't made us be so descriptive, I might not have worked so hard at finding a way to write without it. I'm the perfect journalist, thanks to you."

I rolled my eyes as I stood, with the beginnings of a smile. Inside, though, I was jumping up and down, shouting hallelujah and all that jazz. I'd made a difference in at least one student's life, even if it was slightly convoluted.

"What did you hear about him?" I asked over my shoulder as I reached for a mug. Thank goodness Brent had moved them back to a more sensible shelf. "And how *did* they know to get a hold of Mrs. Goldstein?"

"Well, I was told he had your name listed under 'emergency contact' in his cell phone." Shelby looked at Nora. "So the PD kinda assumed you were a relative, or at least a close friend."

Nora snorted contemptuously, but she motioned for Shelby to continue.

"I can't imagine too many men with a first name like his." Shelby shook her head. "Who ever thought of naming their kid Lazarus, anyway?"

"You have no idea." Nora's tone was dry and self-deprecating. "I had a talent for choosing men whose kids all had strange names. Ask her." She pointed her chin in my direction. "We actually made a list after a couple of 'em came knocking at my door. Sad to say, but Phoebe was probably the most normal of them all, and you got to see her in action, Gwen. She's a walking, talking fruitcake."

"There were certainly some out of the ordinary names." I carefully carried my coffee back to the table. "Besides Phoebe, there were Mercy, Grace, Charity, and Verity, and that's just the girls."

"You must've married a bunch of religious fanatics," Shelby said. "Sounds like the type of names you'd hear way back in the Puritan days."

"Have you asked Marcus if he has any children named Hezekiah or Faith stashed somewhere?" I watched Nora with interest over the rim of my coffee cup. She hadn't mentioned him one time since Shelby and I had arrived.

Nora tossed her head. Some of her hair seemed to be coming back. "That man is the last thing I want to think about, if you don't mind."

Shelby and I exchanged a look. I wasn't sad Nora was feeling this way, but I knew her well enough to know something like this could really get her down. I wasn't looking forward to playing the part of court jester just to keep up her spirits.

"Well, now that we're here, how about dinner?" I glanced from Shelby to Nora, hoping one of them would suggest an evening out. As much as I adored my best friend, I was getting tired of hanging out in her apartment all the time.

"I'm in," Shelby agreed enthusiastically. "I know this little place where they make the best curry in Portland. And I can drive, if you want."

"She's much better than Brent." I nodded in Shelby's direction. "Not one near miss on the way over, cross my heart."

Nora sat in silence, staring at her clasped hands as if they were the most fascinating objects in the world. I could almost see the miasma rising from her thoughts, building into a dark cloud of depression around her. Well, if it was part of my job to keep her emotions balanced, I was determined to do it with all of my might.

"Nora," I began in a firm tone, "you're going to come with Shelby and me, and you *will* have a good time. Whether you like it or not." I crossed my arms in front of me. I was back in teacher mode again, dealing with a recalcitrant student. To my immense relief, Nora smiled.

"Fine. You win this time. But," she held up one finger in warning, "if I hear that loser's name just one more time, I can't be responsible for my reaction. Capiche?"

Assuming the loser she was referring to was Marcus, I promptly agreed. We couldn't say adios to that man quick enough, in my opinion. With a broad smile, I crooked one arm, holding it out for Nora. She took it, slipping her thin arm through my rather padded one, and we were off for an evening of curry and no you-know-who.

You've heard what they say about the proverbial bad penny turning up? Marcus must have been made of pure copper. We'd no sooner been seated when in walked the man himself, all plaid and stripes and swagger.

"Don't look now," I hissed, "but Mar...I mean, you-know-who just walked in."

"Talk about bizarre." Shelby stared across the room as Marcus was seated at a corner table. "Not many people even know this place exists."

I believed her. The Indian Curry Nook was all of a hundred square feet, including the miniscule kitchen, and boasted eight tables. I was born in this town, and I wouldn't have been able to find it without a map. I turned to Nora, ready to comment on the coincidence, when I saw her cell phone on her lap, its screen lit up. The texting screen.

Narrowing my eyes in suspicion, I leaned over. "Some coincidence, right? It's almost as if someone texted the man and told him right where we'd be this evening."

"Sheer craziness." Color crept up from Nora's neck into her face, a telltale sign if there ever was one.

It must've been a brief spat, not a final goodbye.

"We might as well ask him to join us. We can't have you texting through the meal, can we?"

Shelby, bless her heart, looked from me to Nora, a puzzled expression on her face. Maybe she thought age brought with it a kind of code that older people spoke. I wanted to tell her we were no different than the younger crowd, just a bit sneakier.

"Yeah, that's no problem." Shelby motioned to the empty fourth chair at our table, where we'd piled our handbags. "Ask him to come on over."

Shelby gave me a quick wink as she handed my purse to me, and I gave her a small nod in response. Better the devil we knew than the devil sitting across the room shooting daggers at us, to paraphrase an adage.

Marcus wasted no time in joining the three of us, scuttling across the room as if on roller skates. To my disgust and Shelby's surprise, he paused to kiss Nora's upturned face, his lips landing dangerously close to hers. Spat firmly over.

"Evening, Marcus." I was determined to let him know I knew how he'd found us. "At least you two won't have to text back and forth all evening, right?"

"I wouldn't do something like that." He shoved his cell phone into a jacket pocket. "My manners are impeccable, aren't they, honey pie?"

Nora gave an inaudible murmur, leaning closer and depositing the answer in his ear. Judging by the simpering expression on his round face, she'd just made his day.

Honey pie? That was almost as bad as Pookie. Tempted to make a decidedly *not* impeccable rude noise, I focused my attention instead on the laminated menu. An array of delicious-looking dishes were lined up, each one accompanied by a stack of naan bread and golden samosas. This place could become a dangerous habit.

"What do you usually order?" I looked at Shelby, noting that she was still watching the Nora and Marcus show playing out on the other side of the table.

Their chairs had migrated toward each other, creating a two-headed creature seemingly bent on becoming attached as firmly as possible. I wanted to dump my glass of ice water over their heads. If I ever heard the younger crowd commenting on the lack of, um, passion in older folks, I'd just point at Nora. Definitely no lack of anything there except common sense.

We'd just finished our dinner—Nora and Marcus feeding one another, giggling like two loons—when my cell phone pinged. I held it under the table and peered down at the tiny screen.

Miss F. I'm at the apartament. Brent had always been a poor speller. *Rachel says we have, news.* He'd never been one for correct punctuation either.

Indeed. I glanced up to see that my tablemates were watching me with avid curiosity. I held up my phone for them to see.

"Let me answer this text and then I'll tell you what it's about, okay?"

Without waiting for a response, I quickly tapped an answer. I was becoming rather adept at writing with one finger. This new technology world had nothing on me.

At dinner. Will text when on our way.

There. Properly formatted, spelled and punctuated. Maybe Brent would take notice. Somehow, though, I doubted it.

"That was Brent." I slipped my phone back into my pocket. "He said he and Rachel have more news for us."

"Really?" Nora detached her face from Marcus's and sat up straight, her eyes wide with curiosity. "Where is the kid?"

"He's actually waiting at your place. I don't know if Rachel is with him or not."

"Who are Rachel and Brent?" Shelby looked from me to Nora, an inquisitive tilt to her head.

"Brent is—was—a student of mine, like you, but he only graduated last year."

Shelby nodded, leaning toward me as she listened.

"Rachel is another dog walker he met at the Portland Pooch Park. The kicker is that her dad is the lead investigator on the murder case. The *first* murder case," I hastily corrected myself. If this kept up, we'd need to assign them identification numbers.

"Interesting." She pulled out her own cell phone and peered at the screen. "Speaking of murder, Brian just let me know the post mortem will be tomorrow morning. He's gonna hold on to his pending article about the murder until then."

"Will they be able to tell when he died?" Marcus looked suddenly uncomfortable, a sheen of sweat on his forehead. Either Nora's proximity or something else was making him nervous. "It's just that I was, uh, with him earlier in the day, and I wouldn't want anyone thinking I killed him."

"I know. We saw you when we were out walking dogs."

Nora's stiletto made sharp contact with my shin under the table.

"Ow, Nora! Watch where you're putting those things." I frowned at her as I leaned down to rub the spot. I'd have a huge bruise there in the morning. "He needs to know there'll always be someone who'll see something. Nothing is secret in this town."

"My reputation is very important to me, I'll have you know." He drew himself up as tall as his round figure could go, his jaw clenched in irritation. "I regard my name as my bond."

"If that's the case, I can get Brian's article quashed." Shelby spoke in an amiable tone as she broke a samosa in two. "That could definitely do some damage to such a spotless reputation. Just my opinion, of course." She popped a piece of fried dough into her mouth, chewing thoughtfully as she stared across the table at a reddening Marcus. I wanted to clap.

"Well, I think he's wonderful, and that's all that matters in our little world, right, sugar bear?" Nora scooted her chair closer, slipping one hand into the crook of his elbow and leaning her fuzzy head against his shoulder like a love-struck teenager.

Gag. *Sugar bear*?

I wasn't going to be able to finish my dinner after that little display. I pulled the paper napkin from my lap and laid it on my plate. "If everyone's done eating, let's ask for the check and get back to your place, Nora. I don't know about you guys, but I'm dying to hear what Brent and Rachel have to say."

Nora gave a theatrical shudder, clinging even tighter to a now-beaming Marcus.

"Oooh, don't use that word, Gwennie." Another exaggerated shiver, combined with rapid batting of her false eyelashes.

I idly wondered if they'd slip off with all that effort.

"You know how upset I get," she added.

I did? I wisely kept my mouth shut, though, letting Marcus play the role of gentleman gallant to Nora's timid little woman act. Pass the sick bag. I aimed an equally sick smile in Nora's direction. Even Shelby wasn't impressed. Well, if she hung around much longer, she'd probably get to see the entire play, not just one scene.

As usual, I'd be assigned to play the one with common sense.

With Nora still holding tightly to one arm, Marcus said he'd meet Shelby and me back at the apartment. I'd offered to ride with them so Shelby could go home if she wanted, but Nora quickly put the kibosh on that idea.

"Marcus and I have so much catching up to do, don't we, sugar bear?"

This time I didn't bother disguising my gag reflex. She was acting as though it had been months since their last meeting, not mere hours.

Shelby, I noticed, looked amused. Marcus and Nora simply looked like a pair of loonies. Hopefully they'd get all their "catching up" out of the way before getting to her place. I didn't think I could take much more of the billing and cooing.

Brent and a slight girl of about nineteen were waiting at Nora's door, seated with their backs against the wall, both attached to a single cell phone by a pair of earbuds. This would be how the archeologists and sociologists of the future would see us, connected by technology without any human interaction. Giving a dismal sigh, I stood aside and waited for Nora to unlock the front door.

She and Marcus had driven up just ahead of Shelby and me, a mutated shadow with various lumps and bumps that I didn't dare try to decipher in public. They remained practically melded together as they walked ahead of us into the building, completely ignoring Patsy's greeting, still giggling like a pair of randy teenagers.

I gave Patsy a weak finger waggle as we passed her desk. Lord only knew what she was thinking as she stared at the sight that was Nora and Marcus, arms entwined and heads together as they giggled by. I wasn't sure what I thought myself, to be honest.

Shelby, of course, was still grinning from ear to ear as if this was the best show she'd ever seen. I could only hope it wouldn't make her newspaper, complete with a cringe-worthy headline such as "Are We Ever Too Old for Making Whoopie?"

Yes. No. Maybe. At least not in public. *Definitely* not in public.

Glaring at Nora's back as she disentangled herself from an almost-drooling Marcus and fumbled in her leather messenger bag for the key, I saw her jump away from the door, a startled expression on her face.

The apartment wasn't locked.

Call it an impulse or an imp, but I had to ask. "Marcus? Would you like to go first?"

Ignoring the scowl Nora shot in my direction, I looked at the obviously nervous private eye with as much innocence as I could muster. I didn't fool my best friend for one second. Brent, however, was a different matter altogether.

"Maybe we should both go in, you know, being the two men and all." Brent stepped closer to the door, ready to show off his manly skills.

Rachel, I was interested to see, seemed as keen as Brent to go inside. Marcus definitely wasn't.

Nora was not impressed. She was now looking at her beau with something akin to disdain. Nora was nothing if not traditional when it came to her ideal of what a man should do and be, and Marcus clearly wasn't living up to that ideal.

Well, I was her best friend, wasn't I? And if she couldn't see what a complete imbecile the man was, it was my duty to open her eyes.

Giving Marcus a non-too-gentle shove in the back, I sent him caroming into the door, forcing it open as he hit the wood. He went sprawling into Nora's living room, arms flailing like a deranged windmill as he fought to stay on his feet.

Mercy squeaked again and ducked behind Grace, who stood there as if frozen to the spot. They looked and sounded like a pair of trapped mice, and the gray dresses they had on only added to the illusion. It occurred to me just how dowdy both sisters had looked each time I'd seen them. Maybe they *did* need some money. I glanced at Nora, feeling uncomfortable. Of course, that could have been the curry beginning a revolt in my gut. Spices and I had never gotten along that well.

"It was open when we got here, I promise." Mercy peeked out from behind Grace, her eyes opened as wide as they'd go. "And we knocked, didn't we, Sister?"

Grace nodded rapidly again, a mute bobble head doll staring fixedly at Nora.

"Oh." The bluster died away as quickly as it had appeared. Nora took a step back and motioned toward the living room. "Well, sit down. I'm making some coffee."

And with that, she marched off toward the kitchen, her high heels beating an irritated tattoo on the floor.

"I'd better go and help," I offered into the sudden silence. I gestured to the sofas and chairs. "Just, uh, make yourselves at home." With an awkward smile that felt more like a grimace, I hurried into the kitchen.

"What's gotten into you?" I hissed into her ear.

She was standing completely still, gaze fixed on the ceiling.

"Cops or no cops? Coffee for everyone or not?" I gave her arm a poke that was barely this side of angry. "And I'll bet you didn't bother locking up either. In case you don't remember, that's how people get killed around here, girlfriend."

She shoved me out of the way with a pointy elbow. I sat down at the table with a decided thump.

"Sit down and quit spitting in my face." She sounded annoyed. "I'm thinking, all right?"

"I am sitting down, and if you're not making coffee, I will."

"I said I was making it, didn't I?"

"Yes, and you also said to call the cops. And, Nora," I added in wha hoped was a rational tone, "did it occur to you we've got a cop's daugl sitting out there as we speak? She might have already called her for all we know."

"Oh, my word, I completely forgot about those two." She le over and gave me a push. "Get out there and make sure she's not anything stupid."

Chapter 16

Grace, or possibly Mercy, stood in the doorway, one thin hand on her scrawny chest and a befuddled expression on her face as she stared at a red-faced Marcus struggling to upright himself. Her sister stood just behind her, with an identical stupefied look.

Nora was in no mood for checking on anyone's welfare at the moment, however, and I couldn't blame her one bit as she pushed past Marcus. Finding two folks in your home who shouldn't be there in the first place wasn't exactly conducive to polite manners, boyfriend or not.

"You two again! And just how in Hades did you get into my apartment?" Nora stood in front of the two women, hands on hips, eyebrows creating one continuous dark scowl across her forehead. "Gwen, call the cops. I want these two looney birds out of here like yesterday!"

"The cops?" squeaked Mercy.

I knew it was her by the name badge I'd spotted pinned just below a bony clavicle, *Welcome to St. Bridget's—I'm Mercy* printed across it in fancy lettering.

She was breathing so heavily that it bounced up and down, moving as if it had a life of its own. "Please don't call them, Nora. We'll go, won't we, Sister?"

Grace bobbed her head so rapidly I thought her bird's nest hairdo would tumble down. She looked almost pitiful, small and frail next to a very vibrant Nora.

"Marcus, Brent, block the door. No one's going anywhere until I find out who let you in my apartment. Now talk, or someone might get hurt." She leaned toward Mercy, eyes blazing and nostrils flaring.

Mercy squeaked again and ducked behind Grace, who stood there as if frozen to the spot. They looked and sounded like a pair of trapped mice, and the gray dresses they had on only added to the illusion. It occurred to me just how dowdy both sisters had looked each time I'd seen them. Maybe they *did* need some money. I glanced at Nora, feeling uncomfortable. Of course, that could have been the curry beginning a revolt in my gut. Spices and I had never gotten along that well.

"It was open when we got here, I promise." Mercy peeked out from behind Grace, her eyes opened as wide as they'd go. "And we knocked, didn't we, Sister?"

Grace nodded rapidly again, a mute bobble head doll staring fixedly at Nora.

"Oh." The bluster died away as quickly as it had appeared. Nora took a step back and motioned toward the living room. "Well, sit down. I'm making some coffee."

And with that, she marched off toward the kitchen, her high heels beating an irritated tattoo on the floor.

"I'd better go and help," I offered into the sudden silence. I gestured to the sofas and chairs. "Just, uh, make yourselves at home." With an awkward smile that felt more like a grimace, I hurried into the kitchen.

"What's gotten into you?" I hissed into her ear.

She was standing completely still, gaze fixed on the ceiling.

"Cops or no cops? Coffee for everyone or not?" I gave her arm a poke that was barely this side of angry. "And I'll bet you didn't bother locking up either. In case you don't remember, that's how people get killed around here, girlfriend."

She shoved me out of the way with a pointy elbow. I sat down at the table with a decided thump.

"Sit down and quit spitting in my face." She sounded annoyed. "I'm thinking, all right?"

"I am sitting down, and if you're not making coffee, I will."

"I said I was making it, didn't I?"

"Yes, and you also said to call the cops. And, Nora," I added in what I hoped was a rational tone, "did it occur to you we've got a cop's daughter sitting out there as we speak? She might have already called her dad, for all we know."

"Oh, my word, I completely forgot about those two." She leaned over and gave me a push. "Get out there and make sure she's not doing anything stupid."

"Because there's already plenty of stupid right in this room." I got to my feet anyway, ignoring the scathing look aimed in my direction. "What should I do, tie them up and make sure that no one leaves? Or kick them all out and hope for the best?"

"I don't know." She filled the carafe with water. "You figure it out. You're the one who has the degree."

"It's in English Literature, not Portland Idiocy." I headed back to where six people sat immobile as if on display. This wasn't going to be fun.

I'd managed to work myself into a bad mood during the verbal back and forth with Nora, something that usually only happened with my department chair whenever I thought she was being obtuse. Since that had happened quite often, I was thoroughly schooled in verbal volleyball. Plastering on a smile, I walked into the middle of the living room.

"Are we in trouble, Miss F.?" Brent sat next to Rachel on one of the sofas, looking half-dressed without Aggie on his lap. Rachel was glued to her cell phone, probably recording everything for her dad. Great. Unless I knocked the thing out of her hand, which really would get her police officer dad on the warpath, we were at her mercy.

"No, you're not in any trouble." I sat down beside Rachel. "I think we're all just a bit tired, and Mrs. Goldstein was, uh, surprised to see she had company." Hoping that would satisfy the inquisitive teen, I craned my neck to see what his girl was doing on her cell phone.

"Oh, are you interested in cooking shows too?" Rachel looked up to see my gaze focused on the screen in her hand, where a man dressed in a chef's garb was demonstrating how to create something I probably couldn't make if I tried. "I just love this guy. He's so continental, you know?"

To me, "continental" was a style of breakfast that usually came with less expensive motels. But I smiled at her anyway, thankful she was occupied with something besides texting her dad.

She kissed the tips of her fingers a la French chef and then giggled when Brent copied her. Two kids having a normal evening. In a crazy woman's apartment. With several fruitcakes sitting in the same room. Who wouldn't prefer watching cooking videos?

"How long do we have to sit here?"

I looked up to see Mercy sliding to the edge of her chair, handbag clutched tightly with both hands, her lips a thin line of disapproval. Grace was still planted firmly in her seat, eyes as round as coins as she stared around the room.

"You'll stay there as long as it takes to get some info out of you."

We all turned to watch Nora as she walked into the room, carrying a large tray loaded with steaming mugs. Marcus sprang to his feet, but she ignored his outstretched hands, holding the tray down for Shelby to take a cup of coffee. By the time she'd made it around the room with the tray, she was almost smiling. Her hostess reflexes must have kicked in. That was one thing about Nora, she didn't stay in a bad mood for long.

Taking the last cup for herself, Nora curled up on the opposite end of the sofa from Marcus, her gaze fixed on Mercy.

"All right." She took a small sip of coffee as she stared at the truculent woman over the rim of her cup. "Spill it, Mercy. And don't leave anything out."

Mercy's small chin went up in the air, and I could have sworn I heard a small sniff of disdain. "I have no idea what you're talking about."

Leaning forward, Nora stared at her with narrowed eyes, a sure sign she was on the fast track to becoming irritated again. "What I'm talking about is you and your goofy sister breaking into my apartment. Does that ring a bell in that dim brain of yours?"

Grace's chin rose as well. "I am *not* goofy, Nora, and you don't need to be so rude to us."

Nora snorted, settling back against the sofa's cushions. I was beginning to get a neck ache as I looked from Nora to her stepdaughters and back. I really didn't know how folks could watch tennis when I couldn't keep up with a conversation without getting listener's cramp.

"Rude? I haven't even started being rude, missy. For starters, and I'm sure this just slipped that pea brain of yours, but you two trespassed when you invited yourselves inside my home. Didn't that little detail ever cross your mind?"

"But we knocked!" protested Mercy, an expression of indignation on her face. "And the door was unlocked, wasn't it, Sister?"

Grace did her bobble head act again.

"Girls, you two listen to me."

I wanted to laugh at the "girls" reference, especially since both of them were well past forty.

"I want to know what you want from me. And I want to know why you think you deserve whatever it is you want. Does that compute?" Nora spoke slowly, carefully enunciating each word as if she was talking to a pair of children.

To be honest, I wasn't certain they weren't stunted on some level. It sent a shiver down my back as I watched them staring at each other and then back at Nora. If they were putting on an act, they were good, really good.

"You should just ask her, Sister." That was Grace, leaning toward Mercy with an earnest tone. "That way we can leave. I want to go home now."

"Ask me what?" Nora's voice was sharper now, and even Rachel was now fixated on the scene unfolding across from her instead of the cooking video.

Shelby, I noticed, had slipped her cell phone out of her pocket and was holding it out as if she was recording. I could only hope this wouldn't end up in the "Lifestyle" section of the *Portland Tribune* under a headline that said "How Toxic is Your Family?" or some such nonsense.

"Ask me what, Mercy?" Nora's voice was louder now, and Grace shrank back against the chair, putting as much space as possible between her and her ex-stepmother. Interesting reaction.

Mercy lifted her chin even higher, stretching the tendons in her neck into knotted ropes. If she wasn't careful, something might snap.

"We want you to make a donation to St. Bridget's. It needs a new heating system and the kitchen needs to be updated." The words came out in a rush, and Mercy fell back, her bravado deflating like a balloon.

"And we're tired of asking strangers for money," chimed in Grace. "Most folks slam the door in our faces."

I understood that reaction. On the other hand, it would have taken quite a bit of moxie for these two to march from house to house. I was beginning to feel something like respect for the two odd sisters.

"Is that it? You want me to donate to St. Whatchamacallit's?" Nora's expression was one of incredulity, and even Marcus appeared dumbfounded.

What had those two expected to hear? I tucked that thought to the back of my mind for later perusal.

The sisters inclined their heads in unison, both watching Nora with an intensity that was almost scary. Whatever else they had in their lives, St. Bridget's was at the top.

"Mercy," I began gently, leaning into the conversation, "Is there another reason why you want Nora to support your charity work?"

Something about these two women reminded me of the oft-bullied student who finally had had enough. Of course, it could be plain old nosiness on my part, but I'd only posed the same question that was hanging in neon above everyone else.

Marcus and Nora, Brent and Rachel, even Grace—they were all staring at Mercy, waiting for her response.

Finally, she let out a little sigh and aimed her answer at the floor. "When we were, oh, maybe seventeen or so—isn't that right, Sister?"

Grace dipped her head in acknowledgment. The color had slowly begun to rise in her thin face.

"Anyways, we decided to go shopping at one of the nicer stores, the one where all of the other girls would go." There was another pause, this one long enough for Nora to stir restlessly. Mercy looked up quickly and then back down again, addressing her feet. "Our mom didn't get any money after our dad left us."

I stole a quick look at Nora. Her color was now even higher than Grace's, and she wriggled uncomfortably in her seat.

"So, we stole some new clothes, plain and simple. Isn't that right, Sister?"

There was a brief silence before Nora spoke.

"And?" She gave an impatient twirl with her hand, nearly upsetting her coffee cup. "So, you got caught, I'm assuming. What's that got to do with St. Whats-its?"

"That's where we were sent to work our community service hours. Father Tim was kind and helped us see that having things wasn't everything." This time Grace spoke up, sitting up a little straighter as she did, chin jutting out once more. "And we've never left."

"Over twenty-five years of service," Mercy pointed out proudly. "We even got our names engraved on a badge." She reverently touched the white tag pinned to her dress. "Only permanent volunteers get this, right, Sister?"

Nora shook her head slowly as if stunned by what she'd just heard. Brent and Rachel sat openmouthed, and even Marcus looked perplexed. I began applauding softly, not wanting to startle the two pleased volunteers. Call it an automatic response, but I couldn't help it.

When the others joined in, I didn't know who was more astonished, me or the blushing sisters.

After they'd gone, Nora's generous check carefully deposited in Mercy's handbag, the rest of us sat in silence, trying to process what had just transpired. I still wondered about the threatening letters, though. Could two desperate volunteers have done something like that in the name of charity? Possibly. Maybe. That was something else to consider.

"Well, folks, looks like that show's over." Nora startled me out of my thoughts. "How 'bout act two? Or do we need more coffee first?"

"Act two?" Brent's forehead was furrowed as he looked at her, a puzzled expression on his face.

Rachel prodded him gently in the side, smiling across at Nora. I was beginning to like this girl. It appeared she had enough common sense to spare. "I think that's us, silly. And yes, more coffee would be awesome."

"And some cookies too." Brent gave me his patented wide grin. "I saw some in your cabinet the other day when Miss F. made me move the coffee mugs."

Nora glanced at me, and I gave a small shrug. At least I could reach the dang things now.

"Okay. Coffee and cookies it is. And then you two can spill the beans."

When we were finally resettled, Marcus had scooted closer to Nora's end of the couch. I gave Brent an encouraging smile.

"Your text said you had some news for us. What's the scoop?"

Shelby gave a little snort of laughter, and I turned to look at her, my eyebrows lifted.

"And by 'scoop' I mean information that is staying right in this room, not making an appearance in the paper."

"Oh, no way," Rachel exclaimed, her voice concerned. "If my dad knew I was sneaking into his files, I'd be toast."

"Burnt toast," Brent agreed solemnly.

Rachel shot him a sour look, and I hid a smile.

"I won't tell a soul, scout's honor." Shelby held up one hand, her expression appropriately sober. "Does this concern the dead woman or man?"

"The woman, of course." Rachel gave her a condescending glance and then looked at me. "The report Dad got from one of the investigators said the lab was able to lift some good prints off the knife handle."

"That's great news! Have they made an ID yet?" I placed my coffee cup on the small end table and clasped my hands together in excitement. This was better than I had expected.

Rachel and Brent exchanged a quick glance.

"What?" I looked at them, my excitement plummeting. "It's not anyone we know, is it?"

"Worse," said Brent. "They don't have a clue."

"I thought that's what fingerprints were—a clue." Nora's tone was sardonic.

Rachel shrugged. "It is, normally, but the person has to be in the database already."

"Oh." I let that thought sink in. "So, they'd already have to have been printed because of a crime."

"Or because they're a teacher," added Shelby, a mischievous grin on her face.

"Gosh, Miss F., I didn't know you were a criminal. That's kinda cool." Brent's eyes widened with astonishment.

Rachel gave him another jab in the ribs, giving me an apologetic half-smile. If she was going to hang out with Brent, she'd better get used to running interference. "She's not a criminal, doofus. Teachers have to be fingerprinted to get their certificates, right?"

I nodded. "Something along those lines. My concern is we're still no closer to figuring out who killed Linda than we were ten minutes ago."

"Actually," Rachel began, and my pulse quickened. "They did find out something that's pretty telling." She smiled at Brent. "You tell her, okay?"

"Sure thing." Brent wriggled to the edge of the sofa, looking importantly around the room. "What they also found was a little metal thingy in her pocket."

"A little metal thingy?" Nora narrowed her eyes. "What did it look like?"

"Like that thing you stole outta the desk downstairs," was Brent's prompt reply.

I stifled a laugh at the shocked expression on Marcus's face. Shelby simply looked interested.

Nora tossed her head. "Whatever. So, what you're saying is Linda Fletcher had a lock picking tool with her?" She looked across at me, eyebrows drawn together. "Maybe that's how she got into my place to begin with."

"No." I shook my head emphatically. "Remember? It was already unlocked. We didn't lock the door when we left to pass out business cards."

"Oh, that's right." Nora tapped her chin with one finger, looking as thoughtful as Auguste Rodin's famous sculpture, only with clothes. Thank goodness. "So, why would she have it?"

There was silence in the room as we thought about this, and then Brent straightened up, one hand waving in the air as though still in the classroom.

"Yes?" I asked, automatically switching into teacher mode.

"What if it wasn't hers?"

"Huh?" I stared at him in mild confusion. "What do you mean by that, Brent?"

"Maybe whoever killed her put it there."

"That's brilliant, kid." Nora beamed from her spot on the sofa. "You'd make a great detective."

"What about me?" Marcus stuck out his bottom lip, a large child pouting for his mom's attention. "I'm a great detective."

"Hmm," was Nora's reply.

Marcus's lip crept out even farther, forming a pale pink ledge. I was tempted to shove it back into place.

Instead, I chose to ignore him, eager to discuss some possibilities. "Let's say you're right. Shelby, do you think your paper pal might have an idea of where we should go with this?" I glanced at Rachel. "We can't expect you to keep giving us information without your dad finding out."

"Oh, that's no problem." Brent grinned at Rachel. "She's a professional when it comes to sneaking stuff, aren't you?"

I wanted to throw my hands up in the air. First a cat burglar and a wannabe spy, now a document thief. What was next, a safecracker? It was beginning to make Saturday detention with miscreant students sound like a day at the opera.

Chapter 17

"You know," I began slowly, my memory tossing up a piece of forgotten information. "I think I remember Patsy telling me she and her late husband owned a locksmith business. Do you think she might have been our burglar, if not Linda's killer?"

Nora gave a short bark of laughter. "That mealy mouthed woman? I sincerely doubt it. She couldn't swat a fly."

"Maybe." I spoke doubtfully, thinking of the way Patsy had glowered at Nora. She hadn't looked so mealy mouthed then. In my experience, anyone had the ability to do anything if the conditions were right.

For instance, my school's prized senior from a few years back had been up for at least three full-ride scholarships to Ivy League universities, but he'd lost the chance with one poor decision—painting his initials onto one of the biggest rocks that lined Multnomah Falls. Someone had seen him and had called the park rangers, who, in turn, had called the police. And faster than you could say "idiot," his scholarships were yanked and he'd graduated from high school in disgrace. Last I'd heard, he was working part-time in his family's diner and attending classes at the local junior college.

Of course, it was a long way from vandalizing a state park to killing someone. Maybe, however, if Linda and Buddy had uncovered something unsavory about Patsy, she might have killed to keep her job. This world could be a crazy place.

Shelby's cell phone pinged again, and she glanced at the small screen, one eyebrow lifted. "It's Brian again. Is he trying to earn brownie points or something?"

"That's what men do best." Nora's tone was scornful, and Marcus begun sputtering at her side. She shushed him with a wave of her hand. "What's he saying this time?"

"Lazarus—"

"Buddy," interjected Nora.

"All right, *Buddy* had one of those lock pick things in his pocket as well." Shelby looked at me, her expression troubled. "Do you think someone's trying to tell us something, Miss Franklin?"

"You mean like a secret message or something?" Brent sounded excited, and Rachel ducked her head to cover a grin at his child-like exuberance.

Nora looked at him, her expression as sober as a teetotaler's. "That could very well be, kid. It might be a calling card, or whatever it's called. Ask your teacher." She nodded in my direction. "She's the mystery buff in here."

"You make me sound like a one-trick pony," I protested halfheartedly, but I was secretly pleased she'd mentioned it. I'd grab at any chance to talk up Jane Marple's wise observations. "But Mrs. Goldstein is right, Brent. In the books I like to read, the killer sometimes leaves a clue behind to tease the detectives."

"Like a joke? Like maybe the killer's laughing at the police? I don't mean your dad," he glanced at Rachel.

She patted his arm reassuringly.

"Let me put it this way. Sometimes killers can get so confident they think they can outsmart the ones investigating the crime. That's usually when they get caught."

"Agatha Christie, book four, chapter ten, right?" Nora smiled across at me. "Well, if that's the case, folks, we're already one step ahead. My money's on Patsy."

"Just because she used to own a locksmith business doesn't mean she still has the tools," I said sternly. "When she sold it, the new owners most likely got everything."

"Besides, you can get those things right here on the internet. This site sells them in packs of six." Shelby held her cell phone out so we could see the screen. "Wonder if that's even legal."

"Six, huh?" Nora was back in Rodin mode, her gaze fixed on the ceiling, finger tapping her chin. "How many have we come across so far, Gwennie?"

"Well, there's the one I found at my place and one each in Linda and Buddy's pockets. That makes three." I closed my eyes as I ticked off the numbers, trying to remember.

"Don't forget the one that Mrs. Goldstein st—"

"Yeah, yeah, kid. The one I stole." Nora wrinkled her nose at Brent.

Rachel and I exchanged smiles while Brent looked smug.

"And the one the cleaner gave me. That makes five." I held up one hand, fingers splayed. "That's one left, if we assume that's where the killer got them." I pointed at Shelby's phone.

Shelby gave a shudder, wrapping her arms around her middle. "That sounds rather ominous, Miss Franklin. Almost like when we read that short story about that poor black cat, that creepy one by Poe."

Brent's eyes lit up with interest. "I liked that story, except for the part where the cat's owner pokes its—"

"Brent!" Shelby grimaced, covering her ears. "We don't need the details, okay?"

"And I agree." Rachel scowled as she gave him a not-so-gentle shove.

"What'd I say?" He looked from one girl to the other, his voice rising, confusion on his face. "I just wanted to tell you I didn't like that part about—"

"We get it, Brent." I held up one hand, my own voice low and even. I'd discovered long ago that most students modulated their voices to match mine, whether unconsciously or by choice. "It's a story with some rather unsavory descriptions in it. Most animal lovers aren't very fond of it."

"You can say that again," Rachel muttered, giving Brent another jab with her elbow.

"How about we get back to the topic at hand?" Nora glanced over at Marcus and grinned.

He was sitting with his head against the back of the sofa, eyes closed and hands folded across his paunch.

"Some of us oldies need to hit the hay soon."

"I heard that." He opened one eye and immediately closed it again.

"And he's not even wearing a tie." I motioned to his neck, my expression as innocent as a newborn lamb's as I glanced toward the door. "How's that going to work, pal?"

"Mind your own beeswax," Nora replied, but she looked rather pleased, a faint blush on her face.

Marcus's soft snore reminded me it really was getting late. If I wanted to be awake enough to read for a while, I'd need to get going soon.

I turned to look at Shelby. "I'd sure appreciate a lift home, if that's all right with you."

"Not a problem, Miss Franklin. I wasn't going anywhere else tonight anyways." She yawned suddenly, tapping her mouth with her fingertips. "And speaking of getting home, I'm ready whenever you are."

The ride home was silent, except for the shushing sound the tires made on the damp road. Portland was known for its rainy climate, but tonight it was only the backdrop for a cozy night in my own home. I'd put the flannel sheets on my bed only that morning, and I was looking forward to crawling between them and reading a Father Brown mystery.

Saying goodnight to Shelby at the end of my driveway, I fished my keys out and headed for the front door, my mind already focusing on the hot tea I planned on making after getting into my sleep T-shirt and washing my face. I certainly wasn't thinking about having company.

I had just put the key into the lock when I felt something near my ankles, something that was rubbing its damp body all over my legs. I jumped sky high. My visitor let out a yelp.

Once my heart had settled back in my chest again and I could breathe without gasping, I bent down for a closer look. One small dog sat huddled in the corner of my porch, its eyes as large as mine as we stared at one another. Great. It was like the animal rumor mill had announced that a certain retired teacher was now available for shelter.

"Might as well be hung for a sheep as a lamb." I crouched down to get a better look. It definitely wasn't a puppy, certainly not as young as Aggie. From where I was squatting, I could tell it didn't have a collar on either. Double great. I stood up slowly, trying to decide what to do.

It stared at me, its tail thumping hesitantly against the porch floor, and I could swear it had a hopeful expression on its face.

"Fine," I sighed, leaning over and gently picking up the trembling animal. "You can stay with me tonight, but tomorrow you're going to the p-o-u-n-d." I spelled that last word in case the dog recognized it. I didn't like the sound of it myself. "I'll have to double my Benadryl, no thanks to you. And I hope you're house broken."

The dog lifted its muzzle and licked my face.

Was it possible to fall in love so quickly?

Maybe I'd let it hang out for a few days and see if anyone was looking for a lost dog. Besides, I'd read about the pounds and shelters, and I couldn't imagine taking an innocent animal there. And maybe, like Brent had said, I wasn't as allergic to animals as I'd always thought.

I woke briefly during the night to feel soft fur against my arms. Without thinking, I cuddled the dog closer and drifted back to sleep. Neither one of us woke up until my cell phone began buzzing on my nightstand.

"Hello." I spoke groggily into the phone. "Who's calling, please?"

"Hey, Sis! It's already past ten and we've got a ton of jobs for today." Her voice sharpened. "Did I wake you up?"

"No. Yes." I looked at the dog and put one finger to my lips. I could have sworn it understood. Or maybe it was reminding me that it needed to

do its business. I scrambled off the side of the bed, my feet feeling wildly
for my house slippers. "I'll call you back, all right?"

The dog jumped down and let out a small bark. I shook my fist at it. It
licked my bare ankles.

"Is there someone there, you sly thing, you?" Nora asked.

"No, of course not." I shuffled toward the hallway and the front door.
"Nobody here but us chickens."

I opened the door a crack and the dog shot outside. Good. Maybe it was
house trained after all. That also meant it was probably someone's pet. I
promptly shoved that unwelcome thought to the back of the line.

"Hmmm. I could have sworn…all right. I'll see you around eleven
thirty-ish or so?"

"Absolutely." I was eager to get off the line and see what my
guest was up to.

I ran back to my room and slipped on a robe before stepping out on
the porch. The dog was trotting around my small front yard, stopping to
sniff at the various plants and flowers that I'd managed to coax from the
ground. Despite the greenery all around me, I'd never had much luck in
the growing department.

The dog chose a spot in my flower bed and settled down to do its business.
This was the part of animal care that didn't appeal to me. Grimacing, I
turned to go back inside the house to get a bag for poop scooping and
nearly tripped over the small animal as it dashed in between my feet. With
a small bark, it sat down and looked at me expectantly.

"I suppose you want to eat now." Hands on hips, I stared at it, trying
to think of a suitable breakfast. Aggie, I recalled, would eat anything, just
like her owner. Until I was able to get to a store and buy dog food, though,
I'd have to improvise.

In the end, I made toast for both of us, adding a dollop of peanut butter
to the dish I'd used for the dog. It made quick work of the food, its tail
wagging happily as it waited for a refill. I obliged, of course.

There was another immediate problem, of course—what to do with the
dog while I was at Nora's. I wasn't sure she'd appreciate another animal
in her apartment, but I certainly couldn't leave it shut up in my place all
day. I didn't want to leave it outside, either. I finally decided to take it with
me, using an old belt as a collar and some thin rope for a leash. I'd need
to take care of this as well.

I wanted to keep the animal. In the morning light, I could see its
coloring, shiny black fur covering its body with a splash of white on the

chest and the tops of its paws. I took a quick peek at its undercarriage and decided it was male.

"You look like you've got on a tuxedo and spats, almost as dapper as Hercule Poirot. Maybe I'll call you Hercule. Only until your family shows up." I reached down and ruffled his fur.

Hercule gave an excited yip, running the length of the rope and back, a doggy smile on his face. I felt one on my own as well—a human smile, of course, but just as wide. Having a companion, even an animal, was a new experience for me. Maybe Nora only needed a dog, not a man.

Patsy was seated at the concierge when I arrived, carefully picking up Hercule to carry him through the lobby. She looked up briefly from the computer's keyboard as I passed but didn't offer more than a brief greeting. I noticed the dark shadows under her eyes, as if she hadn't slept well. It was probably lonely, living by oneself after being accustomed to having a husband around. In the few short hours that Hercule had been with me, I already dreaded his owners coming to claim him.

"You better be on your best behavior." I ran one hand gently over the dog's back as we stood in the elevator.

He turned his head and licked my hand.

"Nora might not appreciate having two male animals in the house."

Of course, Marcus might not be there, but I wasn't chancing it. This dog was going to behave whether he liked it not.

To my surprise, Nora's apartment door was ajar, sounds of a vacuum cleaner coming from inside. I frowned as I stuck my head around the doorway, Hercule's wet nose on the back of my leg. I couldn't remember her saying anything about the housekeeper coming by today, but I was still half hungover from the double dose of Benadryl I'd taken last night.

"Hello?" I stepped cautiously into the apartment. "Nora? Marcus? Anybody?"

The vacuum abruptly cut off. Marcus, a frilly white apron tied underneath his bulging middle, appeared in the hallway. I was so surprised I forgot to laugh.

"Is Nora here?" I'd also forgotten about Hercule. The dog bounded across the room toward Marcus, jerking the rope out of my hand.

"Now, what do we have here?" Marcus leaned down and gave Hercule's ears a quick rub, causing the dog's tail to wag faster than a professional gossip's tongue. "Is this a client?"

"Actually," I began hesitantly, following the dog to the hallway, "he's kind of adopted me. I found him hanging around my house last night, and well, it was too cold to leave him outside."

"No collar? Maybe he has a chip." Marcus's thick fingers scrabbled under the fur on Hercule's neck, his eyes half closed in concentration. "No, I can't feel anything, but it might have shifted. If he's got one, that is." He gave the dog a final pat and straightened up. "Have you named him yet?"

"Hercule." I smiled as the black and white dog turned at the sound of the name I'd given him. "Although, it might be easier to call him Herc."

"Another nod to Agatha Christie, I suppose."

"Of course. And it goes so well with Aggie."

"What goes so well with Aggie?"

I turned to see Nora standing in the doorway, her arms laden with canvas shopping bags.

"Here, Sis, grab some of these. My arms feel like they're going to fall off."

"You should have told me you were going out," I chided her. "I could have gone with you."

"And you might have thought to tell me you were bringing a house guest, so I guess we're even." She blew a kiss at me as she breezed past toward the kitchen. "And that one had better have more manners than another dog I know."

Marcus and I grinned at each other. With a brief wave, he disappeared back down the hallway and the vacuum cleaner roared to life again. It looked like my best friend had found herself another housekeeper.

"So, does it have a name?" Nora glanced over her shoulder at Herc as he sniffed his way around the room. "Judging by those dangly bits I can see, I'd say it's a boy."

"And you'd be correct. I'm calling him Hercule."

"Hercule, huh? After that funny little detective, the one with the bald head and weird mustache?" She folded up the empty shopping bags and tucked them into a drawer. "Pretty soon we'll have the entire cast if we're not careful."

"Believe me, this wasn't planned, not by a long shot." I patted the side of my thigh and Herc came trotting over, his muzzle lifted. "And yes, he's definitely housebroken, and yes, he's probably someone's lost pet." I lifted the dog onto my lap and he curled up, a bundle of black and white fur.

"Better not get too attached then." Nora handed me a box of fresh pastries. "Eat one of these. It'll take the edge off."

"I'm not edgy in the least." I took it from her anyway. Choosing a large cinnamon roll, studded with raisins and covered with icing, I offered a piece to Herc before taking a bite myself.

Nora watched me, shaking her head. "Yep, I can already tell that you're a goner. What'll you do when his family comes looking for him?"

I gave a small shrug. "I don't know. Guess I'll cross that bridge when I get there. Speaking of crossing bridges, how'd you manage to get Marcus into an apron?" I popped another piece of pastry in my mouth as I waited for her answer.

She slid into the chair across from me, reaching into the box for a cherry-topped Danish. "Let's say he's working off an exchange of goods and services." She bit into the fruit topping, her eyes twinkling at me over the pastry.

"Oh, thanks for the information I didn't need." I made a gagging sound, and Hercule turned his head to look at me. Without thinking, I leaned over and dropped a kiss on the top of his head. Hopefully my Benadryl would keep working for a while longer. "I'm okay, boy. It's my friend here you should worry about."

"Whatever." Nora snorted as she flapped my comment away, but I saw the beginnings of a smile. "And you need to get that mind of yours out of the gutter, Sis. I told Marcus I'd help foot the cost of a new office but he'd have to earn it. He offered to clean my place, so there you go." She raised both shoulders, her head tipped to the side. "To tell you the truth, he's better at it than the gal I have right now. Maybe I'll keep him and let her go."

There was a loud knock at the front door. Nora and I stared at one another, and Herc jumped down from my lap, a tiny growl in his throat.

"Are you expecting anyone?" I hurriedly got to my feet and followed the dog into the front room. "Maybe another stepchild?"

"Bite your tongue." She walked past me toward the door. "Well, here goes nothing."

"Delivery for a Nora Goldstein." A young woman in a drab brown uniform stood in the hall outside the apartment's door, balancing a clipboard on top of a large cardboard box. "Sign here, please."

I gripped Nora's arm before she could reach for it.

"Don't you think we should get Marcus in here first?"

"What for? I'm perfectly capable of handling a box, Sis." Nora lifted one eyebrow as she looked at me. "Besides, it might be some girlie things I ordered a few weeks back, get it?"

I stepped back, my hands held in front of me like a barrier. "All right, all right." I glanced at the curious driver and gave a minute shake of my head. "Don't say I didn't warn you."

Nora simply rolled her eyes and dashed off her signature before grabbing the box and hauling it inside.

I eyed the box with caution. Since getting the anonymous letter, I was definitely jumpy when it came to unexpected deliveries. Bending down for a closer look, I saw a name above the return address that seemed faintly familiar. It was a woman's name. I'd seen that name somewhere before, I knew I had, but where?

"Does that name look familiar to you?" I pointed to the corner of the box. Herc pushed his way under my arm and sniffed at the package, a wide doggy smile on his muzzle.

Nora, however, definitely wasn't grinning as she leaned in for a closer look and did a double take.

"Well, I call that pretty gutsy of her. Pretty gutsy." She stood up, both hands on her hips as she glared at the package. "Hang on a sec." Walking over to the hallway, she raised her voice above the hum of the vacuum. "Marcus! Get your padded fanny out here pronto."

There was instant silence as the machine was turned off, and Marcus appeared, hands twisting anxiously in the frilly apron.

"Did I forget something?" He looked at Nora, his forehead wrinkled as he glanced from her to me and back. "I was getting the vacuuming done before I got to the bathrooms, if that's all right."

"Forget about the stupid cleaning." Nora grabbed his arm and almost dragged him behind her. She jabbed a finger at the box. "Does that name ring a bell?"

Marcus leaned over the box, lips moving silently as he read the return address. With a start, he jerked away from it as if it was alive, dramatically clutching at the front of his shirt.

"I'll take that as a yes," Nora said drily. "Gwen, help old Romeo sit down before he faints on my floor."

I tucked one hand under his arm and led him to the nearest sofa, pushing his head back against the cushions. I knew the proper position for a lightheaded person was to lower their head between their knees, but I wasn't sure I could catch the rather rotund Marcus if he started to fall forward. Better if he collapsed on the sofa where it was soft.

Nora carefully slipped a finger under a loose corner of the packing tape, tearing it away in one yank. Her mouth was a thin line, her expression grim, and I knew that whoever had sent the package probably wasn't going to make Nora's holiday card list.

I watched her begin to lift out the various objects, curious what the box might hold. A pair of leopard spotted briefs or a forgotten toothbrush would be typical, and I wasn't disappointed as Nora held up a pair of boxers covered in a red chili pepper print.

It was the next item she examined, though, that sent a chill down my spine.

Chapter 18

"Well, well, well. Isn't this interesting?" Nora got to her feet, holding out one hand in the direction of the sofa. Something small lay there, something silver and bent and metallic. And familiar. "Have anything to say about this?"

Too stunned to move, I stared from Nora's outstretched palm to Marcus's now sweating face. He was looking decidedly unwell, and I hoped he wasn't going to keel over dead before we got an explanation.

"It's…it's…" Marcus tried to sit up but fell back against the cushions as he ran one finger around the inside of his collar.

I was getting seriously concerned. Was there such a thing as harassing someone to death? Knowing my luck, it would probably come with an incredibly long sentence in a deserted cell with only moldy bread to eat.

My best friend simply waited, arms crossed and eyes fixed unsympathetically on Marcus. "Yes? You were saying something?"

"Nora," I said worriedly, "maybe we should get him a glass of water or something."

"Nope. He's got some explaining to do. Then I'm kicking his carcass out."

"I can explain," Marcus managed to croak out. He lifted one arm and then let it flop beside him.

Herc, who'd been watching this with interest, trotted over to the sofa and leapt onto Marcus's lap. Maybe he was a trained support animal. Wouldn't that make his owners want him back as quickly as possible?

"Spit it out, man." Nora held the lock picking tool between two fingers, dangling it in front of Marcus's ashen face. "You were going to explain this little item, I believe."

"I used it at my last job," he managed to gasp out. "The gas station. Someone lost the keys to the men's room."

Nora straightened up, a perplexed expression in her eyes. I looked at her and gave a small shrug. Maybe he was telling the truth. Stranger things and all that.

"So what I'm hearing you say," Nora said slowly, "is your boss got you this so you could answer nature's call?"

I was relieved to see a bit of color coming back into his face. He nodded, and Herc nuzzled closer, his tail wagging against the cushions.

"We had all guys working there. Supposedly, it was cheaper to get those than it was to change the lock." Marcus began stroking the top of Herc's head. "The owner's a skinflint when it comes to money. At least that's what I heard. None of us actually met whoever owns the joint. I heard it's a cheap woman. I mean 'cheap' as in she doesn't like to spend money." He shifted against the cushions, his fingers still working in Herc's fur, and his eyes looked pleadingly at Nora. "So, does this mean you're not going to help me with my agency?"

A knock interrupted Nora's answer. Brent's head appeared around the door, Aggie clutched in his arms.

When he spotted Herc, a broad smile spread across his face. "Oh, cool, a friend for Aggie." Brent set the small dog down on the floor. "Is it yours, Mrs. G.?" She scampered straight for me, of course, and I drew my bare ankles away from her wet nose.

"He's mine, at least I hope so." I leaned over to give Aggie's ears a quick caress. "His name is Hercule, but I think I'll call him Herc."

The black and white dog stretched out his nose to meet Aggie's, then jumped off the sofa with a thump. The two dogs approached each other like a pair of prizefighters, warily circling and doing that awkward sniffing ritual that animals had. It made me glad humans preferred to shake hands.

Unless, of course, the hand had been used in place of a tissue. I watched as Marcus swiped at his eyes and nose, wiping his hand against his pant leg. He looked downright pitiful, not at all like the Don Juan I'd always thought he was.

Judging by Nora's caustic expression, she was beginning to agree. Turning back to the box, she knelt down and began flinging items about, Marcus weakly objecting as his belongings hit the floor.

"So, what's up with this?" Brent squatted beside Nora, peering with curiosity at the growing pile of clothes. "Are you gonna haul this stuff down to Goodwill?"

"Hey," protested Marcus. "Those are my things, thank you very much."

"So why's Mrs. G. taking 'em to—"

"Brent, focus for a second." Nora stopped going through the box and sat back on her heels. "Number one, this isn't going anywhere. And secondly, did you get the walks finished?"

Brent looked hurt. "I said I did, didn't I?"

"Not that I can recall, smarty pants." Nora glared at him over crossed arms and Brent returned the favor, the pair of them looking as ruffled as two bantam roosters.

"How was Pookie today?" I asked quickly to distract Brent's attention and restore some peace. "And does her owner belong to a motorcycle gang or something?" I remembered the man's rough appearance, the tattoos and leather, juxtaposed against a small fluffy poodle.

"Nah, he just likes to dress like that on his days off. He's a lawyer in some big office downtown."

Nora chuckled and even Marcus gave a halfhearted smile. Brent looked confused.

"Don't I remember something about a book cover? Something you used to tell me about judging?" Nora's eyes twinkled as she looked at me.

I gave in to impulse and stuck out my tongue.

"Fine, smarty pants. I'll remember that." I looked across the room to see what Herc and Aggie were doing.

Nora had tossed a tennis ball she'd taken from the box and now the two dogs were chewing on it. "At least the fur children are getting along."

"Oh, Aggie's good with other dogs." Brent's smile was proud as he watched his puppy play with the ball, her hindquarters in the air and tail wagging furiously. "She's really into sniffing and stuff."

"Better get that one to the vet pronto," muttered Nora from the side of her mouth. "We don't need a houseful of mini Aggies running around here."

"I'll take both of them." I'd already planned on taking Herc in for a checkup and to see if he had the dreaded chip. I really didn't want to find his owners, but I had to make an effort. "Herc could probably do with a little snipping as well."

Brent's eyes were wide as he looked at me. "You mean you're gonna get Herc's—"

"Aaand that's enough, thank you, Brent." I had to laugh at his expression. Even Marcus looked horrified at the idea.

"Men." Nora rolled her eyes in disgust. "You'd think we were talking about them or something."

"Let's move on, shall we?" I reached into the box and pulled out a T-shirt with last year's Portland Fun Run logo on the front. "I didn't know you liked to run, Marcus."

"I don't. I only went because…" He glanced at Nora uneasily.

"Because a girlfriend wanted to go?" Nora's voice was casual, but I could see her shoulders stiffen slightly. "I'm pretty sure I knew you weren't living in a monastery."

"A monastery? Isn't that where all those nuns live?" Brent looked at Marcus with something like admiration. "Just think, Mr. A. You coulda had a *lot* of girlfriends if you lived there."

"Nuns live in a convent," I corrected him. "And that's not what Mrs. Goldstein meant. Why don't you take the dogs outside for a few minutes, all right?"

"You always send me outside when you want to talk about grownup things," he objected, but he did as I suggested.

I heard him complaining all the way to the elevator.

"That one must've been a handful in class." Marcus stood and readjusted his apron. "I really need to get the rest of the place finished if you don't need me anymore." He glanced at the box, color tinging his cheeks again. "Just cram all that stuff back in there. I'll sort it out later."

I waited until I could hear the vacuum cleaner again before I spoke. "I think you're being a little tough on Marcus." I folded the fun run T-shirt and placed it back in the box. "To tell you the truth, I almost feel sorry for him."

Nora snorted, but I noticed she was folding the various pieces of clothing, not just tossing them in willy-nilly. "I'm beginning to think he sees me as his personal ATM."

I'd already been thinking along those lines, but I'd also seen something in his eyes just a few minutes ago that tugged at my heart. I had a soft spot for the underdog. I'd always been that way, even as a child, and I never hesitated whenever I spotted someone who could use a little TLC. Still, I'd never dealt with someone who was an accused murderer. Was there a special protocol, or did I ignore his status as a suspect?

"The way I see it," I said slowly, "is here we have a man who's what, fifty-five or so? He's working at a gas station to make ends meet because he can't make enough at the job he really wants to do. He hasn't had any luck in the long-term relationship department either."

"And what does that tell you?" Nora closed the flaps on the box and reaffixed the tape. "Sounds like a loser all the way around to me."

"That's what I'm trying to say. I don't think he's ever had someone believe in him." I stood up carefully, shaking my right foot to get the blood flowing again. "I taught students like him, the ones whose home life was nil. Something about Marcus reminds me of them, just forty years down the road."

Nora stayed kneeling on the floor.

It seemed I'd struck a chord in her and now she needed time to process her thoughts. I left her to it, heading into the kitchen. Besides, I needed coffee. And a cookie or three.

I'd gotten a fresh pot of coffee made and was rummaging around for the sweets when I heard the front door open.

"Miss F., look what that lady downstairs gave me," Brent called.

I hurried to the living room, curious to see what it was. He held up a small dog, its fur curling over a plump body. With a short tail and flat face, it looked like a mishmash between a poodle and a pug.

"What do you mean, she 'gave' it to you?" I could hear the quotes in Nora's voice as she frowned at the little dog in Brent's arms. "We absolutely do not need another four paws in this place."

"Well, she didn't actually give it to me," Brent admitted sheepishly. "She only asked me to pet sit while she runs some errands."

"Are we talking Patsy Reilly here? The concierge?" I couldn't imagine her owning a pet. She'd never mentioned one, not even when she'd seen us with Aggie.

Brent nodded. "She said it's not really hers. It belongs to another person who lives here but she's watching it while he's away on a business trip or something."

"Well, I'll be sending her the bill." Nora's voice was firm. "No freebies in life. That's not how you get ahead."

"There's a little problem, though." Brent looked down at his over-sized shoes. "I have to leave real soon 'cause I told Rachel I'd pick her up from college."

"Has she ridden with you before?" I had to ask, especially since I couldn't imagine someone willingly getting in the car with him.

"Yeah, why?" Brent looked at me with a puzzled expression.

"No reason." I reached down to pat Herc's ears as he nuzzled around my feet. "You drive safely with her in the car, alright? And don't forget her dad's a cop."

"I'm not a kid, Miss F." He snapped his fingers at Aggie. "Come on, girl. Let's go for a spin."

"Hey, wait a sec, Lothario." Nora got to her feet, groaning as she rubbed her back. "Good Lord, I need a massage."

"I'm not gonna rub your back." Brent hastily backed toward the door. "I walk dogs and that's it."

"No, idiot, not you. I only meant…oh, forget it. Listen, did she say when she'd be back? Patsy, I mean. Will she be gone a long time?"

"Nah. She said it's only for an hour, maybe an hour and a half." He paused, twisting the toe of one shoe into the carpet like a child trying to explain his behavior to Santa Claus. "Maybe I shoulda told her no."

"It's alright," I assured him. "One of us will watch him."

"It's a her," Brent said. "Wanna see?"

After Brent and Aggie had left, thankfully without any gender demonstrations, Nora and I stared at each other. I certainly didn't want to volunteer to dog sit, but money was money, as Nora had pointed out.

"I can do it." Nora leaned down and picked up the dog, gently running her fingers through its thick fur. "My word, but that's a lot of hair. I'll bet your owner has to keep you brushed all the time, doesn't he?" She dropped a quick kiss on the dog's head and winked at me. "Maybe I'll have to get a dog as well and call it Captain Hastings or Jane Marple."

I had to laugh, surprised. "I had no idea you were so familiar with Agatha Christie's books, Nora."

"I'm not a complete Neanderthal, you know." She gave the dog another squeeze and set it back on the floor. "I just prefer my stories to come with pictures. You know, the kind that move and talk and everything."

"I believe that's called a movie." I had to smile. I wouldn't have expected her to answer any other way.

"Guess I'd better see if Romeo is about done with the cleaning, then I'll take this little gal for a walk. Want to join me?"

"Actually, I think I'll take Herc and head home. His owner might be out looking for him." I watched the black and white dog give our visiting canine an obligatory sniff and then go back to gnawing the tennis ball. "Maybe I should get something for him to play with at home."

"Take that with you. I'm sure it's too soggy for Marcus to keep now anyway. I suppose I'll need to replace it."

"If you're sure." I stood a moment, watching Herc chomp down on the ball. If he kept that up, there wouldn't be much left to play with. "Please tell Marcus thank you for me."

Nora waved her hand. "Will do. So, I guess I'll see you and *you*"—this was directed to Herc, along with a scratch behind his ears—"tomorrow. Maybe a little earlier than today?"

"I'll try to keep the Benadryl intake down to a bare minimum," I laughed. "Come on, Herc. Let's get the rope back on you."

"You need to get a real leash, Gwen. That rope makes you look, I don't know, like a..."

"Like a retired teacher on a budget?" But I was only teasing, and I kissed her cheek as I passed her on the way out. "If I get to keep him, I'm sure I can find one at the Goodwill or at a yard sale."

Nora rolled her eyes. "You and your shopping habits. Remind me to be busy that day."

"You'll most likely be too busy playing house with Marcus to go anyway." I ducked out the doorway as she shook her fist at me. I saw her smile, though. Maybe things *would* work out for the two of them.

The walk home was on the chilly side, and I hurried as fast as I could, anxious to get back to my warm house. Herc, on the other hand, had other ideas, and he stopped at nearly every plant, tree, and fireplug on the way.

"It's like a dog's internet café." An older man walking two Golden Retrievers stopped to talk to me as I waited yet again for Herc to finish sniffing around a flower bed. "They get the lowdown on all the other dogs in the area and then leave their own message." He nodded as Herc lifted a leg. "Smart creatures, dogs."

"They certainly are. Actually, he isn't mine, at least not yet." I leaned down and patted Herc's head. "Do you know of anyone missing a dog?" I mentally crossed my fingers that he hadn't.

"I'm new to the area, but I'll keep my ears open, Mrs.—"

"Miss." My face warmed. "Miss Gwen Franklin."

"Miss Gwen," he repeated, and smiled. "And I'm Roger Smithson. I hope we'll run into each other again."

"Indeed." I pulled on Herc's temporary leash. "Let's go home, boy."

What was it that Mark Twain, that venerable wit and writer, had said about dogs? Something about them being gentlemen, a word I found myself applying to Roger and his companions as Herc and I finished the walk home. Well, I'd heard about matches being made in the grocery store, so why not out walking with a dog?

Good grief, Gwen. I got the front door opened, nearly tripping over Herc's eager dash inside. *Having a dog has turned your brain to mush.*

I fed Herc another piece of bread and peanut butter and was settling down for an afternoon with my ever-growing "to be read" pile when my cell phone began chirping. Glancing at the screen, I saw it was Nora. She probably wanted to talk about the next day's work or Marcus. Either way, it could turn into a marathon, so, with a sigh, I set my book aside and pressed the "answer" icon.

"Nora, I saw you less than an hour ago. What's up?"

"It's Marcus."

I sat up straighter, a timpani beginning to pound its way through my chest. Call it a gut feeling or years of being her friend, but something suddenly felt off. "Where's Nora?"

"That's what I'm calling about, Gwen." There was a snuffling sound on the other end of the line and I held the phone away with a grimace. I was never a fan of someone sniffling in my ear.

"She's not here, if that's what you wanted." I reached over to pat an inquisitive Herc. "Maybe she stepped out with Patsy's dog for a moment."

"I already checked, and Patsy said she hasn't seen her or the dog." More sniffling. "I'm getting kinda worried. This isn't like her, especially going somewhere without her phone."

I thought for a moment. Marcus was right about the phone. Since Nora had started tucking it inside her bra, for reasons that still went over my head, she was never without the thing.

"Give me a few minutes to get ready, Marcus, and I'll head back there. I'll be walking so it'll take some time."

"I can come get you." His words came out in a grateful rush. "Thanks, Gwen. I was beginning to feel a bit panicked."

He was in my driveway in less than ten minutes. Herc leapt into the open side door of the minivan without any coaxing, another sign he'd been a part of a family. Closing the door behind him, I shot a furtive glance around my street to see if anyone had noticed. Since I didn't see anyone running toward me screaming "pet thief" or "homewrecker," I felt safe for at least another day. With a sigh of relief, I buckled into the passenger's seat.

Marcus, on the other hand, looked anything but relaxed. Nora's disappearance, if that was what it truly was, had him in a frazzled state of mind. Maybe I should have volunteered to drive.

"You really think there's something wrong?" I turned to look at Marcus, noting his hands clamped firmly on the steering wheel, knuckles blanched like a first-time driver. "Did you try looking around the building's property? She might have stepped outside."

"Sure did. And across the street at the dog park. No one's seen her, at least not today."

"And you said Patsy hasn't seen her either? I thought she was out running errands, by the way."

Marcus nodded, his eyes fixed firmly on the road. "She'd just gotten back when I spoke with her. She didn't seem too worried, though. I think she was regretting having that dog to take care of and is glad someone else has it."

"Could be." I tried to think where Nora might have gotten to. Was there another pet sitting job I'd forgotten about? "Did you check her phone to see if she'd received a call for another job?"

Marcus slowed the van as we pulled into a visitors' parking space in the building's parking garage. Shutting off the engine, he turned to face me and now I could see exactly how worried the man was. Nora was going to get a lesson in manners when I caught up with her.

Chapter 19

"Look, Marcus, we'll find her. You know Nora. She's loud enough for the entire building to hear her when she gets going, so someone will spot her." I reached over and patted his arm.

Herc stuck his nose between the seats, and I patted him as well.

"Let's go back to her apartment. She might even be there already, wondering where you've gotten to." I tried to smile, but my mouth felt strangely stiff. I don't think I believed myself.

"Yeah, you're probably right." Marcus gave Herc's head a scratch and opened his door. "I think I'll suggest we cook in tonight instead of going out. This little episode has really taken it out of me."

"Oh, you're probably beat from doing all that housework." I kept my tone light as I walked beside him to the main entrance, Herc's rope securely in one hand. "I had no idea you were such a homebody."

"It's one of my dirty little secrets." He grinned at me, and I was relieved to see it was genuine.

Nora had better be waiting for us with bells on and coffee ready.

Her apartment was empty. I let Herc run through it, thinking that perhaps he'd unearth Nora behind the laundry basket or basking on the small balcony. No such luck, though. I looked at Marcus, my own anxiety mirrored on his face.

Nora really was missing.

"All right." I drew in a deep breath, both to calm my heart and to steady my thoughts. "I'll take a jaunt around the building, see if I can spot her or someone who's seen her. Sound good to you?"

He shrugged dejectedly. Herc nuzzled up to him, his tail wagging hopefully. Marcus reached for the dog, running one hand over his coat as he sat silently thinking. With all my heart, I wished Herc's owners had moved out of the city. Out of the state would be preferable.

"You know Nora. I'm sure she's fine." I sounded almost too perky, so I toned it down. "Besides, if she's still got that dog with her, she'll turn up just to give it back to Patsy, along with a bill for services rendered."

Herc scooted in closer, resting his head on one of Marcus's knees.

"Yeah, she's most likely out with the dog. I probably missed her." He gave a half-smile. "And don't tell her about me panicking, all right? She'll tease me forever."

"I won't. Can I leave Herc here with you? I'll have my phone in case she turns up before I get back." I waggled my cell phone in the air.

"Sure. I appreciate the company, to tell you the truth. This place is kinda empty when she's not here."

I had to agree. Nora, as small as she was, filled every place she was with her huge personality.

"But please be careful, Gwen." His face became somber. "If something's happened to Nora, it could happen to you as well. And listen to your gut. That's the best system in the world for detecting trouble."

That sent a shiver down my spine.

"I'll keep my eyes and ears opened. Nothing will get me, especially not in this place. It's got to be the deadest spot in Portland." Whoops. I'd used the "dead" word. Another set of chills took a trip from my head to my toes.

Snap out of it. With a wave and a promise to call him if I found her, I headed down the hall toward the elevator. I'd start at the top and work my way down.

By the time I'd gotten back to Nora's floor, I was both irritated and beginning to become frightened. This wasn't like my best friend. Yes, she'd always loved playing hide and seek when we were younger, but I was fairly certain she'd outgrown that nonsense a few decades ago.

As I stepped out of the elevator, I thought I heard something coming from Linda's empty apartment. If Nora was hanging out in there to make a point or to send Marcus into a tizzy, she was going to answer to me. I'd much rather be home, curled up on my couch with a pile of books and a cup of hot tea, Herc at my feet.

Sidling up to the apartment, I put my ear to the door but heard absolutely nothing. All was quiet. Absolutely silent. I wanted to find Nora so badly my mind must be playing tricks on me.

I was about to walk away when I remembered the lock picking tool still in my pocket. I was kind of old to start a new career in felonious behavior, but I was willing to give it a try. Pulling out the lock pick from

my pocket, I silently slipped it into the key hole, eyes closed, as I listened
for the magic click.

"Can I help you?"

The voice behind me, its words underpinned with curiosity, made me
jump sky high, and the lock pick fell silently to the carpeted floor.

"Patsy. You startled me."

"Still looking for your pal, I take it? Seems to me someone as obnoxious
as she is wouldn't be that difficult to locate." She gave a short laugh, and
I offered a half-smile I definitely wasn't feeling.

What I did feel was a sudden uneasiness. For someone who was supposed
to have the needs of the building's inhabitants foremost in her mind, Patsy
was acting quite the opposite.

And I didn't put up with anyone criticizing my best friend, except me.

I tried again, crossing my fingers she was only teasing. "Is there any
way we can make a general announcement? Maybe have each floor check
stairwells, empty apartments, that sort of thing? I'd sure appreciate it."

"We aren't equipped with an all-call system, but I'm sure I can send
out an email, ask the residents to keep their ears peeled for a yappy dog
and a yappier woman."

She sounded amused at her own words, but there wasn't an ounce of
warmth in her voice.

Suddenly, I was frightened, wishing I'd listened to Marcus about gut
feelings and all that jazz. The man was actually sensible, if you could get
past his womanizing flamboyance. If I lived to tell the tale, the first thing
I'd do, besides finding a bathroom, which I suddenly needed, would be to
apologize for not taking him seriously.

"I...I thought I heard someone in there." I pointed to the door behind
me. "And since I know it's supposed to be empty, well, you know..."

Her gaze was very intent. I'd never noticed how dark her eyes were.
Maybe it was just a trick of the light.

"Well, let's take a look together, shall we?" She pulled out a set of keys,
with a thin smile. "I think these might work better than that." She kicked
the lock pick away from me and bent down to get it. "I'll hang onto this,
if you don't mind." She gave a chuckle that sounded anything but jolly.
"It matches the one I slipped into your pal's pocket."

Of course I minded. It provided the only proof I had of Patsy's involvement
in everything. Besides, the warning prickles of caution had begun to slide
up and down my spine. I needed to watch my back. And my front.

The door opened with a soft click. I hesitated for a moment, not wanting
to trap myself inside with this nutcase. A shove from behind sent me

staggering through the doorway and into the empty apartment. It was damp and chilly inside, and I hugged myself with arms that were covered in goose flesh. No one had turned the heat on in here for a long while, and it felt as though I were underwater, staring up through half-light and trying to find the bottom. An unexpected wave of vertigo hit me and I swayed, eyes closed, as I reached out for support.

Instead, I found myself lying face down on the carpet, Patsy kneeling next to me as she quickly bound my ankles and hands. I turned my head to the side, trying to breathe without sucking in a lungful of dust mites and God only knew what else. What a lousy time to be thinking about my allergies.

"I trust you're nice and cozy down there." Patsy's foot gave me a nudge, and I tensed, waiting for more. Instead, she walked off, leaving me lying there in the middle of the living room, trussed up like a Thanksgiving turkey. Ready for…what? *Don't say the "slaughter" word.*

This was one time my teacher voice wasn't working. I laid there and began to cry. What an idiot I'd been. I should have listened to Marcus. Round and round, vicious circle thinking. I should have called the police first. I should have had a plan.

Should have, would have, could have. I used to say the same words to students who didn't turn in an assignment. In my world, my tiny, one-faceted academic universe, school came first. I'd forgotten all about life. If I ever got out of this situation, I promised myself I'd take out the largest full-page ad in the *Portland Tribune* and offer a public apology.

Shelby. Her name came flying through the air and smacked me right upside my head—metaphorically, of course. And I had her number in my cell phone.

"You never know when you're gonna need someone to run over in the middle of the night, Miss Franklin," she'd said and, without another word, had programmed her number under my "favorites" and set it up to be the first one on the call list. "See? All you need to do is open the list, like this, and tap the number. It'll ring straight to me, and I'll be here before you can say headlines."

If I could reach my cell, I was pretty sure I could follow her instructions and alert her to what was happening. If I could reach it. My hands were tied behind my back like some cheap B movie scene, and I didn't have the first idea of how to get them loose.

Footsteps sounded behind me. Patsy was coming back into the room from wherever she'd been, so I kept still, my eyes open enough to see through my eyelashes.

"Your bestie seems to still be out of it, shall we say, so I think it's probably safe to leave you gals alone for a while."

She gave a cackle of laughter that made me squeeze my eyes closed. If she was going to start the head-spinning portion of her transformation from kindly concierge to wicked witch, I didn't want to see it. I'd heard enough about *The Exorcist* to know I would never be able to sleep again if I had to watch something like that.

Without another word, she left the apartment. I heard the keys jingling against the door as she locked it behind her and the sound of her now-cheery voice calling a greeting to another tenant. And then silence.

Maybe I should call out to Nora, see if she could hear me. Then I did just that, wincing at the crackling in my voice.

"I sound like the old lady Brent thinks I am," I muttered and tried again. This time I got a response of sorts, or maybe I was hoping so hard to hear something that I'd conjured it out of thin air. Whatever it was, it gave me incentive to get busy and get the two of us out of here, preferably alive.

How I was going to do that, I had no idea. The only possible move was to somehow get my hands unbound so I could get to the cell phone I'd placed in my front shirt pocket. Of course. The one place I couldn't reach, which was probably why the head-spinner had left it behind.

I'd never been one to exercise, not even in my, ahem, younger days, so I had to really think through what I needed to do to get into the kitchen. I figured that would be the most likely place to find something that could help me free myself. Perhaps a conveniently placed knife–newly sharpened, of course, or the razor sharp edge of an opened tin can. You know. All those things that empty luxury apartments were likely to have.

In your dreams, Franklin. I rolled over toward the nearest wall. If nothing else, this place was famous for its cleanliness and orderliness. Nothing out of place, nothing out of line.

Except for the killer staff, of course.

That last thought struck me as hilariously funny, and I had to force myself not to laugh. I couldn't afford to go hysterical, not even for a second.

I managed to push my feet against the wall so I was able to sit up, legs still angled out because of the ties around my ankles. Closing my eyes and willing myself to move, I got onto my knees, fingers braced against the wall, and pushed out as hard as I could.

Teachers had notoriously strong fingers. No kidding. It was due to all the things we had to carry while juggling a coffee cup and keys, all while trying to open a locked door. If there was ever a competition to see which career produced the strongest fingers, I'd vote for teachers every time, hands down.

And they didn't fail me now. I was standing, still tied up, of course, but on my own two feet. I took a moment to catch my breath, gearing up for the next part, hopping into the kitchen. And to be honest, I didn't know if my knees could handle it.

Something flashed into the back of my mind, something I'd read or possibly seen on television, perhaps on something along the lines of *CSI*. A woman who'd found herself in about the same situation I was in had managed to get her hands from in back of her to the front. Of course, she'd been impossibly thin–no stomach to work around—and she'd probably trained as a contortionist at some time in her life. But she *had* been able to help herself. That was the main thing.

I stood still for a moment, half-listening for returning footsteps as I went through the movements in my mind. It was possible, but I'd have to sit back down first. Great.

Leaning back against the wall, I gradually slid down, wincing as my shirt rode up and exposed my back to the cold stucco. I'd probably given myself both a case of friction burn as well as frostbite; it was cold enough to take my breath away.

Now for the contortionist bit. I'd need to get my arms under me and around my legs in order to get them in front. I found myself cursing that last Voodoo Doughnut I'd eaten. Alright, I'd had three. I held my stomach in as much as I could while squeezing my knees next to it. Tucking my head and muttering my over-used bedtime prayer, I inched my arms under my comfortably padded tush and over my legs. If I ever got out of here, I'd not only place that ad in the *Trib* and apologize to Marcus, I'd also join a gym. My penitence list was getting longer by the minute. Maybe that was what a sorta-near-to-a-near-death experience did to you.

I felt like I'd conquered Mounts Everest, Kilimanjaro, and Hood all at once. Bending forward and grasping the rather clumsy knot Patsy had tied on my ankles, I quickly untied the thin cord and stood up, smiling from ear to ear. My strong teacher's fingers had saved the day once more.

But my finely tuned teacher's ears had caught the sound of footsteps, and they were headed this way. As quickly as my numb feet could hobble, I headed for the back bedroom. I figured that was where Nora would be held, the farthest spot from the front door.

She was.

Nora was lying as still as a corpse (*not* a corpse, I firmly told myself) and I closed the door, locking it behind me before hurrying to her side. I leaned over her and examined her chest for any signs of breathing. I felt a rush of relief when I saw her tight shirt rising and falling in a steady rhythm. At least she was still alive. Now I needed to get help here before Patsy discovered I'd made it to Nora. My hands were still tied and my fingers had passed the tingly point, but I was fairly certain I could still dial 9-1-1.

That was, I might have been able to if my phone had been charged. Frustrated, I threw it down and watched it come to rest near the open closet door.

And then I saw a way out.

There was something to be said for the mega-rich. They could be quite paranoid at times, even of their own family. Linda Fletcher, it would seem, was as fearful as they came. For that I was grateful. Very grateful.

I managed to get both of us into the closet and bolt the door. Paranoid Linda had turned her walk-in closet into a panic room, complete with a separate phone line and a bulletproof interior. Wherever the woman had gone, whatever patch of the Great Beyond was now hers, I needed to remember to send her a great big thank you.

My list was growing, and I didn't care one bit. Heck, I'd even consider tossing in a "thank you" to Nora's stiletto manufacturer. If push came to shove, those babies would make awesome weapons.

After checking to see Nora was still breathing, I grabbed the phone from the wall and could have fallen over with relief. There was a dial tone. With shaking fingers, I carefully pushed in the number for emergency services.

Chapter 20

It was always possible that memory came with a bit of readjustments. Things that really happened were turned around and appeared differently and words that people said were abridged, edited down to the bare minimum.

But there was no way on God's green earth that would happen to me. Not only did I witness most of the action, I also—*ta dah!*—managed to record it. My cell phone, the one I'd tossed down in disgust? Well, apparently it *was* charged. The back had come loose and the battery had been moved. When I threw the little darling, it fixed itself. And somehow, don't ask me how, it began to record the sounds in that back bedroom.

After Nora and I were safely locked inside Linda's panic room slash closet, Patsy had come charging in, screaming at the top of her lungs. Her voice on the recording had sounded spooked, and I guess she thought we'd performed some type of magic and had vanished—*poof!*—into thin air. She'd gone running out of that bedroom as if the hounds of hell were on her heels.

And, in a way, I suppose they were.

* * * *

What it came down to was this. Patsy, or to give her the name she'd been born with, Prudence Patricia Wainwright, was the oldest child of Nora's first husband, Thomas Biddle Wainwright. The man had been married one more time than he'd admitted to, and that brief first marriage had produced a daughter. When his wife had finally gotten fed up with his

Uriah Heep ways, always acting so holier-than-thou in public but being a devil at home, she'd taken little Patsy and moved away.

"So, I'm assuming Tom didn't like being the dumpee." I used a finger to mash sugary crumbs on my plate as I waited for Nora's reply.

The four of us were seated in the kitchen, Aggie and Herc prowling under the table for treats. Brent was silent for once, but I'd say it was due to the Voodoo Doughnuts Marcus had brought more than a burning desire to listen. Besides, as he had told us smugly, he'd already gotten the scoop from Rachel.

Marcus was too busy holding Nora's hand to pay much attention to the strawberry frosted Homer donut that lay on his plate, but he looked much happier than he had the last time I'd seen him. Who knew? Maybe another wedding wouldn't be such a bad idea after all. Then again…

"Got it in one, Sis." Nora looked at me over the rim of her coffee mug. "And when I left him, well, let's just say he nearly had a fit of apoplexy. Tom didn't appreciate being mocked in public by a mere woman." She set the mug down and picked up the Bacon Maple Bar with the hand that Marcus wasn't clinging to. "When I got that nice-sized cash settlement, it about did him in for good. Last I heard, he'd sold his share of the business and moved to an abandoned lighthouse in the San Juan Islands."

"And Patsy really thought you'd stolen the money from her and her mom?" I shook my head slowly as I took a bite of donut. "I don't see how that even made sense, considering the business was built with his second wife's money. If anything, Grace and Mercy had more of a say in that, right?"

"Absolutely." Nora nodded in agreement, her gaze fixed somewhere above the table as if seeing the past. "But, as you know, Patsy *isn't* in her right mind. Officer Taylor let it slip that she's been taken to Cedar Hills for a nice, long rest. She'll most likely get away with killing Linda and Buddy, although I don't think that's right, and won't be charged with attempted murder and kidnapping either."

When it came right down to it, the only person who could have committed the laundry list of crimes was the concierge herself. Trustworthy, competent, and…insane. Like a waiter or a department store salesperson, there but a part of the scenery, Patsy was able to become "visibly invisible." What a perfect disguise for someone wanting to commit a crime!

Linda Fletcher had simply been in the wrong place at the wrong time. Patsy had slipped into Nora's apartment to see if her little sleeping pill Danish topping had worked and had spotted Linda, looking enough like Nora to a deranged Patsy to make her think she'd actually killed her.

Poor Buddy. When had I started thinking of him as "poor Buddy"? He had presented a threat simply by talking to Marcus. It turned out that Patsy was the absentee owner of the gas station, inherited from a kindly stepfather, and she'd recognized Marcus right off the bat the first time he'd made an appearance. Somewhere in her twisted mind, she'd thought Buddy and Marcus were conspiring against her and were going to spill the beans to Nora.

"And here's the kicker, she's been telling whoever will listen to her that this building is haunted." Nora smiled at me with something of her old archness. "Something about a room where people can disappear without a trace. I have no idea what she's talking about, do you, Sis?"

I had to laugh. That panic room was a marvel all on its own. Not only were the walls and door constructed of bullet-proof material, it was also insulated well enough that no sound could be heard from the outside. That was why Patsy hadn't heard me making the emergency phone call.

I'd thought about creating my own panic area in my little bungalow and then stopped the thought in its embryonic tracks. I'd go on doing things the Miss Marple way—chair wedged under the doorknob and maybe a spray bottle of strong vinegar next to the bed. Besides, who'd want to break into Miss Gwen Franklin's house? Of course, a dog might not be a bad idea either. I'd just need to take my allergy tablets and carry lots of tissue along with the poopy bags.

"Miss F., the lady I got Aggie from? She says she's got another dog you can have if you want, maybe company for Herc." Brent shoved the last piece of donut in his mouth and leaned down to gather the excited puppy into his arms. "Of course, it won't be as cute as Aggie because it's an old dog that sleeps all day and only goes out to do its business." He looked directly at me and I saw a twinkle in his eyes. "I told her it would be perfect for this old retired teacher I knew."

We finally sent Brent and Aggie home and managed to convince Marcus that Nora would be fine on her own.

"I'll call Gwen if I need someone to stay with me." She smiled as she detached Marcus's hand from hers, and I had to turn my head so he wouldn't see my smile. The man really had it bad for my best friend.

"You run along and get some rest, Marcus. You've got a big day ahead of you tomorrow."

Marcus brightened at her words. His newly purchased office space, backed by a certain gal who liked to wear stiletto heels with everything, was holding its grand opening the next morning. Along with free hot dogs and canned sodas, also provided by Nora, Voodoo Doughnuts would be there as well, selling its famous sweet treats out of a food truck painted in the company's iconic pink.

"I think Marcus Avery, Detective at Large has a nice ring to it, don't you, Gwen?" Nora gave me one of her patented winks and then turned to give Marcus a not-so-gentle push toward the door. "And who knows? Maybe someday we'll add a few words about Two Sisters Pet Valet Services on the door as well."

Not if I can help it.

But I smiled at her in response. Despite needing a slug of Benadryl as my breakfast coffee chaser, I'd really enjoyed these past few weeks. And Herc, bless his furry little heart, had gotten his paws firmly around mine. Maybe I'd been missing something my whole life. All of the pet owners I'd met through our business had seemed like perfectly rational folks with one difference—they provided a place for a pet to live safely, and, in return, had gotten a bundle of unconditional love.

It sure beat having to switch husbands so often. That was only my humble opinion, of course. Nora, on the other hand...well, that was a story for another day. Maybe wedding bells *were* in her future, and maybe not. Either way, we had Two Sisters to keep us busy and grounded, and Portland could breathe easier knowing one particular driver had handed in his Uber sticker.

As for me? Well, I always fell back on my fictional pal Miss Jane Marple for wisdom and advice. I couldn't recall the words exactly, but I'd once read something along the lines of "making your own happiness" in one of Agatha Christie's books.

And that was exactly what I intended to do. Retirement, I'd discovered, wasn't only about getting to ignore the alarm clock or reading all night. It was also about making time to discover more about the real "me."

Of course, I'd never be as flamboyant as Nora or as spontaneous as Brent, but I *had* uncovered a real love for animals, something I'd never thought was possible, and I'd acquired a roommate whose furry tux really dressed up the place.

Miss Jane Marple, in all her spinsterish wisdom, once said folks shouldn't live lives full of "cannots." I won't, Miss Marple, indeed I won't.

ACKNOWLEDGMENTS

It would be impossible to acknowledge every person who has contributed to my love of reading and writing. There are several, though, who deserve my sincere thanks, beginning with my late mother. She consciously made time for reading in our home, and trips to the library were a weekly ritual. My agent, Dawn Dowdle, has honed my craft to a fine point, and for that I thank her, even when I get cranky (wink, wink, Dawn!). My dear friends Mary Karnes, Susan Furlong, Gemma Halliday, and Kate Young have all encouraged me to keep writing, even when I felt that perhaps it wasn't my game. And finally, my husband, Greg has given me the space and time to pursue my dream of writing, and that has been the biggest gift of all. Thank you all from the bottom of my heart.

If you enjoyed **DOGGONE DEAD**
by
Dane McCaslin
Be sure not to miss the next book in the

The 2 Sisters Pet Valet Mysteries
CAT'S MEOW
Turn the page for a quick peek at
CAT'S MEOW
Enjoy!

Chapter 1

"Run it by me one more time, Sis. Who all's been invited to this get-together?"

Nora Goldstein, my best friend since kindergarten and the closest thing I had to a real sister, was sitting cross-legged on one of her over-stuffed sofas, working on one nail (fake, of course) as though her life depended on it. I watched as she held up the nail tip for inspection and then began sawing at it again in earnest. I'd never worn anything false in my entire life, unless you counted the time I stuffed wadded up tissues in my bra for the eighth grade dance.

"Hang on a minute and I'll double check."

As co-owners of the 2 Sisters Pet Valet Services, we'd received an invitation to the annual Clear the Shelter fundraiser, a really big deal in our town. Picking up my newish smartphone, I opened the Google app and carefully tapped in with one finger: Greater Portland Shelter Association. A colorful banner featuring adorable dogs and cats floated across the top of the page, their cute little faces making me smile.

"What's making you grin like the Cheshire cat?" Nora glanced up from her nails, a tiny pucker between her carefully shaped eyebrows. "See any good lookin' men on that page?"

I ignored the comment and tapped on the menu icon. The event's list was there, and I spotted our names in the lower third.

"Looks like Miss Oregon will be there, along with the mayor, a few television personalities, and a handful of minor Portland celebrities." I held up my phone for her to see the screen. "And us, of course."

It felt like a dream to see my name there alongside those of well-known Portlandians. Gwen Franklin, retired teacher, mingling with local celebrities!

Nora snorted as she leaned in closer to inspect her nail, but I could tell that she was pleased. When she'd received the invitation asking us to participate in Portland's annual Clear the Shelters fundraiser, both of us had been bowled over at first and then tickled pink. Our pet care business was small but thriving, thanks to word of mouth advertising and the fact Nora lived directly across the street from Portland Pooch Park.

"I think I remember hearing something about the glorious Babs Prescott doing some of the presentations, but that could be wishful thinking." Nora shot me an amused glance as she said this and it was my turn to snort. Babs was only glorious to those who mattered, namely herself.

Babs Prescott, one half of the evening news team on the local station, had the requisite big hair and big teeth, plus a big personality to boot. The problem with her, though, was she was a legend in her own mind. Whenever she appeared on television or out in public, I did my best to avoid her. I tended to break out in hives around folks like her.

"So, you gonna try to sit at her table?" Nora glanced at me as she tucked the emery board back into her clear makeup bag. "Or is that a definite 'no' I hear?"

"What do you think, smarty pants?" I crossed both arms over my chest and scowled at the image on my phone's small screen. Even in miniature, Babs managed to appear colossal, filling the display with her big toothy smile. Of course, it could have simply been the way she'd turned to face the camera. With big hair and even bigger, uh, female assets, she made sure she was the center of attention whenever an opportunity presented itself.

Like the time she'd come to the school I taught at to raise awareness about the pitfalls of social media. Needless to say, by the time she'd finished her speech at the assembly, I was *not* her biggest fan.

Of course, it might have had something to do with the way she managed to turn the presentation into a slide show starring none other than a certain blonde news anchor, and some of the images were, in my opinion, not appropriate for the younger crowd. Judging by the frequent outbursts of whistles and cat calls, I'd say I was right. When the principal decided to shut the whole thing down and send the students back to class, I was relieved the show was over.

I was also very irritated because she'd pre-empted a great lesson on rhetorical devices I'd worked on for days.

"Sure you're not jealous?"

Nora's voice was teasing, but I wasn't in the mood. Just thinking about Babs Prescott was enough to turn me into a grump the size of Mount Hood.

"Positive," I said firmly. "Now, what's up with next week's schedule?"

"It's on my iPad." Nora unwound herself from the sofa and stood up, lifting both arms over her head and arching her back in a feline stretch. "By the way, is Brent back from his trip down south?"

Brent Mayfair, one of my many ex-students and our official dog walker, had taken a road trip down through California with his girlfriend Rachel and precious dog Aggie in tow. I missed him horribly, but only because I'd been stuck with most of the dog walking duties while Nora took on the various pet sitting assignments. Too much of Brent on any given day was grounds for sainthood.

"The last text I got from Rachel said they should be back in town sometime late tomorrow." I glanced at my phone and opened the message. "Says here they're staying at Mount Shasta tonight."

"Nice." Nora nodded in approval as she walked over to her desk and retrieved the tablet. "I'm glad to see them having fun together."

I laughed. "And I'd love to have been a fly on the wall when Rachel told her folks she was going on vacation with Brent."

"Right? Especially that tough cop dad of hers." Nora curled back up on the sofa, reaching up to pat her blonde curls. After a disastrous escapade with a perm-happy hairdresser last year, she was finally able to go out in public without scarves or hats.

"Speaking of tough, what's the latest on Marcus?"

Nora tossed her head, losing one hoop earring in the process. "If I never see him again, it won't be too soon for me."

Same song, second verse. Or perhaps verse five. Nora and Marcus Avery, her on-again, off-again beau, were the talk of the luxury apartment building where she resided. I made sure to drop a few juicy tidbits now and then for the new concierge to share with the other residents. I saw it as my duty to liven up the place, especially since the average age was well over sixty-five. I saw it as my contribution to the collective heart and circulation health of Nora's neighbors.

"Well, you'll have to see him tomorrow." I scooted closer to her so I could see the iPad's screen. "Isn't he coming by to drive us to the fundraiser?"

"We could Uber it."

Taking an Uber was something of a private joke between us, thanks to Brent and his one and only attempt at being an Uber driver. We liked to say we'd single-handedly saved the good folks of Portland when we hired him and got him off the road.

"Or I could drive. Of course," I added doubtfully, "I'm not sure my car will start. It's been in the garage since I retired last year."

"That's all right. I'll handle Marcus."

Smiling, I read over the upcoming pet walking and sitting jobs. It was clear our business was growing, and it was probably time to hire another walker. I wasn't fond of the end result of a walk and having to clean up after the little darlings. My own dog, Hercule, was another matter. He was home at the moment, living it up with the newly installed doggy door that led out to my rather minuscule backyard, probably enjoying the good weather and barking at the squirrels.

"Have you thought about taking on another employee to help Brent with all the dog walking jobs?" I glanced up from the tablet and swiveled around to face her. "Maybe Rachel?"

"Maybe. Isn't she still in junior college?"

"Yes, but only two days a week. And the dog walking job she had last year ended a few months ago, so she might consider joining us."

"I'm sure Brent would love that, but it's tough enough keeping the kid focused on his duties as it is."

"Rachel wouldn't mess around," I sounded more confident than I felt, but I was determined to get myself free of the walking end of our business. "That girl has more common sense than most folks twice her age."

Nora nodded. "True. Particularly one certain private investigator I know. He's such a nitwit, Gwen."

"Amen to that," I muttered as I looked at my phone. I'd received another text, this time from Brent. "Hang on a sec. I need to check this message from the boy wonder himself."

Hey Miss F We're having a good time except maybe Aggie since she got stung by a bee. Ok see you tomorrow.

Dear goodness. Had the boy been absent the day I taught punctuation? How he'd managed to graduate was a puzzle, but he had, and now he and I were coworkers in one of those weird universal flips.

"Well? What'd our resident genius have to say?" Nora's words might have been sardonic, but her tone was soft. She'd really taken to Brent, something that never ceased to amaze me, especially since I'd never known her to suffer fools gladly. That might have had something to do with her five—or was it six?—marriages.

"They're enjoying themselves, but it sounds like Aggie might be under the weather a bit. Blame it on a bee."

"Oh, poor baby." Nora grabbed the tablet and began scrolling. "Can dogs die from bee stings?"

I shrugged. "If she has an allergy, she probably could. Brent didn't seem too upset about it, though."

"Wonder if Marcus has any allergies?"

I stared at her, one hand on my chest. I'd love to say "on my bosom," but that part of my anatomy had recently begun its own trip south and hadn't returned. "I hope you're kidding."

"About what? I only said—"

"Oh, forget it. You'd better play nice tomorrow, though. We might need a ride home as well."

She wrinkled her nose at me but turned her attention back to the tablet.

I absentmindedly reached down to pat Hercule and then remembered I'd left him at the small bungalow he shared with me. I'd finally gotten brave enough to have a doggy door installed after a couple of break-ins last year. Of course, one had been perpetrated by my best friend, trying to prove a point, but I still hadn't wanted to give anyone else carte blanche to my house. Waking up to Nora skulking in my dark living room had been more than enough to turn my gray hair white.

Hercule was something special, though, and well worth a doggy door. He'd come into my life one rainy night and had never left. With a sleek black coat and a white front and paws, he looked as dapper as the fictional detective Hercule Poirot, hence the name. Having a dog could be a chore at times, but I wouldn't have traded Herc for anything in the world.

"Earth to Gwen—come in, space cadet." Nora snapped her fingers in front of my face, and I jumped. "I asked if you wanted to take a walk to The Friendly Bean."

"The Friendly Bean?" My mind was still on break-ins and bee stings. "Right now?"

"Yes, Gwen. Now." Nora mimed drinking a cup of coffee. "We need caffeine, and lots of it."

"Sure. I guess." I pointed to the iPad. "Shouldn't we make up our minds about another employee?"

"We can do that on the way." Nora jumped up and headed down the hallway toward her bedroom. "Give me a sec, all right?"

I sighed and settled back on the sofa. A "Nora sec" could be anywhere from two minutes to thirty, depending on how dolled up she was getting. My friend loved heels, the higher the better, and any clothing made from stretchy material. Her typical outfit of black yoga-type leggings and neon-colored tight tops was in direct contrast to my preference for cotton capris and loose, flowy shirts.

And Birkenstocks. I did love my sandals, no matter the weather. Rain in the forecast? Add thick socks. Snow? Even thicker socks. Going by the amount of similarly shod feet I saw around town, I wasn't the only one who felt this way.

"Hurry up," I called out. "You've got me craving a latte. And a croissant."

Or three. I loved my food as well, that was for sure, and our local coffee hangout made the best croissants this side of the Columbia River: buttery, flakey, and absolutely delicious.

As I waited for her, I idly thumbed through my social media accounts. I'd only recently joined Instagram and Facebook since those seemed to be the common platforms my ex-students used. Call me nosey or unable to let go, but I loved being included in their postings and commentary. Seeing the pictures of their own sweet kiddos made me feel nostalgic.

And old.

I was about to close my Instagram account when something in the feed caught my eye: a picture of none other than Miss Babs Prescott herself, one tanned arm slung over the shoulders of a sullen looking Shelby Tucker. Shelby, also a former student, was a journalist with the *Portland Tribune* and my go-to for help in all things digital.

"Catching flies, are we?"

Nora, dressed in all black Lycra, came teetering into the front room in the highest pair of heels I'd ever seen.

I snapped my mouth shut and silently held out my phone to her. Taking it, she peered at the screen and her own mouth gaped open in shock.

"Holy guacamole, Sis. What in the world was Shelby doing with that piece of work?"

I shrugged. "No idea. I'm thinking we need to give the girl a call."

"Indeed we do. And there's no time like the present." Reaching into the front of her top, Nora pulled out a slim cell phone and began scrolling through her contacts.

I had to shake my head. Why a woman of fifty-something would carry a cell phone in her bra was beyond me, especially since her clothing was usually tight enough to reveal even the smallest freckle.

"Shelby, this is Nora Goldstein." Nora gave me a thumbs-up, perching on the edge of the sofa as she spoke. "Listen, Miss Franklin saw something on Instagram that has us both a tad curious." She paused, listening, one eyebrow lifted slightly. "That's right. Any idea why she would post that?" Nora's eyebrows rose and her eyes widened as she listened to Shelby's response. "I see. Well, isn't *that* a hoot, considering the source. I wouldn't give any credence to a word that woman says." Another pause.

I could hear Shelby's voice clearly, although I couldn't make out anything she said. Maybe I needed to have my prized supersonic teacher's ears checked.

"Well, keep your chin up, girlie. Karma can be a powerful you-know-what-in-the-you-know-where."

By the time Nora had ended the conversation and replaced the cell in her secret carrying case, I was wound up tighter than an eight-day clock.

"And? What did she have to say?"

"You're not gonna believe it."

"Until I know what it is, I have no idea whether I will or not." I gestured impatiently. "Spit it out already, slowpoke."

"Don't get your panties in a wad, woman. I'll tell you on the way to get coffee."

"Fine," I grumbled. "And don't forget we still need to discuss hiring another dog walker, so get busy talking."

Nora, much to my chagrin, chattered about insignificant topics until we exited the lobby of the luxury apartment building.

When I was beginning to think that I couldn't stand it any longer, she reached over and clutched my arm, stopping me in mid-shuffle. I was wearing Birkenstocks, after all, and that required a slight toe curl to keep them in place as I walked.

"Okay, Sis, listen to this. The Wonderbra Woman of television has dissed our sweet Shelby so badly she's considering murder."

"Who is? Wonderbra or Shelby?" I couldn't picture Shelby killing anyone, not really, and certainly not Babs Prescott. It might wrinkle her Botoxed face and designer dresses.

Nora poked me in the side irritably. "Shelby, silly. Babs had the nerve to suggest Shelby needed to book herself into a spa for a makeover. She even suggested one, some place called the Fabulous Fattie Farm."

I had to hand it to her: Babs certainly had some nerve. Knowing her, she'd probably flashed her teeth and wiggled all the way through the conversation. No wonder Shelby had been glaring in the Instagram post.

"Well, I don't blame her for being upset." I nodded a greeting to a pair of whispering women and pulled my arm from Nora's grasp. "And let's start walking. People are beginning to stare."

Shelby, in my opinion, was far from overweight. Sure, she'd never be found on a catwalk or wear a size triple zero, but she definitely wasn't in need of a makeover. What had possessed Babs to make such an idiotic suggestion?

As if reading my mind, Nora said, "Apparently Shelby was at the state capitol at the same time Babs and her cronies were, covering a new bill about food labeling. Isn't that the craziest thing you've ever heard?"

"I'm not sure I'd call it crazy. More like commonsensical. Don't you want to know what's in the food you're eating?"

We'd reached the corner across from the coffee shop, a light breeze coming in from the river and ruffling my hair.

"Of course I do." Nora spoke impatiently, jabbing one finger on the button to activate the walk signal. "What I'm talking about is why those two were sharing the same oxygen, Babs and Shelby. I call that crazy."

"Probably because both of them are in the news business. You know, television and newspaper?"

"I know that, goofy. I meant I've never heard of The Great One actually speaking with other reporters before. Something must've happened to cause that. Or not happened. Maybe she didn't get her daily dose of public admiration or something."

The light turned green and the sign lit up, allowing us to cross safely. I trudged along as I normally did, but Nora was giving every driver an eyeful of undulating black Lycra and strutting heels. I ignored her, hoping no one could tell that we were together. She could be an entire headline herself, and I wanted no part of it. Retired teachers didn't cavort with people like that.

"Hey you," she called out loudly, and I groaned, turning around to watch her prance the last few steps. "Mind waiting up for me?"

"Trust me, there are times I wish I didn't have to." I headed for The Friendly Bean's entrance, stepping aside to let a giggling gaggle of teens exit. "Do you always have to walk that way when we're in public?"

Nora preened, patting her curls and putting one hand on an outthrust hip. I held back an eye roll, pushing her inside ahead of me. Apparently Babs Prescott wasn't the only publicity hound in these parts.

"And deprive the good folks of Portland? I think not." She grinned over her shoulder, dropping one eyelid in a playful wink. "Now, how 'bout that coffee?"

I snagged an empty table near the rear of the café while Nora placed our orders. In our town, coffee was almost a religion, one I tended to follow with unwavering devotion. I liked my coffee dark and black and hot, although I'd recently ventured into the froufrou land of cappuccinos and mochas. By the time Nora had swayed back to the table, carefully balancing a pair of steaming lattes, I was ready for my daily dose of caffeine.

"The barista says she'll bring our croissants over when they're heated." Nora took a sip from her coffee cup and closed her eyes. "Ah. That hits the spot. Nothing like a latte made with almond milk."

I paused, holding my mug in midair. "Please don't tell me you put that stuff in my drink."

Nora merely smiled.

"Fine. I'll handle it this time." I glared at her over the rim of my cup. "Next time I'll order my own coffee, thank you very much."

"It's much better for you, Gwennie. You know, healthy and all that jazz. Don't you want to live to be a hundred?"

I snorted. "Not if it means drinking milk made from nuts. If God meant us to drink almond milk, he'd have given them little almond boobs."

"Here're your croissants." The barista slid a thick white plate between Nora and me, her eyes wide as she stared at me. "Miss Franklin? Is that you?"

I could have kicked myself for that last comment about almonds and body parts. Forcing a smile onto my mortified face, I looked at the young woman, trying to recall her name. "Yes, it is. And it's Kate—Katelyn, right?"

She beamed at me and I gave a small sigh of relief. I'd had well over one hundred students per year throughout the twenty plus years of teaching, and it was almost impossible to remember each and every name. Unless, of course, they'd done something to stand out, like plagiarizing a paper or leaving tacks on my chair.

"I'm getting ready to graduate from college." She leaned one hip against the table and smiled proudly. "And guess what? I'm going to be an English teacher like you."

"Oh, honey, you're a brave soul." Nora reached over and patted Katelyn's arm. "Look at Miss Franklin here. That's what happens after being in high school for fifty years."

"It was twenty." I spoke through gritted teeth, my lips curled up in what I hope would pass for a smile. "And ignore my friend here. She doesn't get out that often. Issues, you know." I tapped the side of my head.

Katelyn flashed a look of sympathy at Nora. "That's all right. My grandma's got that too, the disease that makes you forget your name and say all kinds of crazy things." She glanced over her shoulder at the front counter. "Whoops, I'd better get back. It was great talking to you, Miss Franklin."

"Well, thanks a bunch, best friend." Nora leaned over and snagged a steaming croissant, juggling it between her hands. "You made me sound like a raving imbecile."

"And you made me sound like a drooling old hag, so we're even." I held up my coffee cup. "Here's to another fifty years of friendship."

We clinked our mugs together, smiling at one another with real affection. We'd been inseparable since kindergarten, and nothing as petty as name calling would ever break us apart. At least it hadn't yet.

We were in the midst of discussing Rachel as a possible employee when the television hanging on the wall behind us flashed the latest news bulletin from around the greater Portland area. It was the best way to find out what was happening in our part of the city and usually focused on local farmers' markets and craft fairs. I glanced causally at the screen, waiting to see what they'd say about the Clear the Shelter event.

The first item, however, caused me to gasp and Nora to sputter around a mouthful of croissant, sending a shower of crumbs across the table.

"We begin this broadcast with sad news." The earnest young man seated at the news desk looked appropriately solemn, and I sipped my latte as I waited to hear the bulletin. "Shortly after a press conference at the state capitol today, the body of news anchor Babs Prescott was discovered in a nearby parking garage. This is a breaking story, and we'll bring you all the details as soon as they come in. In other news, members of the local garden club…"

We looked at each other and said in one voice, "Shelby."

About the Author

Dane McCaslin, *USA Today* bestselling author of the Proverbial Crime mystery series, is a lifelong writer whose love of mysteries was formed early in life. At age eight, she discovered Agatha Christie—much to her mother's dismay—and began devouring any and all books she could find that featured murder and mayhem. After retiring from her career as a high school and community college English teacher, Dane now devotes her newly found freedom to writing mystery novels…and reading for pleasure.

Printed in the United States
by Baker & Taylor Publisher Services